CHANGING FORTUNES

CHANGING FORTUNES

Pamela Oldfield

This first world edition published in Great Britain 2002 by
SEVERN HOUSE PUBLISHERS LTD of
9–15 High Street, Sutton, Surrey SM1 1DF.
This first world edition published in the USA 2002 by
SEVERN HOUSE PUBLISHERS INC of
595 Madison Avenue, New York, N.Y. 10022.

British Library Cataloguing in Publication Data

Oldfield, Pamela, 1934–
    Changing fortunes
    1. Great Britain – Social life and customs – 19th century – Fiction
    2. Historical fiction
    I. Title
    823.9'14 [F]

ISBN 0-7278-5702-9

Typeset by Palimpsest Book Production Ltd.,
Polmont, Stirlingshire, Scotland.
Printed and bound in Great Britain by
MPG Books Ltd., Bodmin, Cornwall.

One

1890

'So, Miss Blake, tell me a little about yourself.'

Aware of the importance of this interview, Chloe sat a little straighter in her chair. It was eleven o'clock in the morning. Thursday the fifth of June. Outside the sun shone but had yet to penetrate the room in which they sat.

'I'm twenty and in good health . . . sir.' She knew she was looking her best. Her wavy brown hair was fastened back neatly and the dark jacket and skirt showed off her trim figure to advantage. 'I can read and write, Mr Maitland, and I have nursing experience.'

Oliver Maitland leaned forward a little. 'Which amounts to what exactly?'

'I nursed my own mother until she died recently.' Immediately Chloe saw the alarm in his face.

'It wasn't consumption, I hope.'

'No, sir. It was dropsy.'

She watched him appraisingly as he scanned her letter, which lay unfolded on the desk before him. His smooth dark hair was parted in the middle and behind his steel-rimmed glasses his brown eyes were friendly.

Chloe asked, 'How ill is your mother?'

He sighed. 'We hardly know any more. She hates to leave her bed and almost never leaves her room. Our family doctor can find nothing physically wrong with her but she seems to have no strength. No interest in the world around her. She has no appetite and apart from reading she has no pleasures.'

1

How boring, thought Chloe, but kept the thought to herself. She had heard her brother-in-law complain about the idle rich. Presumably Mrs Jessica Maitland fell into that category. Chloe was assuming they were rich. Fairfield House was a large, well-established property, brick under a tile-hung first storey with a peg-tile roof. It was set amid rambling grounds close to Icklesham on the Hastings side. Not that it was very well maintained. Chloe had noticed that the low wall that fronted the road was crumbling in places and the railings were rusty. Perhaps the family was living in what her brother-in-law called 'genteel poverty'. On the other hand they could afford to employ staff and a companion. They were certainly wealthy compared with her own family.

Oliver Maitland was rereading the letter of application over which Chloe had laboured long and hard. She had no qualms on that score, for it was perfect. No ink blots. No alterations. No misspellings. She had used her sister's dictionary to good effect. She wondered what he did for a living – if he did anything. A solicitor, perhaps, or a gentleman farmer.

He said, 'I see you live with your sister and her husband.'

'Yes sir. But it's only temporary – since my mother died.'

'And you can't stay there?'

'I could, sir, but I have no wish to be a burden. Not even to my sister. They have only been married for four years and they need to be on their own. They have their own problems and I don't want to add to that. I want to earn my own living.'

She thought briefly of the shabby but comfortable rectory where her sister, Dorothy, lived with her husband, the Reverend Parks. For a moment her doubts resurfaced. Should she be leaving them? But she had to be independent, she reminded herself. She wanted not only to earn her keep but to save money. Chloe Blake had plans for the future.

Oliver Maitland was eyeing her intently and she promptly gave him her undivided attention.

'Miss Blake, you say in your letter that your father is absent. What does that mean?'

For the first time she hesitated. How much should she tell?

'He quarrelled with my mother over another woman but she forgave him. Then he said he was going to America to make his fortune. He left and we never heard from him again.' Not quite the truth but it would do. 'I was eight and my sister was twelve.'

'You seem well enough qualified, Miss Blake. Have you applied elsewhere for employment?'

A lie was required, she decided. 'I have another appointment, sir. Tomorrow afternoon at four.'

'Ah!' He nodded. 'Then perhaps I should tell you that I am offering you the position.'

Chloe hid her relief. 'Thank you, sir. I hope I shall feel able to accept.'

If her answer surprised him he hid it well.

'Let me tell you a little about our family. My unmarried sister, Bertha, lives here as does my great-uncle, Matthew Orme, on my mother's side. So you wouldn't bear all the responsibility for Mother's care. We are adequately provided for financially. There is also a housekeeper and a maid, Hettie, who answered the door to you.'

'She seems a very cheerful girl.'

'Does she? I suppose she is . . . You know the wages we're offering and you would have three free meals a day. Do you have any questions, Miss Blake?'

'Yes sir. Would I have my own room?'

He pursed his lips. 'The choice is between sharing a large room with the maid and having a small room to yourself. From your question I assume you would prefer the latter.'

'I would.' Her mind was racing through the questions she had planned to ask. 'Where would I eat?'

3

The question obviously surprised him. 'How do you mean?'

'Would I eat with the staff or the family?'

'Ah!' he said again. 'I see . . . To be frank, I hadn't thought about it.'

'I'd prefer to eat with the staff.'

'I'm sure that would be possible although as Mother's companion you might well eat the midday meal with her in her room. Perhaps you could vary it.'

'I suppose that's best. And what exactly does a nurse companion do?'

He shrugged lightly. 'You would read to Mother, maybe, and find books for her to read.' He waved a hand to indicate the library shelves. 'Take an interest in her needlework. Help her in and out of bed. See that she changes her clothes regularly and takes her medicine—'

'I thought there was nothing wrong with her.'

'Mother has trouble sleeping and occasionally a very debilitating sick headache. We feel she is too inward-looking, Miss Blake. She needs distractions. Try to . . . to entertain her. Cheer her up, Miss Blake, in any way you can.' He sat back in his chair. 'Be there when she needs you. Someone she can rely on. The truth is that my sister is weary of the problem. Poor Bertha has coped for too long with Mother's moods and desperately needs a break. It was my suggestion that we employ a companion.'

Chloe nodded. 'You haven't told me the hours, Mr Maitland.'

'Haven't I? I'm sorry. Let me think . . .'

So he hadn't interviewed anyone else, thought Chloe. If he had he would already have decided these matters. Interesting.

He said, 'Suppose I said you could have Sunday after-noons to yourself and all of every second Monday. You live locally, I believe.'

'In Icklesham, sir.'

'Then you'd be able to visit your sister on your day off.'

4

Chloe also sat back, considering. This was the only job on offer and it sounded reasonable. Dull but reasonable – but she needn't stay too long. A twelvemonth would be fair. If she disliked it she would then start to look for another position. Time to make a decision. She looked round the room, playing for time. A large mahogany desk and two well-upholstered armchairs stood beside the fireplace. There was a carpet on the floor and the heavy lace curtains were clean. She had smelled polish as she came up the stairs and the maid had seemed likeable enough.

'After six weeks, if I prove satisfactory, would my wages be increased?'

He smiled suddenly. 'Possibly a small increase.'

'And after a year?'

'We would look at the matter again.'

He seemed to think she had said something humorous. She said, 'Do you also live here, Mr Maitland?'

'I suppose I do but I'm in lodgings in London most of the time.' He gave her a long look. 'So what do you say, Miss Blake? Will you join us?'

She smiled. All things considered the interview had gone very well. 'I think I will, Mr Maitland. Perhaps I should meet the rest of the family.'

Moments later she was following him out of the library and along the passage to be introduced to Jessica Maitland.

As they entered the large bedroom, Chloe's eyes were drawn to the enormous bed in which an elderly woman lay propped among the pillows. She looked smaller and frailer than Chloe had expected. Her thin auburn hair lay in two plaits and a small mob cap covered her head. She was wrapped in a blue woollen shawl from which small neat hands protruded. Her face was pale and faintly freckled but to Chloe's surprise she appeared younger than she had expected. Perhaps fifty-five.

Jessica watched their entrance with obvious irritation.

5

'Mother, I've brought Miss Blake to meet you. She will be your companion.'

Chloe made a small but courteous bob. Smiling, she said, 'It's a pleasure to meet you, Mrs Maitland.'

Jessica glared at her. 'This is all nonsense, Miss Blake. I don't need a companion. I have my daughter.'

Her son stepped forward. 'Now please don't be difficult, Mother. We've talked about this. Miss Blake is—'

'A companion?' She tutted. 'It's a waste of money. There's nothing she can do for me that Bertha cannot do.'

Chloe could see an argument developing. She smiled. 'I can't help admiring your hair, Mrs Maitland. My mother had auburn hair and I always envied her. But she always wore hers curled. I could curl yours for you, if you wished.' She studied Jessica Maitland with her head on one side. 'Maybe if I took a little off the sides. I'm good with scissors.'

She had the feeling that Oliver Maitland was holding his breath. Jessica Maitland was staring at her.

'Bertha says plaits are much easier,' she said at last.

'Easier? Oh yes, but not prettier. It's not as though you're an old lady.'

'Not old, maybe, but not well either.' Green eyes challenged Chloe's.

Her son, it seemed, had been forgotten.

Chloe said, 'A few side curls and a pale green shawl. The blue doesn't do justice to your eyes.'

For a moment Chloe thought she saw a spark of interest but then Jessica waved a hand dismissively. 'I don't feel up to all this,' she told her son. 'I was awake half the night with indigestion. Do pull the curtains for me, Oliver dear. You know how I hate the afternoon sun.'

Oliver made a move to obey but Chloe darted across the room to the window. She looked out and saw a lawn with deckchairs. As she pulled the curtains she said, 'What a lovely garden. Do you spend much time outside?'

Oliver said, 'Mother feels the cold so.'

6

Jessica said, 'I am easily chilled. The sun goes in so suddenly and Bertha has no sooner—'

'But there's a charming little summer house,' Chloe told her. 'I can just see the two of us snug as dormice, tucked up with a jug of raspberry cordial. You can work on your embroidery while I read to you!'

Jessica muttered something that sounded suspiciously like 'I don't think so' as she slid down into the bed. She closed her eyes against any further conversation and after a moment Chloe and Oliver tiptoed from the room.

He said, 'I'm afraid Mother is rather delicate, Miss Blake.'

Chloe, busy with her thoughts, wisely said nothing.

Downstairs she was shown into a spacious drawing room so filled with large dark furniture that it appeared smaller. The ornate mantelpiece housed an assortment of china and glass ornaments and below it an embroidered fire screen hid the empty hearth. The table was draped with a tasselled chenille cover and the walls were hung with pictures of varying sizes. In one of the armchairs an elderly man was smoking a cigar while he read a newspaper.

'Ah! Here is my uncle, Matthew Orme.'

Thus alerted, the man threw down his paper, rose and held out his hand. He was small and plump and his face was smooth. Almost a baby face, thought Chloe. He wore a brown velvet smoking jacket over pyjamas and his feet were thrust into shabby leather slippers. In the middle of the morning? Chloe hid her surprise but Oliver allowed his disapproval to show.

Matthew Orme said, 'Ollie, old lad. Who's this vision of loveliness, eh?'

Oliver said, 'This is Miss Blake, who is to become Mother's companion.' To Chloe he said, 'This is my uncle, who must be one of the laziest men in Christendom!'

'If not *the* laziest,' he agreed, taking the cigar from his mouth with his left hand. He appeared totally unruffled by the slur. Beaming, he clasped Chloe's hand and pumped it up and down. 'Come to save us, have you, Miss Blake? Well, good luck to you, m'dear. We could do with a bit of saving although I say it myself. My sister's not the easiest person in the world but you look tough enough for the job!'

Tough enough? Chloe wasn't sure how to take that remark but Oliver intervened.

'You mustn't mind him, Miss Blake. He prides himself on plain speaking – among other things.'

Chloe didn't know how to take that remark either. On what else did the man pride himself? she wondered, but he was still eyeing her with obvious admiration so she put him down as a possible ally.

He went on. 'Not a real uncle, as it happens. A stepuncle, if you see what I mean. I'm Jessica's stepbrother. The black sheep of the family. That's me, eh Oliver?' He roared with laughter and then winked at Chloe. 'But don't worry. I'm more grey than black. Bark's worse than my bite. Call me Uncle Matty. Can't stand formality.'

At least he's cheerful, thought Chloe. I think I might get along with this particular grey sheep. She smiled at him and he roared, 'That's the ticket, young lady! Thank God for someone with a sense of humour. Poor old Ollie carries the cares of the world on his shoulders, poor devil.' He took a draw on his cigar, blew out the smoke then carefully laid the cigar on the edge of a heavy glass ashtray. 'And poor old Jessie!' He thrust his thumbs into the pockets of his waistcoat. 'That's Jessica to you, of course. She hates being called Jessie so I do it to tease her.'

Oliver took Chloe firmly by the arm saying, 'Pay him no attention, Miss Blake. He's a bad influence. We must find Bertha and—'

But the uncle went on. 'And poor Bertha. Show me a woman crossed in love and I'll show you—'

Oliver gave him a warning look. 'Miss Blake doesn't want to hear all that, Matty.'

'Doesn't she? I'd have thought it essential preparation for taking on this family!'

Oliver turned back to Chloe as though he hadn't spoken. 'Then we'll meet Mrs Letts, the housekeeper. You've already seen Hettie, the maid.'

Chloe said, 'Goodbye for now then, Mr . . . Uncle Matty,' and allowed herself to be led away. They passed a pleasant dining room dominated by a huge mirror and a small breakfast room which smelled of kidneys and bacon.

'Bertha's probably in the garden,' Oliver told her. They retraced their steps to the drawing room and went out by way of the French windows. 'Poor Bertha was betrothed once but it was an ill-starred romance.'

'Ill-starred?' Chloe repeated, her heart at once going out to the unfortunate Bertha. 'What happened?' Several possible scenarios presented themselves to her. 'She wasn't jilted, was she?'

'No, no. Nothing like that. He was a soldier, a lieutenant with the Royal Horse, but Father wasn't keen on the match. Bertha thought he might change his mind but before that could happen the poor devil was killed.' He turned and put a finger to his lips. 'Not a word to Bertha.' Raising his voice again he cried, 'Bertha! I've brought Mother's new companion to say hello.'

A tall thin woman in a dark skirt and blouse was kneeling beside a bed of geraniums. She glanced up as they approached and Oliver offered a hand to help her to her feet. Chloe saw that her auburn hair was swept back and tied with a black ribbon. Her face was pale and serious, with fine cheekbones and a slight dusting of freckles. Very much her mother's daughter, Chloe thought with approval and not a little envy.

Bertha was eyeing her from top to toe and finally appeared satisfied with the results of her scrutiny. Chloe felt amused rather than offended. This was what it meant to be 'in service', she told herself. A servant. Or a paid help. What was she exactly?

'I'm pleased to meet you, ma'am,' she said with a small bob.

9

'Don't call me ma'am. I'd prefer Miss Maitland.'

'I'll remember that.'

'So you'll be living with us at Fairfields,' she said. Then, noting Chloe's blank expression, she added, 'Here, in other words. This is Fairfield House – because of the view. We call it Fairfields. Didn't you know that?'

'I'd forgotten.'

'Is your memory generally poor?'

'I don't think so.' Chloe kept her tone neutral and her gaze steady. No need to let her ruffle you, she told herself. Establish your right to be here from the very beginning. She said, 'The geraniums look very sturdy. And that glorious red! Quite dramatic.'

Bertha was willing to be distracted. 'They are doing rather well. I grew them from cuttings.'

'Bertha has green fingers and she loves the garden.'

Bertha nodded. 'Binns, a local lad, helps out with the lawns and any heavy digging. He also drives the dog cart and acts as handyman. Not bright but willing.'

Chloe smiled. 'With me here you will have more time for your gardening.'

Bertha pulled off her gloves and laid them neatly together. 'That depends. Will you be full-time or part?'

Before she could answer, Oliver said, 'Full-time with Sunday afternoons off and every second Monday – but not carved in stone.'

Bertha gave a cursory nod. 'Have you met Mother, Miss Blake?'

'Yes I have. I'm sure we'll get along.'

'Are you really?'

Again Chloe met her gaze without flinching. Strange, she thought. She had expected Bertha to be glad that she was being relieved of the burden. Instead she almost seemed to resent the fact. Had brother and sister agreed the change or had Oliver insisted on it?

Bertha turned to Oliver. 'Where is she going to sleep?'

'Miss Blake chose the small room. She likes her privacy.'

10

Bertha raised her eyebrows. 'Mother's companion sleeps in the attic while the housemaid has the larger room on the first floor? A little topsy-turvy, wouldn't you say?'

Oliver looked crestfallen. 'I hadn't thought about it like that.'

Chloe said, 'I don't mind. Really.'

Ignoring her, Bertha said, 'Honestly, Oliver, you must think these things through. Miss Blake ought to be near Mother in case she needs help in the night. I suggest Miss Blake has the guest room next to Mother, Hettie's present room is converted into a guest room and Hettie moves upstairs to the attic.'

Oliver looked at Chloe, who said, 'It makes sense to me.'

'Then I'll see to it.'

Bertha put a hand to her back. 'I think I've done enough for today,' she said and picked up a trug into which she dropped her gloves, secateurs and trowel. As the three of them walked back towards the house she asked Chloe where she was going to eat.

Oliver said, 'Sometimes with us, sometimes downstairs.'

Bertha glanced at Chloe. 'Don't get too involved with the domestic helps. Avoid tittle-tattle. You are a companion, not a servant. There is a distinction, Miss Blake, which we would like you to observe.'

'I'm sure I can manage that, Miss Maitland.'

'We shall see.' She looked sharply at Chloe to see if she intended any impertinence and then glanced at her brother. Chloe had the feeling that there was some animosity between them. It might be simply the normal relationship between older brother and younger sister. On the other hand there might be more to it. Perhaps life at Fairfield House wouldn't be quite as dull as she had expected.

The kitchen was a large, gloomy room with whitewashed walls hung with copper saucepans and wooden sieves. A large window looked out on to a small yard overshadowed by a huge lime tree which cut out the sunlight. There was a sturdy iron range, a walk-in larder and an enormous Welsh dresser which almost groaned under an abundance of plates and dishes. A well-scrubbed table took up much of the remaining space. Chloe couldn't help contrasting it with her sister's cosy kitchen. Even now Dorothy would be preparing something for their supper and suddenly Chloe longed to be with her sister, recounting her morning's adventure.

The housekeeper, a heavily built woman, was elderly and rather breathless, although Chloe couldn't tell if this was caused by the heat or was her normal state of health. She was wearing a clean apron over a dark green dress and was stirring something savoury in a pot over the stove.

At that moment a bell rang and Hettie came flying along the corridor towards them. She beamed at her employer.

'Please, sir, it's George Brier to see about the front gate.'

'Oh dear!' Oliver frowned. 'You'd better tell him to wait. I'll be about ten minutes.'

She looked disconcerted. 'He says he's in a hurry, sir. He says you told him to be here at eleven and he's been waiting for you.'

Bertha gave her brother a challenging look.

'He's right,' he admitted. 'I forgot Miss Blake was coming today.'

Bertha said eagerly, 'Suppose I see to it, Oliver, while you deal with Miss Blake. I've already met Mr Brier and we've discussed what's wanted.'

'Are you sure?'

'Of course I'm sure. We've discussed it enough over the past week.'

Hettie said, 'He says the brickwork's crumbling worse than he thought and you should maybe pull them down and—'

'That will do, Hettie!' Bertha told her. 'You concentrate on your own work.'

Oliver said, 'They are in a bad state, I'm afraid.'

'I'll talk to him,' Bertha said. 'If you'll excuse me, Miss Blake.'

And she hurried away. Hettie, red-faced, slipped past Chloe into the kitchen and resumed the washing-up. After the introductions Mrs Letts asked where Chloe would take her meals.

Oliver spoke for her. 'Miss Blake will eat in the kitchen some of the time, probably for breakfast, and she may occasionally dine with the family or alone with Mrs Maitland.'

Mrs Letts smiled at Chloe. 'And you're a nurse, are you?'

'No. I'm a companion for Mrs Maitland but I do have some nursing experience.'

'Well that's nice.' Leaning over the pot she sniffed hard then reached for a pot of salt and added a generous pinch to the stew. 'Mutton does need a good bit of seasoning,' she informed them. 'My first mistress used to say, "Never spare the salt." Not that we had mutton that often. The master was partial to game and duck, pheasant . . . Oh and before I forget, the window cleaner came and I paid him. Not that he's worth it. Poor Sam's getting that slow with his rheumatism. I still reckon Binns could do the whole job—'

'He could,' Oliver Maitland agreed, 'but Mother likes Sam and he's been doing the job for years. She's sorry for the old chap.'

Mrs Letts tutted. 'She's too soft-hearted! My first mistress—'

'Binns does the second floor and it works well enough,' he told her firmly. 'Now, we mustn't keep you from your work.'

He led Chloe from the room. Lowering his voice, he said, 'Mrs Letts likes to dwell in the past. She once worked for Uncle Matty's mother before she was widowed. They were quite wealthy. Then she married Thomas Maitland. And Mother was born. I suspect Mrs Letts feels we can never quite compare!' He laughed ruefully. 'It's all a bit vague. Mr Orme doesn't care to speak of the past.'

'But Mrs Letts does!'

'She doesn't actually tell us anything but she likes to toss in these snippets. You mustn't be tempted to listen. It's ancient family business and nothing to do with you.'

'So where is Mrs Letts' husband?'

'She never married but she likes to call herself Mrs Letts. It's harmless so we go along with it. I think she feels it gives her more authority.'

By this time they had regained the hall and Chloe realised they were heading for the front door. So the interview was at an end and she had got the job. She would be leaving the comfort of her sister's home and stepping into the unknown. For better or worse? she wondered, but didn't for a moment fear the answer. It would be a new experience and Chloe found that exciting.

That evening Chloe, Dorothy and Albert sat together over the supper table. Dorothy was like Chloe in colouring but shorter by an inch and nicely rounded. Chloe reviewed her morning.

'The son, Oliver Maitland, is rather quiet but well meaning, I think. He may even be lonely. He lives in London for much of the time but he didn't say why or where.'

'Something in the city,' Albert suggested. He was tall and spare with thin features. Chloe found him unemotional but she loved him for Dorothy's sake.

'Are they rich?' Dorothy looked hopeful. As a struggling vicar's wife she was fascinated by wealth and the owners of wealth.

'Not particularly. Fairfields is rather isolated but quite handsome in a shabby way. There is something wrong with the front gates—'

'Fairfields?' cried Dorothy. 'You mean the place that stands back from the road, with the lime trees?'

'That's the one. There's another garden at the back and the sister was planting geraniums and there were masses of rhododendrons and dark shrubbery under sycamore trees.'

'Any children?'

Dorothy had spoken without thinking and there was an immediate tension in the air.

'None.' Chloe avoided their eyes. Her sister and Albert had been married for nearly four years and there had been no children. Dorothy was heartbroken and Albert mortified. It was usually a topic the two sisters avoided. Now Chloe frowned, searching for more interesting information in order to change the subject.

'The mother's a bit fragile,' she told them. 'They say she's bedridden but I can't see why. Bertha's the unmarried daughter. She seemed a little frosty but maybe she's reserved.'

'If she was unpleasant towards you . . .' Dorothy sprang to Chloe's defence. As the older sister she had always been protective towards her.

'Not exactly unpleasant. More cool. She has an unhappy past.'

Dorothy shook her head. 'It's not that. It's because she hasn't married and you're young, pretty and marriageable!' Dorothy glanced at her husband then back at Chloe. 'She's probably jealous of you.'

Chloe shrugged. 'There's a sad story about her lost love, a soldier, killed in an accident. I feel sorry for her.'

Albert smiled. 'You feel sorry for all lame dogs, Chloe.'

Dorothy rounded on him. 'Hark who's talking!' she cried. 'Under that gruff exterior you have the kindest heart in the world!'

'It goes with my calling,' he protested.

Dorothy took hold of his hand. 'Everyone's a lost lamb to you, Albert.'

Chloe was amused to see that this small show of affection embarrassed him. He said, 'They sound a somewhat troubled family, Chloe. You can change your mind, you know. We love having you with us.'

'I know but you know me, Albert. I like a challenge. Oh, then there's Mrs Maitland's stepbrother. Matthew Orme.

15

He's a bit jollier. He describes himself as a bit of a grey sheep.' Chloe smiled. 'He says—'

Dorothy frowned. 'Grey sheep? I don't like the sound of that. Has he done something dreadful?'

'I don't think so but I'll tell you whatever I find out.'

Her sister's frown deepened. 'You watch your step with him. He might be one of those men . . . You know what I mean, Chloe. They . . . they dally with the servants.' She gave Chloe a meaningful look. 'It would be your word against his, remember.'

Chloe shook her head. 'I can't imagine anything like that.'

Albert frowned. 'Dorothy's right though. He might try to take advantage of your youth. I take it he isn't married, this uncle or whatever he is.'

'No. At least there's no sign of his wife.' She grinned. 'And I doubt if she's locked up in the woodshed!' She at once regretted this attempt at humour as Dorothy and Albert exchanged a worried glance.

Dorothy put a hand on Chloe's knee. 'You must be on your guard with all of them. Not everyone is as innocent as you.'

'I can take care of myself.'

'But can you? You've never lived alone.'

'I shan't be alone. There are—'

'Dorothy means that you'll be among strangers and they do sound rather odd.' Albert shook his head. 'If you're determined to go ahead you must promise to keep us informed. Don't hide anything from us or we won't be able to help you.'

Dorothy said, 'And why isn't the son married?'

Chloe laughed. 'He didn't tell me. Do you think I should flutter my eyelashes at him?'

Dorothy groaned. 'No I *don't*! And I do wish you'd be serious, Chloe. Couldn't you go daily? I don't like the idea of you sleeping there. The night brings out the worst in some people.'

'I'll lock my door.'

'If there is a lock.' She looked at her husband for support.

'We must wait and see, Dorothy,' he told her. 'She'll be in God's hands, remember. And she's not a million miles away.' Turning to Chloe, he said, 'If there's any trouble you must leave at once and come home. Forget about earning money. Forget about being independent. The main thing is your safety and well-being.'

With a barely muffled sigh Chloe promised. They were both very sweet but she thought it a huge fuss about nothing.

Thursday the fifth of June. So it is settled. I shall start Monday and we shall see what Fairfields has to offer. It will be strange to be away from my family. Since childhood I have lived at home and even when Ma died I moved in with Dorothy and Albert. Now I shall be free to make my own way in the world. I shall save every penny, for without money I shall always be beholden to someone else. For me that will not be good enough. Dorothy hopes the Maitlands will like me but my hope is that I shall like them. That's where Dorothy and I differ.

Two

Chloe moved in to Fairfields the following Monday and by Friday she was beginning to feel at home. The faces around her had become familiar; she had learned the layout of the house and the daily routine. Her own room pleased her and she was in the process of adding the personal touches. The sampler her mother had made as a child hung on the wall alongside a plaited raffia cross which Albert had given her years earlier. Her sewing basket, left to her by her grandmother, rested on a small table inside the tall deep window and a big brass alarm clock stood on the bedside table.

She was also becoming accustomed to her duties and finding them the challenge she had wanted. So far Jessica Maitland had stayed firmly in bed, refusing even to sit in her armchair. Sheer laziness, Chloe decided, and made up her mind that things were going to change. Friday was *the* day. As soon as she had helped Jessica on to the commode Chloe began to strip the bed, pulling off the sheets and pillowslips at a great rate and dropping them on to the floor.

Jessica reacted immediately. 'What are you doing, child? That's Hettie's job.'

Chloe hid a smile. She was growing used to being addressed as 'child'.

'Not any longer,' she said. 'I've offered to do it. I want you to have a well-aired mattress and Hettie is too busy to see to it properly.' She gathered up the laundry and laid the pile to one side. She then tugged the mattress from the bed and propped it against the side. 'Now both sides can air,' she said briskly and departed with the laundry before Jessica could protest further. Returning with the fresh bedding, Chloe left them on the bed still folded and, seeing that Jessica was ready, helped her to the armchair.

'Now to make you comfortable,' she smiled and tucked two cushions behind her companion's head.

'I can't stay here!' Jessica cried, a hint of petulance in her voice. 'I am only truly comfortable in bed. I hate armchairs, especially this one. It's overstuffed and quite unyielding. I've told my daughter time and again but—'

'I'll have another one brought up tomorrow,' Chloe improvised hastily. 'There's no way I shall allow you to be uncomfortable, Mrs Maitland.' She tucked a blanket around Jessica and stood back admiringly. 'I certainly prefer you without the plaits,' she said. 'My grandfather used to say there wasn't a woman alive who didn't look prettier with a few curls.' It sounded quite convincing, she thought.

For the moment it seemed Jessica would persist in the protest but abruptly she gave up. She sank back into the armchair and surveyed her room from this new angle.

'What's it to be?' Chloe asked. 'Your book or your embroidery?' She fetched them both and put them on a nearby table well within her companion's reach.

'Neither. You've confused me with all this nonsense.'

Chloe busied herself with the various pills and bottles on the bedside table, lifting each one and dusting beneath it.

'Miss Blake! I want to go back to bed.'

'You will, of course – as soon as it's properly aired.' Chloe smiled at her. 'I'm surprised your doctor hasn't insisted on it before now. So, you don't want to sew or read . . . Then you might as well enjoy the view.' Ignoring the inevitable protests, Chloe grabbed the back of the armchair and heaved and tugged it into position beside the window.

'For heaven's sake, Chloe! Are you trying to shake me to death?' Jessica clung to the arms of the chair as though she were on a dangerous rollercoaster. 'And don't answer that!' she continued. 'I might not want to hear it.'

Chloe regarded her with surprise. Had she detected a spark of humour in the last comment? Was it possible that there was more to her tetchy employer than she had first thought?

'I'm off now to post your letters,' she said. 'Is there anything I can fetch for you from the village store?' She smiled. 'A stick of licorice or some mint humbugs? They used to be my favourites. Do you have a sweet tooth?'

Jessica thought about it. 'I used to like chocolate but I'm not able to digest it these days.'

'Who says so?'

'At my age—'

Chloe put a finger to her lips. 'I'll bring you a bag of chocolate drops and you can just eat a few. A little treat. No one needs to know but us.' She smiled. 'May I take Binns for the dog cart? I shall soon be able to handle the horse on my own but I'm not quite ready for that yet.'

Jessica shook her head. 'I don't know why you want to go all the way to Icklesham when Binns can do it on his way home.'

'There's method in my madness,' Chloe answered. 'In time all will be revealed. I'll be back in two shakes of a lamb's tail and will pop you back into bed.'

'But how long will you be gone?'

Ignoring the question, Chloe hurried from the room. Now Jessica would be in her chair for nearly an hour. A good start, she thought. Poor woman. She really deserved a few chocolate drops.

Ten minutes later Bertha made her way to her mother's room and knocked on the door. She was surprised to see Jessica sitting in the armchair by the window.

'Whatever are you doing out of bed, Mama?' she asked.

'I'm admiring the view. I have no option, it seems.'

Frowning at the upended mattress and the bedsprings, Bertha said, 'What on earth is going on?'

'You'd better ask my newly appointed companion,' Jessica told her. 'She's determined to air the bed properly. Or so she says.'

'Air the bed? What nonsense! When are you supposed to get back into it?'

'When she gets back from Icklesham. She's posting my letters for me. Don't ask me why, Bertha, because I don't know. You chose the girl. I didn't.'

'Oliver chose her, Mama. I had no say in the matter. If you remember, I did not approve of the idea from the beginning and I was certainly not consulted. Oliver has been very high-handed over the whole affair.'

'I had no say in the matter either.' Jessica's mouth tightened. 'Oliver made it clear that you found looking after me tiresome. That you were always complaining about your dreary life.'

Bertha's expression hardened. 'You mean I'm hardly the dutiful daughter! Perhaps you're right there. Perhaps I would rather be a married woman with a home of my own but you seem determined to—'

'Don't!' Jessica cried. 'I cannot bear any more fruitless discussion on that subject. I am only thinking of your happiness.'

'If I had married when I wanted to you would have needed a companion by now. At least Oliver can see that I need some time for myself.'

Jessica breathed rapidly, one hand to her heart. 'Oliver gave me to understand that *you* thought I should have a companion – presumably because you had tired of the job.'

Bertha felt herself flush under her mother's renewed criticism. 'I may have said that I felt like a paid companion. That is not quite the same as wanting one. I'm not sure that the experiment is going to prove successful. Miss Blake's presence irritates me and her constant cheerfulness is becoming wearing in the extreme. Also, we seem to have no privacy.'

Jessica gave her a triumphant smile. 'Well, she's here now and you have only yourselves to blame. We'll just have to make the most of a bad job.'

Bertha suddenly saw that it was in her own interest to keep Miss Blake. Unbeknown to her mother she now had another suitor and was once again hoping to escape the claustrophobic confines of Fairfields. Bertha thought quickly. She pulled up a chair and sat down beside her mother. 'So you don't like Miss Blake.'

Jessica hesitated. 'You're putting words into my mouth. I have an open mind.'

'You said originally that you liked the look of her.'

Jessica rolled her eyes. 'I didn't know she was going to be so . . . so forceful. She's beginning to bully me.' Her lips quivered.

Bertha recognised the signs. Her mother loved the role of long-suffering victim and there was only one way to deal with that. 'Then Miss Blake must go,' Bertha said quickly. 'I'll tell her when she gets back. She can pack her things.'

Jessica looked startled. 'Go? You can't sack the girl. She's only been here a few days!'

'But if she's bullying you, Mama . . .'

'Oh don't be so foolish, Bertha. I was exaggerating. You know me. She means well, I daresay.'

They lapsed into silence. Jessica turned to stare out of the window and Bertha watched her curiously. The idea of a companion had been Oliver's but it was true he'd been goaded by Bertha's constant complaints. Somehow the idea had taken shape with the result that Chloe was among them, for better or worse. The reality was strangely disturbing. She was a stranger in the house. A cuckoo in the nest. Well meaning, perhaps, but what did they really know about her?

'Do you trust her, Mother?' she asked.

'What an odd question . . . Do I trust her? I suppose so. Don't you?'

Bertha frowned. 'Binns says he's promised to teach her to drive the dog cart. I can't think why.'

'She's making a big secret out of it, I know that much.'
Jessica tutted. 'She says it will make her more useful and I
daresay that's true.'

'Useful? But what's the point when we have Binns?
Where will she go? What will she do?'

'Perhaps she's going to kidnap me!'

With surprise Bertha saw that her mother was smiling. It
made her look so much younger.

She found herself returning the smile. 'Maybe she'll elope
with Oliver!' she suggested.

Jessica's smile broadened. 'Or your Uncle Matty!'

They both laughed aloud at the vision this created and
Bertha wondered how long it had been since they had shared
a joke. Too long, she thought guiltily. Over the past few
years the relationship between them had soured, turning to
the beginning of resentment on both sides.

Jessica said, 'Pass me my sewing bag, Bertha.' When
this was in her lap she pulled out the small tapestry she
was working on and said, 'Since you are here you might as
well thread my needle.' While Bertha did this her mother
went on. 'I know Miss Blake is a trifle unpredictable but
I think we must give her a fair trial. Oliver mentioned a
six-week period. After that she either stays with us or she
leaves.'

'She's very young.' Bertha realised, even as she said
it, that she envied Chloe her youth. She also envied her
freedom, her obvious joy of life and her prospects of
marriage. When she did find a man that she could love
she had no mother to dissuade her from her choice. No
father to insist that she was too young to know her own
mind or advise that she wait for a better offer. With a
bitter twist of her mouth, Bertha pushed back the unhappy
memories raised by this line of thought. Was there a young
man eager to marry Chloe Blake? Maybe when she knew
her better she could ask her.

'Her brother-in-law's a clergyman so I daresay she's
honest enough.' Bertha handed over needle and thread and

23

stood up. 'I must check the menu with Mrs Letts. Did you know, Mama, that you're to have meat roll today like the rest of us?'

Jessica's eyes widened. 'Meat roll? But it's Wednesday. I have an omelette on Wednesday. I never have meat roll. It's much too rich for my digestion.'

Bertha was enjoying her mother's startled expression. 'Miss Blake says your diet is too bland and that's why you have no appetite and no stamina. So today you'll have meat roll, creamed potatoes and carrots like the rest of us.' Whether you like it or not, she added silently. Miss Blake was certainly a force to be reckoned with, but was that necessarily a good thing? Life at Fairfields had progressed smoothly for many years and no one had questioned the familiar routine.

She turned back at the door. 'Kill or cure, Mama!' she said and went downstairs with a smile on her face.

Chloe climbed into the dog cart with Binns' help. The cart was painted a sensible brown and the horse, an elderly roan, was a near match except for a streak of white on one foreleg.

Binns beamed at her. His round face was ruddy, his hair dark beneath his cap. The sleeves of his jacket were too short and he seemed to be bursting from his clothes. Perhaps Mrs Letts was feeding him too well, Chloe thought with amusement. Gardeners were traditionally offered most of the leftovers.

'I been awaiting for you!' Binns told her in a slow drawl. 'Poor old Neddy's been that fidgety.'

'Neddy?' Chloe laughed. 'Not a very original name.'

It was such a warm day and their journey so short that Chloe had not bothered with her jacket but had tossed a lightweight shawl around her shoulders. As the horse trotted along the road the breeze whipped at her hair and touched the high lace collar at her throat. From the corner of her eye she saw Binns take more than one sly glance at her.

Was Binns walking out with a young lady? she wondered. He was cheerful enough and seemed good-natured but a certain vagueness in his eyes suggested that he might not be very bright.

'What's your Christian name, Binns?' she asked.

'Alfred, after my pa.' He seemed flattered by her interest. 'I be nineteen come Christmas and my great-grandfather was a gipsy. Caravan, he had, an' everything. But his son, my grandfather, he married out of the tribe, see. They never forgave him. He became a butcher.'

'How interesting. I don't suppose you ever met your great-grandfather.'

'Never, more's the pity.' Binns reined in to let a small herd of cows cross the road. A farmhand brought up the rear. 'He was dead afore I was born. Killed in a knife fight with his cousin. Right tearaways, the Binns. We're a very warlike family.'

He said this proudly and Chloe decided he must be a throwback. Anyone less warlike than Alfred Binns would be hard to find.

The farmhand touched his cap by way of salute and Binns said, 'Hey there, Tom!' As the man fastened the gate the dog cart rolled forward once more.

Binns said, 'He's one of Denbury's men. Tom Widden. Used to be postman in Rye 'til they found he was on the take and sacked him.'

'You know him, then?'

'Went to the same school, didn't we.'

She nodded her understanding. 'So are you walking out, Binns?'

He blushed. 'I'm giving it some thought,' he told her with a shy grin.

'I thought perhaps you and Hettie . . .?'

'She's a decent little body and I daresay she's smitten with me but I don't know. Ma says I shouldn't be in no hurry yet awhile.'

'Very wise. You must take your time.'

Chloe felt by this time that she had done enough prying and fell silent. Her mother had told her many times that she was too inquisitive but she could rarely deny her natural curiosity. Now, however, she turned her thoughts to the mysterious envelope Uncle Matty had thrust into her pocket.

'Give it to the postie in Icklesham,' he had whispered. 'He'll know what to do with it. And not a word to anyone or I'll be for the high jump!'

Holding the envelope to the light had revealed nothing because the contents were so thin. One folded sheet of notepaper, she supposed. Perhaps Uncle Matty was courting the postman's sister. She smiled at the thought.

'Uh-oh!' Binns muttered.

Chloe saw a burly man coming towards them. He was carrying a shotgun and a grey lurcher dog ran beside him. He scowled at Binns as their eyes met and then gave Chloe a quick glance. Despite the mild weather he wore a long shapeless coat and a large brimmed hat.

'That's Sid Jakes,' Binns volunteered. 'Gamekeeper to the Denburys.'

'Does everyone work for Denbury?'

'Mostly. He's the biggest farmer in these parts, that's why.'

'Jakes looked rather mean.'

'He's a nasty piece of work. I wouldn't like to get the wrong side of him.'

'You know him as well, then.'

'Know of him, more like. Bit of a ruffian on the quiet, he is. Used to be a wrestler but he half killed a man and was locked up in the Ypres Tower in Rye. Then he got six months.'

Chloe turned to watch the man and was disconcerted to see that Jakes had turned and was watching them. When he caught Chloe's eye he raised a fist.

She said, 'What a horrible man. Do you know many like him?'

Chloe had meant it humorously but Binns shook his head. 'Not many. There's plenty of better folk hereabouts. Met the blacksmith, have you? He's a decent sort of chap.'

'Not yet. Is he good at his job?'

'Good enough. Doing our gates at Fairfields, he is, and the railings. Leastways he will if the mistress says he may knock down the old wall.'

'It does look the worse for wear,' Chloe agreed. 'So he doesn't just shoe horses.'

Binns laughed. 'No he don't. Fact is he don't ever shoe them. See, he's not a farrier. 'Tis the wrought iron he likes. Make anything out of iron, he can. I've watched him in the forge, hammering away like his life depended on it.' He turned to offer her a gap-toothed grin. 'I knows a thing about him. I've seen him looking at her. Looking at her in that special way.' He waved his whip in the direction of the horse and it flicked the animal's flank. 'Come up, Neddy, you lazy devil!' For a few seconds the horse moved at a faster pace but soon dropped back to an effortless trot.

'Looking at who?' Chloe prompted, intrigued in spite of herself.

'Miss Hoity-Toity!' He laughed. 'Miss Maitland. Who else?'

Chloe was torn. Oliver had warned her not to gossip with the servants but this was irresistible. 'So he admires her,' she said.

'Admires? Huh!' He tossed his head. 'Soft on her, I'd say. Mooning over her. Can't see why. I mean, Miss Maitland's no spring chicken and she—'

'Binns!' She felt reluctantly obliged to protest. 'You shouldn't speak of her that way. It's disrespectful.'

'Disrespectful? How can that be? She can't hear me.'

His logic defeated her and Chloe thought she had better change the subject, but before she could do so he went on.

'Mrs Letts says as how she should have wed long ago. A soldier, he was, and they was made for each other.

Leastways that's what Mrs Letts says and she should know. She was here when he was killed.'

'I heard. Poor Miss Maitland.'

'Poor him, more like. 'Twas him that died. Not that she could have wed him, for they said he wasn't near good enough for her. Not by a half!'

'In what way not good enough?'

Binns touched his cap as they passed a governess cart containing three young men. Chloe nodded politely.

'Not a real officer,' Binns told her. 'Leastways not a high-up officer. Not a gentleman.'

Chloe tried to imagine a younger Bertha struggling unsuccessfully with her mother over her suitor. She was still thinking about it when they reached the small hamlet of Icklesham and the horse slowed to a halt outside the post office. Chloe climbed down and thrust Jessica's letters into the pillar box.

Mr Cross came hurrying out of the post office.

'Miss Chloe! What are you doing in these parts? I thought you'd left home?'

'I have,' she told him, 'but I haven't gone far. I'm a companion to Mrs Maitland at Fairfield House.' She indicated Binns with a wave of her hand. 'This is Mr Binns, the gardener-cum-groom.'

Binns doffed his cap and the two men exchanged nods.

Chloe said, 'I want a penn'orth of your chocolate drops for Mrs Maitland,' and followed him back inside the little shop. Inside it took a moment for Chloe's eyes to adjust to the gloom after the brightness of the June sunshine.

The post office was nothing more than Mr Cross's parlour, decked out with shelves and a counter on which stood a pair of scales and a cash box. Tin kettles hung from the ceiling alongside watering cans. In the corner of the floor dust pans and brushes jostled with bundles of kindling wood, and a large tortoiseshell cat slept on top of a sack of corn meal. The air was scented with dry wood, candles and peppermint. The shelves groaned under the weight of sweet jars – humbugs, pear drops, violet cachous, aniseed balls, licorice strips, broken toffee and much more. Mr Cross reached for one of the jars and weighed out the required chocolate drops.

'Your sister was in this morning,' he told her. 'Still keeping cheerful, is she?'

'Oh yes! Dorothy rarely gets downhearted.'

They both knew this to be untrue. Dorothy's inability to have a child was a great sorrow to her and in a small village everyone knew everyone else's business. It was common knowledge that she had failed to give her husband children.

The chocolate drops were tipped into a twist of paper and the penny duly paid. When Chloe glanced at the post office clock she frowned.

'Oh no! It's taken longer than I thought. I shan't have time to call in on Dorothy, but I must find the postman.'

Leaving Binns to wait in the dog cart, Chloe hurried along the lane opposite the church. At the third cottage she stopped and unlatched the small gate. She ran down the path and knocked on the door. It was opened by Daniel Cobbet, who delivered the post.

'Miss Chloe!' he cried. 'I thought you'd gone into service.'

Chloe explained again and then produced the envelope Uncle Matty had given her. 'Mr Orme asked me to give you this and to say he might be along tomorrow or he might not and that you'd know what he means.'

He laughed as he took it then put a finger to his lips. 'Oh I know, don't you fret. Tell him I'll see to it same as usual.'

'All very mysterious!'

'Men's work!' He winked. 'Less you know the better, Miss Blake.'

As Chloe hurried back to Binns she wondered afresh about the envelope and its contents then resigned herself to the fact that she might never know.

'We'd best get a move on,' she announced as Binns hauled

29

her back on to the seat beside him. 'I told Mrs Maitland I'd only be gone half an hour.'

He grinned as he urged the horse to a trot. 'You might want to hurry and so might I, but the horse don't never want to.'

He was right. They arrived back at a leisurely trot, ten minutes late.

Later that afternoon, while Jessica was taking her nap, Chloe found Bertha in the garden with a large sacking apron covering her dark skirt. Binns was weeding on the far side of the lawn while Bertha wielded a large watering can.

'The cuttings need regular watering,' she told Chloe, straightening up and putting a hand to her back. 'They don't have much in the way of roots until they get established. Are you interested in plants?'

'My family originally lived in Hastings and we only had a backyard. Of course Dorothy has a garden now that she's married.'

'Ah yes. The rectory garden.'

'It's mostly shrubs so she does a bit of weeding. That's all.'

Bertha looked round. 'It's a never-ending task with a garden this size. I've told Oliver we need a second gardener or a lad to help Binns but he won't make a decision. But that's Oliver for you. What does he care? He's in London most of the time. If he were here more he could help me.' She pursed her lips. 'I sometimes wish he didn't have this place in London. He's gone back again today. Caught the two seventeen from Rye.' She drew off her gloves and regarded her hands, flexing her fingers. 'Oliver can be very selfish. He never shares the flat. He says it's not big enough or he's got a friend staying. Grandfather left him money for an allowance so he can do what he likes within reason.'

They began to walk in the direction of one of the garden seats and, reaching it, sat down in the welcome shade. The rhododendrons brightened the area with splashes of pink and crimson and on the far side of the garden a jay strutted across the grass.

'What's it like?' Chloe was curious about Oliver's 'other' life. She liked what she knew of him but she had no idea how he lived his life when he was absent from Fairfield House.

'I've never even seen it. He calls it a studio. Apparently it's rather poky but has a large north-facing window which is ideal for his painting.'

'Oliver's an artist?'

'He studied art but he doesn't sell much – or if he does we never hear about it. His work's not bad, in fact, but he can't be bothered to sell it. No business sense.' Bertha sighed. 'The portrait over the mantelpiece in the drawing room is one of his.'

'The seated woman?' Chloe was surprised. It was above average in her opinion although she was no expert when it came to art. Changing the subject, she said, 'I caught a glimpse of the blacksmith by the gate when we came back from Icklesham. He looked very smart.'

Was it her imagination or was Bertha blushing?

'George Brier is extremely talented,' Bertha told her. 'He works with his elderly uncle but he'll take over the business before long. Mama wanted him to repair the gates – they're rusting away and don't close properly. But I told her we need more than that. He's designed a new pair of gates and railings. Even the wall is in a poor way and may have to be knocked down. It could be a lot of work but it would transform the approach to the house.'

'Is Mr Brier doing drawings?'

'He's done them. Oliver offered to design something simple but I talked him out of it. He'd take forever and they wouldn't be as good as Mr Brier's. He's an expert and the work's already under way. Oliver would still be thinking about it!'

Chloe sprang to his defence. 'Poor Oliver. What do they say about prophets? They are without honour in their own country!' She suddenly recalled what Binns had said

31

about George Brier and Bertha, and decided to return to the subject. 'I could see something happening down there when we drove back.'

Bertha's expression changed into one of eagerness. 'He's working down there now. Would you like to see what he's doing? I could take you down there.'

Minutes later they were standing beside George Brier, who held a rolled blueprint in his hand. Bertha introduced them and Chloe saw a man totally at odds with her image of a blacksmith. George Brier was a slight man with pale blue eyes and smooth fair hair. He had a small clipped moustache and a pale complexion. His voice, too, was soft. The arms of his white shirt were rolled to the elbows and he wore a plain dark tie. His waistcoat was neatly buttoned.

He and Bertha seemed quite at ease with each other, Chloe noted. Plenty of smiles.

He willingly unrolled the plans and he and Bertha held one corner each as they pressed it flat against the gate so that Chloe could study it.

''Tis hardly a set of railings,' he told Chloe gently. 'More a wrought-iron screen – though a short one, 'tis true. Miss Maitland thought . . . That is, the family thought a brick column at the outer ends would be enough as we're now lowering the height of the wall to allow higher railings, which will form the screen. Much more elegant.' He stabbed a slim finger at various points on the plan and then pointed to a chalked cross on the existing wall.

Bertha said, 'It will be much lighter in construction yet will last longer.'

'Does Oliver like the design?'

Bertha exchanged a glance with George Brier. 'I didn't ask him because he wasn't here. He doesn't take much interest, to be truthful.'

'And yet he's artistic. You'd expect him to—'

'If it isn't in London, Oliver doesn't get involved.'

The blacksmith said, 'Miss Maitland has done most of the work. She has a good eye and we've taken our time over it. No point in rushing something that's going to last for hundreds of years.'

'Certainly not.' Chloe smiled.

He went on eagerly. 'Two panels of palisades here and here . . . then the gates with a frontispiece and—'

'Please!' Chloe protested with a laugh. 'I don't understand.'

'I'm sorry. Palisades are probably railings to you. A frontispiece is the design on the entrance gates themselves. Something in the middle of each gate and then the motif will be repeated above the gate. On the rest of the screen there'll be a decorative frieze.'

He was obviously – and justifiably – proud of the design.

Bertha said, 'Not so grand as to appear pretentious but good enough to enhance the property.'

She and Brier exchanged what Chloe could only consider a conspiratorial look and for a moment she felt a stab of envy. These two shared confidences. She was sure of it.

Chloe said, 'And you, Miss Maitland, will be overseeing the work, presumably.'

Bertha nodded. 'I'll be a terrible taskmaster.'

The blacksmith looked unimpressed by the threat and Chloe saw that this way the two of them could spend time together without arousing adverse comment from the rest of the family. Clever Bertha.

Later, as they walked back along the gravelled drive, Chloe said, 'What a charming man – and so talented.' Bertha's sigh was heartfelt. 'Where did he learn his skills?'

'He was apprenticed to his uncle for seven years. During that time he won several prizes for his work. Now he's setting up on his own. He needs this type of commission – partly for the money, of course, and partly for the prestige. He needs to be able to show future clients previously completed work. He's still quite young.'

Chloe was beginning to suspect Bertha's dilemma. 'How young?' she asked innocently.

33

There was a pause until Bertha said quietly, 'He's five years younger than me.'

A fact which Bertha's mother has no doubt mentioned, thought Chloe. 'But he's obviously got a splendid career ahead of him.'

'Try telling that to Mama!' Bertha clapped a hand over her mouth but the words were out. From the corner of her eye Chloe saw Bertha give a startled look in her direction.

After a moment Chloe said, 'That sounded like a cry from the heart.'

As one, the two women stopped, yards from the front steps. Slowly their eyes met.

'I shouldn't have said that,' Bertha stammered. 'Please forget what I—'

'Why should I, Bertha? I'm a woman too. I understand these things.'

Bertha clasped and unclasped her hands. 'You have an admirer, I suppose. A young woman like you.'

'No one. I don't wish to marry just yet. I have other plans . . .'

'You don't wish to marry? But why? What can you—'

'I have to travel first. I have to go to North America. That's all I can say. After that I may well hope to settle down.' She smiled. 'If you ever need someone to confide in you can trust me, Bertha.'

She saw indecision, even reluctance, in Bertha's eyes but with it a longing to share her hopes and fears. As the silence lengthened, Bertha glanced guiltily towards the house as though she feared her mother's watchful eyes.

Chloe said, 'It's a mild evening. Shall we take a look at the rhododendrons?' and rolled her eyes meaningfully.

When Bertha didn't answer Chloe thought she had gone too far but suddenly she said, 'Very well.'

They walked in silence. Chloe knew what a step it would be for Bertha to confide in her mother's companion – a virtual stranger – but she obviously had no one else to whom she could talk. Chloe, aware of her own close relationship with Dorothy, felt a wave of sympathy for the lonely woman. Oliver was presumably unwilling to listen to her problems. Maybe he had some of his own, which he played close to his chest. The Maitlands seemed less a family and more a group of separate souls.

Bertha stared straight ahead as they crossed the lawn. 'George – we're on first-name terms – is very . . . fond of me. And I feel a great deal for him. We met three years ago when I visited friends in Rye. He was making them a weathervane and a sundial and they told me how clever he was. We met again at a local fair where he was exhibiting some of his work. I'd persuaded Oliver to take me.'

She looked at Chloe with shining eyes. 'We just knew immediately that we were attracted to each other. Then, for a few months, I didn't see him again and I felt so desperate. When he wrote to me, asking if we could meet somewhere, I didn't dare say yes without Mama's permission. She was horrified, of course.' They stopped beside the old swing and Bertha clung to one of the ropes. 'She said she couldn't allow it. He's too young. He's too poor. He's not "our sort of person". The same old story.'

Chloe said nothing about the earlier relationship because she was not supposed to know. 'I'm so sorry,' she said, genuinely touched by the woman's plight.

Bertha faced her. 'We write to each other. I have to make sure that I get to the letters first. Of course Mama doesn't come downstairs but Oliver would disapprove on principle. He's Mama's darling boy! Oh dear!' She covered her face briefly with her hands then looked at Chloe. 'That was unkind of me. I'm sorry. But it's true. Oliver is the favourite. He can go off to London and do whatever he pleases because he's a man while I am . . .' She swallowed hard. 'I'm needed here. That's the phrase. There was another man, years ago. He would have been promoted in time but my parents refused to consider him. I'm the daughter. I was born to make the sacrifices. It's so terribly unfair!'

'It is. I agree.'

Bertha began to twist the ropes of the swing together. 'I wouldn't mind quite so much if I were truly needed but Mama isn't ill. She took to her bed when Papa died and that was understandable. Grief needs careful handling and the doctor recommended bedrest.'

'But she stayed there.'

'Yes. Days became weeks and then months.'

'I'm doing my best to get her out of it,' Chloe told her, a wicked glint in her eye.

Bertha smiled. 'I've noticed a few changes.' The smile broadened. 'The meat roll must have come as a shock!'

Chloe laughed. 'Actually she enjoyed it but she couldn't bring herself to say so. But she cleared the plate and so far there have been no ill effects.'

'You seem to have a way with you.'

'My mother was a genuine invalid for four years. Anyway it's always easier for a stranger. There's a natural distance between us. I'm just doing what I'm paid to do so there's nothing personal. Except that I like your mother.'

Bertha released the twisted ropes and the wooden seat began to spin and instinctively both women stepped back out of range. Leaving the swing to its own devices, they began to retrace their steps.

Chloe said, 'Would you marry George if he asked you?'

'He has asked me and I said I would – if ever I could persuade Mama to allow it. But I'm sure she will never agree. Too demeaning to see her daughter married beneath her! She was the same when I was a girl and wanted to bring home my school friends. They had to be vetted. Poor Evelyn. Her father was a baker so she was discouraged. Oh, she came to tea once but Mama gave her such a difficult time. Asking awkward questions. You can imagine. Evelyn never came again.' She sighed. 'Parents can be a trial.'

'So did she say no? Your mother, I mean.'

'I haven't dared to ask her. She is still hoping I'll change my mind about Miles Sandford. He's the son of an old friend of the family but such a bore. If I accepted him Mama would be delighted but it's out of the question.'

'Is he rich? Is that it?'

'Rich and well-connected. Hunts, mingles with the aristocracy . . . and is fat, forty and bald!'

Chloe laughed. 'I see your point. But all the time your mother hasn't said no there's a chance for George Brier, isn't there?'

Bertha shrugged. 'I'm afraid that once I ask her she'll say no and maybe cancel the gates. Then how can we meet?'

As they reached the steps for the second time Chloe said, 'Do you need her permission, Bertha? You're not under twenty-one, are you?'

'How I wish I were!' Bertha stopped in her tracks. 'Defy Mama? Is that what you mean?'

'That's exactly what I mean. If I were in love I don't think I'd let anyone come between us. What could she do to you?'

'She'd do plenty! You don't know her yet. She wants me to stay at home and look after her.'

'But you're not doing that any more. I am.'

'You might leave.'

'She could find another companion.'

Bertha shook her head. 'It's out of the question.'

Chloe smiled. 'I'm sure we can think of a way. I'll put on my thinking cap – and you do the same. And see if Mr Brier has any ideas.' Her smile deepened. 'He really is a most charming man. Don't give up so easily, Bertha. There's always a way.'

They went up the steps into the house and separated. Bertha went to her room and Chloe went to see how her companion was getting on without her.

Jessica had fallen asleep with her book open on her lap. Chloe regarded the slumbering figure with a calculating eye.

'I'm going to bring you back to the land of the living,' she whispered. 'Whether you like it or not!'

* * *

Friday the thirteenth of June. But not an unlucky day, thank goodness. I'm going to like it here. Plenty to think about. I can manage Jessica, and even Bertha is beginning to trust me. George Brier seems a very suitable man for her. If only Bertha wasn't so cowardly where her mother is concerned. The new gates are going to look wonderful. At least I think so. Haven't seen much of Uncle Matty but he seems harmless enough. Poor soul reminds me of a fish, with his wide mouth and slightly bulbous eyes. I took a mysterious letter for him to the postman in Icklesham. Oliver is off to London again. I doubt if I shall see him much, which is a shame because I do find him attractive. He lives alone but no doubt he has plenty of lady friends. I tell myself not to harbour any ideas. I am only a glorified servant. I wonder why he doesn't paint in this area. Plenty of beautiful scenery not to mention Rye and the harbour. Perhaps he only paints portraits. I wish I could think of an excuse to visit him in his London studio and find out for myself. It's strange that his mother doesn't want him to wed. He might provide her with grandchildren. As matters stand, the Fairfield branch of the Maitland family could possibly die out!

Three

Saturday was very quiet. Oliver had returned to London and his artistic endeavours. Jessica grumbled about his absence but without much real conviction. When he was around she complained that he was wasting his time and should be painting but when he was away she missed him. Bertha and Uncle Matty were around somewhere and Jessica and Chloe were busy with a large jigsaw of Westminster Abbey.

Jessica was sitting at a small table with Chloe opposite. The corners of the jigsaw had been completed and the top of Big Ben was coming into view when, just before twelve, there was a knock on the door.

Mrs Letts came in looking very red in the face. 'It's Hettie, ma'am. I'm a bit worried . . . That is, she's behaving . . . I mean, that girl's in trouble.'

Chloe stood up. 'I'd better leave you two alone,' she suggested.

'Don't be silly, child!' Jessica indicated that she should sit again. 'I tell you whether to stay or go.' She turned to Mrs Letts. 'You're not making much sense. Start again, please.'

It seemed that Hettie was behaving in a very suspicious manner.

Jessica's eyes widened. 'Suspicious? You mean she's *stolen* something? Hettie? Are you sure?'

Mrs Letts folded her arms. 'I almost wish it was that, ma'am, but it's worse.'

Chloe closed her eyes. It could only be one thing.

'Worse? Well, go on for heaven's sake, woman. What has the girl done?'

'It's not what she's done it's . . . what a gentleman has done to her. She's been putting on weight for some time and now I hear that she had some sickness on and off. It suddenly came to me . . . what might be the trouble. I think Hettie's . . . well, to put it bluntly, is in a certain condition, ma'am, or I'm a Dutchman!'

There was a long shocked silence. Then Jessica said, 'Hettie? But she's not courting. Not to my knowledge.' Slowly Jessica turned to Chloe. 'Is it possible?' she asked. 'The girl's hardly a woman. How old is she – seventeen? Eighteen? She doesn't *know* any men.'

Mrs Letts shrugged plump shoulders. 'Girls these days . . .' She left the rest to their imagination.

Chloe said, 'Has Hettie agreed that she might be with child? Has she agreed that she has been with a man?'

'No to both questions,' Mrs Letts told her. 'Either she doesn't believe me or she's very ignorant. Or she's pretending to herself that it hasn't happened.'

The three women looked at each other and Jessica put a hand to her head.

'I feel a trifle dizzy,' she murmured. 'I think I am going to need my sal volatile.'

Chloe hurried to the bedside table to find it, her mind busy on possibilities. Who were the weekly tradesmen who called at the servants' quarters? The butcher's lad – no more than sixteen years old. Possible. The fishmonger – a man in his thirties with a wife and child. Hardly likely but who knows? The coalman – never allowed to set foot in the kitchen for fear of the coal dust he shed as he walked.

Perhaps it was someone she met on her days off when she allegedly returned home.

Chloe held the small bottle beneath Jessica's nose and said, 'Don't breathe too deeply.' As a child she had experimented with her own mother's sal volatile and had never forgotten the effect it had had on her. After a danger-ously deep sniff, the young Chloe was soon coughing and spluttering and her eyes had streamed tears for what seemed hours afterwards.

Fortunately Jessica's recovery was speedy and she sat up again, a hand to her heart. 'I don't feel able to deal with this,' she said. 'Chloe, go and find Bertha. She must talk to Hettie. You'll probably find her talking to that dreadful blacksmith.'

Chloe stared at her with exaggerated shock. 'The black-smith? George Brier? I thought him a most charming man – and very talented. I'll certainly look there first.'

As she left the room she heard Jessica berating the housekeeper for 'not keeping an eye on the girl'. A tri-fle unfair, she thought, but certainly no one could blame Jessica herself.

And there was Binns, of course. Why had no one thought of him? He was around all the time and had every oppor-tunity to lead Hettie astray. Not that I'll mention your name, she told the absent Binns. But if he was responsible there would be further heartache. How could any young woman face life with a man like that? And what kind of father would he make?

As Jessica had predicted, Chloe found Bertha talking to the blacksmith and an older man she had not seen previously. Taking Bertha discreetly to one side she passed on the message from Jessica.

Bertha's face fell. 'Why should *I* have to deal with it?' she cried. 'Mama is so unfair. I am not to meddle in the affairs of the staff – until something unpleasant occurs. And then suddenly I'm expected to deal with it.' She glanced at the blacksmith as though reluctant to leave him. Brier was concentrating on the work at hand, which was the beginning of the demolition of the wall.

Chloe saw that the older man now wielded a huge mallet. Each thundering blow sent up dust and fragments of brick and created new cracks in the brickwork.

41

Bertha's mouth tightened. 'Please tell Mama that I am supervising this work but I will speak to Hettie later.' She glanced at the blacksmith again and whispered, 'Much later.'

This reply, when passed on to Jessica, did not go down at all well. Jessica clutched her heart and gasped for breath. 'Oh that daughter of mine! She does this to annoy me. She knows the state of my health yet she persists in this perverse behaviour. Well, you will have to talk to Hettie, Chloe. I am going back to my bed. This has been a shock and I need to rest.'

To Chloe's surprise she then stood up and took the five steps back to her bed unaided. Chloe made a mental note of this startling progress but said nothing.

Downstairs she found Hettie sulking in the kitchen and took her into the drawing room for the tête-à-tête that Jessica had decreed. Not that Chloe felt qualified to discuss such an intimate matter, for she herself was very untutored in sexual matters, but she had never been one to dodge difficult issues.

She sat Hettie down in an armchair and took her place opposite her. Hettie's eyes were red-rimmed but the rest of her face was pale. Chloe was fascinated by her. Had this young maid actually discovered the mysteries of a man with a woman? The word 'sex' had never passed Chloe's lips although she had tried more than once to imagine what went on between Dorothy and Albert in the privacy of their bedroom.

'Nothing's happened,' Hettie insisted in answer to Chloe's first question. 'I never did anything and nor did anyone else. Mrs Letts has got a nasty mind to think such things. When I tell my ma she'll take it very hard.'

'You may be right, Hettie,' Chloe told her quietly. 'Maybe nothing has happened. Maybe you are not with child. Would you like to know for certain?'

'Nothing's happened. He said nothing would—' She stopped abruptly and colour flooded her face.

42

Chloe sighed. 'So something *has* happened. Who is it, Hettie? We have to know sooner or later.'

Hettie's small mouth tightened stubbornly. 'I'm not saying. I have to talk to him. I have to tell him first.'

'Is it Binns?' She crossed her fingers.

Hettie cried, 'Binns?' and her expression was sufficient answer.

'Then is it one of the tradesmen?'

Hettie shook her head.

'Look Hettie,' Chloe said patiently. 'Whoever it is we have to know what has happened. The doctor can put your mind at rest.'

'The doctor? We don't have no truck with doctors,' Hettie protested, her voice rising. 'My ma says they're no better than—'

'I'll speak to your mother . . .'

'She won't listen.'

'Hettie!' Chloe counted to ten. 'Do you want to lose your job?'

'Lose my job?' Hettie regarded her indignantly. 'Course I don't. My ma—'

'Then you must go to the doctor. I'll come with you if you like. If nothing's happened to you the doctor will know. Then we can all forget about it.' That was a lie, Chloe thought, but it must suffice for the time being. 'It's a very serious thing, Hettie. Mrs Maitland is responsible for you while you work for her. She can't ignore what Mrs Letts has said. And if you are going to have a baby we must tell the baby's father so that you can be married. You'd like that, wouldn't you?' She expected some enthusiasm at this prospect but Hettie's expression had changed to one of sullen resentment. 'Will you see the doctor, Hettie? If not we'll be forced to speak to your mother.'

'No! She'll tell Pa and he'll wallop me! My sister—' She stopped abruptly.

'Did your sister have a baby?'

Hettie nodded.

'But we must tell your mother, Hettie. She'll want to help you.'

Faced with this prospect, Hettie's face crumpled and tears spilled from her eyes. Chloe gave her a handkerchief and watched while the girl dabbed at her eyes.

'Don't worry, Hettie,' she said gently. 'Whatever happens you'll be looked after. Tell Mrs Letts that we're going to the doctor on Monday. A baby isn't the end of the world, you know. Many young girls like you have babies and they get used to the idea – and they love them.'

The ghost of a smile appeared on Hettie's face and Chloe's heart ached for her. With a sigh she sent her back to the kitchen and made her way upstairs to make her report to Jessica Maitland.

Later that afternoon Chloe had an idea which she believed was a modest brainwave. She asked Mrs Letts if she knew her employer's birthday.

'Birthday? Well, now you've got me.' Mrs Letts paused in her work, knife in hand over a bowl of sliced apples. 'I know it's in the summer . . . Yes, because one year we had a birthday picnic. I'm going back years, of course, when she was fit and able. It must have been July but when I couldn't say. Ask Miss Bertha. She'll know.'

Chloe hadn't wished to disturb Bertha and George Brier – who had little enough time together – but now, reluctantly, she made her way along the drive towards them. Work was continuing on the demolished wall. Two men were extricating the old railings from the pile of broken bricks and loading them into a small wagon. The blacksmith was drinking lemonade from a jug Chloe recognised from the kitchen and Bertha was talking to him with obvious animation.

Chloe smiled at both of them and said, 'Good morning, Mr Brier. You're making headway here, I see.'

Bertha said, 'He was here at seven this morning.'

The blacksmith glanced at the sky. 'I reckoned we'd have rain later.'

Chloe nodded and turned to Bertha. 'I'm wondering if I could have a word about your mother's birthday.'

Bertha looked surprised but tactfully the blacksmith wandered away to inspect his ruined wall.

Chloe began in a rush. 'I thought that if you and Oliver could commission her portrait, as a birthday present, she would be obliged to rise and dress regularly so that she could sit for the artist.'

Bertha looked blank. 'A portrait of Mama? I doubt she'll agree. She was very beautiful in her youth apparently but now that she's older . . .' She shrugged. 'What put this idea into your head?'

'I'm doing whatever I can to help her forget that she's bedridden,' Chloe explained. 'When your brother interviewed me he suggested there is nothing actually wrong with her. Don't you think she should recover her strength and enjoy everyday life with the rest of us? The only reason she needs a companion is because she believes herself to be helpless.'

Bertha frowned. 'I see your point but we mustn't presume too much. I wouldn't like to put Mama under any strain. Any sudden shock—'

'Why would she have a sudden shock? She may appear fragile but I'm not totally convinced. And if she *were* to have a shock, the stronger she is the better, surely.'

Bertha found no answer to this logic and Chloe continued.

'She would only need to be taken downstairs to sit in a chair and look elegant and be fussed over by the artist. I think she might find it exciting. Something new to think about. If we appeal to her vanity . . .'

'You may be right.' Bertha's initial caution was giving way to be replaced by optimism.

Chloe raised her eyebrows. 'It might also occupy her mind. Less time for her to wonder what her daughter is up to!'

Bertha laughed. 'Chloe Blake, how persuasive you are!' she cried. 'But I do agree that we should put the idea to Oliver. I'll speak to him as soon as he returns.'

'When is he expected?' Chloe hoped she sounded casual. The truth was that she much preferred him to be around. She had no real hopes in that direction but a good-looking man was always interesting and, if she was honest, something of a challenge.

Bertha shrugged. 'There's no knowing with Oliver. Once he stayed away for three weeks and Mama was furious. Furious and frightened. She always thinks she may never set eyes on him again. When he didn't come home Mama suggested I should go to London in search of him. I wasn't happy about making the journey but a friend of mine from Rye was going up to do some shopping in Regent Street so we went together.'

'How was the train?' Chloe was curious.

'I wasn't exactly enamoured. Very busy, very noisy and too many fellow travellers. They warn against pickpockets at the stations and I did see some rough-looking men who looked thoroughly untrustworthy.'

'And London?'

'More of the same but I hailed a taxi to Oliver's place.'

'It's a studio, isn't it?'

'Apparently. Oliver's terribly secretive about it, which makes me suspect it's nothing more than a glorified attic and he's ashamed of it. I rang three times and eventually a foreign woman answered the door to me and seemed a little abrupt.'

'An elderly woman?' Chloe imagined her making her slow way down several flights of stairs.

Bertha shook her head. 'A rather handsome woman, probably a little older than Oliver – but she must have been the landlady, because Oliver lives alone. She pretended I had the wrong address but I checked when I came home and it *was* the right place.'

'So why the mystery?'

Bertha shrugged.

'Perhaps you should have waited around a little longer to see if he appeared.'

At once Chloe wanted to unsay the words but it was too late. She was being impertinent – a fault for which her mother had often criticised her. It was not her place to tell Bertha what she should have done.

Fortunately Bertha did not take exception to the remark but said, 'I did think about it but it was raining hard and I was tired so I gave up and came home.'

Chloe frowned. 'If her birthday is in July we don't have much—'

'July? No, Mama's birthday is the fourth of August. We could manage it.'

Inspiration struck again. Chloe said, 'I could go up to London and talk to Oliver. I know how busy you are with the supervision of the new gates.' She gave Bertha a conspiratorial smile, which was returned. 'We must persuade Oliver to help us. He might even know a portrait artist who would do it.'

Now that she had suggested a trip to London, Chloe was suddenly full of enthusiasm for the idea and anxious to be on her way. She would insist on being allowed in to Oliver's flat and would be the only person to have braved him in his lair!

After a short discussion of how it could be achieved it was decided. Bertha would pretend that Oliver wanted to see Chloe urgently in London. She would hint that it concerned Jessica's birthday – which it did. They would pretend that the portrait had been Oliver's idea.

'Mama will let you go,' Bertha assured Chloe. 'As long as the idea is his. I told you, he's her favourite.' She regarded Chloe with something approaching awe. 'Aren't you nervous about travelling alone?'

'Should I be?'

'I suppose not. There's a regular service from Rye or you can go from Hastings. Are you used to rail travel, Chloe?'

'Hardly. It will be my first train ride,' Chloe admitted, 'but I'll copy your example and take a taxi from the station straight to the studio.'

47

It was settled and Chloe began the walk back to the house. She was halfway across the lawn when she heard a low whistle which came from the direction of the shrubbery. She stopped, surprised. Was it Uncle Matty playing a joke? Or Binns? Assuming it to be one or the other Chloe gathered up her skirt and made her way across the lawn to the rhododendrons, which now lay in the deep shadow cast by the overhanging sycamores. 'Where are you?' she asked, peering into the gloom.

Without warning rough fingers grabbed her left arm in a painful grip. As she opened her mouth to protest a hand was clamped over her mouth and she was jerked sideways. She lost her balance and before she knew what was happening she was being dragged deeper into the shrubbery. She stumbled and fell to her knees on the damp leafy soil but now her attacker clutched a handful of her hair and dragged her painfully back to her feet.

The shock was total. Her heart pounded and fear flooded through her. Her legs scarcely supported her. The hand round her mouth relaxed and she stammered, 'Who are you? What—'

'Shut up and listen!' The voice was low and full of menace. 'And listen good!'

The voice was very close and the man's breath reeked of ale. He was drunk, she thought. Or mad? Was he going to kill her? 'Please don't—'

'Shut up! I'm doing the talking. You just listen.'

He was holding her so that her head was twisted away from his face and she had no chance to look at him but she saw a shotgun propped against the nearest tree and was filled with dread.

'You tell that blackguard Orme that I'm on to him,' he hissed. 'Tell him he's had his chance. His time's run out. Got that?' The hand tightened once more over her mouth so that she could only nod. 'Tell him I'm out here and I want to see him and sharp. If I don't get to talk to him, he'll regret it.'

Then he pushed her, stumbling and terrified, back towards the lawn and with a final shove sent her sprawling. As she fell she caught a glimpse of his face but almost at once he stepped backwards into the gloom and vanished.

For a moment she stayed where she was, desperately trying to recover her wits and allow her heart to resume its normal pace. Then carefully she dragged herself to her feet and took several deep breaths, thinking. The man had seemed vaguely familiar but she couldn't put a name to the face. Uncle Matty!' she whispered. 'What on earth have you got yourself into?'

With a quick glance behind her to make sure that her attacker was still out of sight, Chloe walked shakily towards the house, brushing leaves and grass from her clothes and telling herself that tears were inappropriate. She didn't think she had ever been so frightened. The sound of the coarse voice still echoed in her mind as she drew a handkerchief from her pocket and rubbed at her mouth, remembering with disgust the feel and smell of his hand.

By the time she regained the safety of the house she had recovered a little of her dignity and her fear was giving way to anger. Perhaps she should make a telephone call to the police, she thought. But how would that affect Uncle Matty?

So much for the 'grey sheep', she reflected. Perhaps he *was* more black than grey. Whatever he was, he had no right to involve her in his problems.

When she found him dozing in his armchair she longed to shake him.

'Wake up!' she demanded and waited, arms folded, for him to open his eyes. Seeing her, he smiled broadly.

'My dear Miss Blake—' he began.

'I'm not your dear anything.' Her eyes flashed. 'I've just been grabbed and shaken and pushed and . . . and *terrified* by a hulking great thug who wanted to give me a message for you!'

His smile vanished. His mouth fell open and he stared at her. 'A message for me?'

'Yes. Whoever it is says he's on to you and he's waiting under the sycamores . . . oh, and you've had your chance. So you'd better stir yourself and get down there or you'll live to regret it.'

Still trembling, she turned on her heel but Uncle Matty cried, 'Wait! Please!'

Something in his voice made her turn back. He had covered his mouth with one hand and his eyes were wide. 'This is very bad,' he told her. 'I can't go down there. You don't understand. That man's a thorough bounder. A rotten apple. He was born mean. He'd as soon shoot you as look at you!'

Chloe glared at him. 'You don't need to convince *me*. I've just discovered for myself what a nasty piece of work he is. He nearly pulled my hair out! And it's your fault. I don't know what you've done but he's very angry and he's waiting.'

Uncle Matty heaved himself from the chair and tiptoed to the window. He peered out from behind the curtain. 'I don't see him. Perhaps he's gone.'

'Of course you can't see him. He's hiding under the trees in the middle of the shrubbery. But he's there and he's demanding to see you.'

He turned, nervously rubbing his fingers through his hair so that it stood up in tufts. In a different situation Chloe would have found it comical.

He swallowed and Chloe saw how pale he was.

'I seem to be in a spot of bother here . . .' he said, clutching the back of the chair by way of support.

'What have you done to annoy him?' Chloe tried to sound brisk but she was beginning to appreciate his predicament.

'Nothing,' he protested. 'That is, not much really. A bit of a loan, that's all. Nothing to make a song and dance over.'

'You mean you owe him money and you can't pay it back?'

To Chloe, this was the stuff of nightmares. Her parents had been scrupulous about the family finances and Dorothy and Chloe had been brought up never to buy anything that couldn't be properly afforded. Friday evenings had seen the checking of the household accounts. Every missing penny had to be discovered before the ledger could be closed, with a long sigh of contentment from her father.

Now, she looked at Uncle Matty with deep dismay. 'How did it happen?' She sat down heavily.

It had crept up on him, he told her, joining her on the sofa. He had borrowed a few shillings when his funds were low and had then run into further problems. He hinted that this involved helping out an old friend who was taken ill and needed medical attention.

'You mean you gave the money you owed to this friend instead of paying off the debt?'

He nodded. 'What could I do? A friend in need is a—'

'And this so-called friend didn't pay *you* back?' It was sounding very suspicious, she thought.

'He couldn't. It was a doctor's bill. For his surgery. He was somewhat strapped for cash . . .' He rolled expressive eyes.

'I don't believe a word of it!' Chloe told him.

'My dear Miss Blake!'

His air of injured innocence was well done but Chloe raised her eyebrows. Without a word she continued to challenge his story until at last he gave in.

'No, you're right,' he conceded. 'I maybe . . . Indeed I *am* bending the truth a little. The little white lie . . . It's one of my faults. The truth is I used the money for a little business venture which went wrong. Badly wrong, in fact. I borrowed a little more—'

'And didn't pay that back either.'

He shrugged. 'That's about it.'

'And is that the man – the man in the shrubbery?'

'No. That's someone who collects for him. You'd call him a debt collector but he's actually a gamekeeper. A nasty brutish man. I dare not go out there, young lady.'

51

Chloe stared at him as the name sounded alarm bells in her mind. 'Not Sid Jakes?'

'I fear so.' He sighed heavily.

'We passed a rough-looking man when I was out with Binns. He shook his fist at me. The man, I mean. Now I know why. Somehow he knows that I work here.' She remembered the shotgun and another jolt of fear went through her. 'Yes, it was Sid Jakes. I thought I recognised him.'

'Most probably. My dear Miss Blake, you'll have to tell him I—'

'Me?' Chloe's eyes widened. 'I'm not going out there again. He's hurt me quite enough already. Sid Jakes is your problem.'

Uncle Matty seemed to shrink before her eyes. 'I daren't,' he whispered. 'Look here, Chloe, he won't hurt you if you tell him I'll settle up next Saturday. On my word as a gentleman. Tell him I'm in bed with . . . with gout but I'll be fine in a few days. Say I'll see him in the White Hart on Saturday around six.'

'Gout?' Don't listen to him, Chloe urged herself. He's brought this on himself and he must sort it out. 'More little white lies?' she said.

'I do have gout from time to time.'

'But not right now! You must go and face him. Promise the money and then keep your word as a gentleman. If not I shall be forever frightened to pass the shrubbery for fear he's lurking there. Suppose he had grabbed Bertha – or even Mrs Maitland.'

'My sister never goes into the garden.'

'But that's going to change.'

Uncle Matty shuddered and laid a hand across his heart. 'I will pay him. You have my word on it.'

'Then go and tell him so. You've brought this on yourself and I'll have nothing more to do with the wretch.'

'And if he kills me? You'll be full of regrets.'

'What nonsense!' Chloe tossed her head. 'Kill you indeed.

Now are you going to him – or do I have to mention this to your sister?'

'I'll go,' he said, 'but I hope you never regret your share in this.'

'I hope neither of us regrets anything.'

Hardening her heart, Chloe flounced from the room. She hurried upstairs to the library, from where there was a clear view across to the sycamores. She watched for ten minutes but there was no sign of Uncle Matty crossing the lawn towards the shrubbery. So he had had second thoughts. He fell even further in her estimation. Still, there had been no retaliation from Jakes. Be thankful for small mercies, she told herself. Perhaps Sid Jakes had thought better of it. Perhaps he hadn't intended to hurt her. Some men didn't know their own strength. Feeling a small measure of relief, Chloe made her way into the kitchen to supervise Jessica's tea tray.

Five minutes later, however, she was forced to revise her opinion when a small rock was thrown through the drawing room window, shattering the pane. In stunned silence she and Uncle Matty gazed in horror at the shards of glass which littered the floor. Chloe ran to the window and, half hidden by the heavy velour curtain, looked across the garden for a glimpse of the perpetrator. There was no one to be seen.

She turned from the window and said shakily, 'This is your fault. You should have heeded his warning. You should have gone out there. You should have promised him the money.'

'I'll settle up with the blighter. I promise on my honour. Just keep this between ourselves.'

She nodded reluctantly. 'What are we going to tell the others?'

Visibly shaken, the old man swallowed hard. 'We'll clear it up and . . . and send Binns for a glazier double quick. We'll say a bird flew into the window. They do sometimes. They see the sky reflected in the glass and they—'

'Please! You're being ridiculous. A bird wouldn't break the glass – unless it was an eagle!'

'A pheasant might.'

'A *pheasant*?'

Chloe regarded him with something approaching despair. This was a man to whom lies came all too easily. She sent for Hettie, who brought a dustpan and brush and between them they removed all the broken glass. The glazier lived locally and came within the hour. Fortunately Bertha showed little interest when told of the incident but Chloe went to bed that night with a heavy heart.

Sunday the fifteenth of June. Poor Hettie might be with child but who is the father? Not Binns I hope, for both their sakes. It seems so unfair that Dorothy has waited so long for a child and Hettie doesn't want one. At least, she certainly didn't plan for this one. I wish I hadn't offered to take her to the doctor but I shall now have to go through with it. Perhaps Doctor Bell can persuade her to tell us the father's name. Better news is that I shall be going up to London shortly to visit Oliver. I shall be alone with him in his studio. Perhaps he will ask me to pose for him. Sadly I would have to refuse. The journey is all part of the plan to get Mrs Maitland up and about. Part of the cunning 'birthday portrait plan' I've dreamed up. Mama used to say I was so sharp I'd cut myself! 'Too smart for your own good!' Dear Mama. Strange to think that if she were still alive I'd never have met this family. I think she would have liked Oliver. On second thoughts, she would have classed him a 'dark horse'.

Chloe lay awake for hours and at last her conscience began to prick her. Should she have told Jessica about the situation with Sid Jakes? It might be that she was used to Uncle Matty's reckless ways and could deal with it. If anything worse happened, the event might well come to light and then her part in the deception would be known. Jessica

Maitland would not take kindly to the fact that Chloe had been disloyal. She would claim, with some justification, that Chloe's loyalties lay with her employer and not with Uncle Matty. But he had promised on his honour that he would deal with the problem so there should not be any chance of discovery.

Chloe found herself wondering why she was willing to shield the old man. He didn't deserve her help and yet she hadn't been able to refuse him. He was far from perfect but in a strange way he was a likeable rogue. Honest about his own failings and tolerant towards others'. She smiled into the darkness. Dorothy would have a fit when she heard what had happened – and it might be best to keep the entire matter from Albert.

Restlessly she turned over. By the light of the moon she saw from her clock that it was twenty past one and still she was wide awake. Resigned to another sleepless hour, she turned her attention to Hettie's dilemma. She thought it likely that whoever was responsible for her condition had convinced her that what they did was quite innocent. Or if Binns was the father, Chloe could imagine how naive *he* could have been, faced with an excitable housemaid. Had Hettie been willing? Perhaps he had tricked her into it . . . or lured her with promises.

Chloe tried to imagine how the doctor would know whether or not Hettie was with child. In her imagination it promised to be rather embarrassing but maybe he could tell from an examination with his stethoscope. She hoped so.

Chloe had never been enthusiastic about the prospect of motherhood and had exasperated her mother by refusing to plan her life around wedded bliss. Unlike Dorothy, who had longed for a home of her own, Chloe had always pushed the idea to the back of her mind. She had had one offer of marriage – from Henry Larkin, a distant cousin. She had met him when she was sixteen and he was twenty and he had fallen in love with her. Hopelessly, he had plied her with letters, flowers and gifts but all to no avail. Chloe told him as kindly as she could that she had other plans although she did not enlighten him further. Don't wait for me, she had told him. It might be a long wait.

She began to wonder why Uncle Matty had never married. Or had he? Was there a secret in his past that involved a woman? Had a woman ever found him attractive?

Uncle Matty? She sat up in bed as a terrible thought occurred to her. 'No!' she whispered, frowning. 'Not *you!*'

Could Uncle Matty be the father of Hettie's child? She felt a rush of shame for even thinking such a thing. She hardly knew the man and yet she was suspecting him of misbehaving with a servant – although Chloe knew from her sister that such things did happen. Albert had spoken to Dorothy on occasions and Dorothy had passed on the information on the strict understanding that Albert should never find out. But it was unlikely a young girl like Hettie would find Uncle Matty attractive. Wasn't it? Unless he had forced his attentions on the girl . . . or promised her money.

'No!' she repeated. Not Uncle Matty. He might be an eccentric rogue but Chloe couldn't believe such a thing of him. She lay down again, confused. They would find out eventually, she told herself, and made a determined effort to put Hettie and her problem out of her mind.

She would think about Oliver instead. She smiled into the darkness. He obviously liked her or he would never have employed her but was there any more than that? she wondered. Probably not or he wouldn't have gone back to London without a goodbye. But at least he must have trusted her because he had confided a few indiscreet remarks about members of his family. She would like to believe that he was spending more time than usual at Fairfields but even that seemed improbable. Perhaps she would casually ask Mrs Letts or Hettie or Binns. It would be too risky to alert one of the family by such a question. Bertha, in her present state of heightened awareness, would certainly suspect her motive. She sighed. There was something about Oliver's thin face with its dark eyes that appealed to her. She even approved of the spectacles. They gave his eyes a hidden quality as though he had deep thoughts which he would not share with the rest of the world. Chloe tried to imagine the feel of his hair beneath her fingers and sighed again.

'Why aren't *you* married?' she asked his image. Bertha had once hinted that he was too idle to fall in love. Uncle Matty had suggested that Oliver hated commitment.

'Just as well,' she muttered sleepily. 'I've no plans to marry anyone.'

But as her eyes closed in sleep she did wonder if that were true.

Monday brought the dreaded visit to Doctor Bell's surgery with a trembling Hettie in tow. Chloe felt sorry for the girl but she also felt put upon by the family and slightly resentful as she waited in the gloomy room set aside for the patients. It was small and stuffy, filled with a motley assortment of people needing advice or treatment. A babe in arms whimpered, a small boy ran about while his mother nagged him to behave. An old man with bleary eyes coughed incessantly and a middle-aged woman crocheted as though her life depended on it. Chloe was immensely thankful that she was not here on her own accord, for the atmosphere was dispiriting to say the least.

Hettie clutched her arm suddenly. 'If I tell you who it was can we go home?' she whispered.

'No Hettie, we have to stay. Telling me his name won't change anything – but you can tell me if you like.'

'Only if you cross your heart and promise that you won't tell a soul.'

'You know I can't do that.'

The surgery door opened and the doctor appeared. With him was a mother leading a toddler. The mother looked worried and this sight unnerved Hettie, who began to cry.

'Miss Hettie Leeming?' The doctor looked round enquiringly.

He was small and elderly but his expression was kindly. Seeing the tears he held out a hand but Hettie flinched and Chloe had to take hold of her arm and urge her towards the door. The consulting room was somewhat airless and Chloe noticed that the window was closed in spite of the mild weather. There was a desk, several chairs and a high long table covered with several blankets topped with a white sheet.

Hettie, after a quick glance round the room, refused to say a word so Chloe explained briefly what seemed to be the problem. During the doctor's examination, Chloe stared firmly out of the window, preferring not to see anything and wishing she need not hear Hettie's anxious cries of discomfort and humiliation.

'Well now, Miss Leeming,' he said when she was once more fully dressed. 'You're going to be a mother in a few months' time and someone is going to be a father. The two of you must wed as soon as possible.' He reached for his pen and dipped it carefully into the ink and began writing. 'The father's name, please.'

Hettie shook her head violently. 'I'm not saying. Not until he knows. And he won't know until he comes back.'

'Ah! He's gone away.' The doctor cast an enquiring look in Chloe's direction. 'But he is coming back, I take it. He's not a military man, by any chance?'

'Course not.' Hettie clamped her lips firmly together and stared down at her clenched hands.

Chloe and the doctor exchanged looks and he said gently, 'Will he be pleased, d'you think? Many men are, Miss Leeming. You mustn't assume that he will be angry with you.'

After a pause Hettie said, 'I'm angry with him. He said it wouldn't happen.'

'Well my dear, it has happened and there's nothing anyone can do about it.'

'He'll think of something. He'll know what to do.'

'There's nothing he can do. Nothing he can suggest that

is legal. You get my meaning?' The pen moved slowly across the page. 'The child is due in three months' time. Or thereabouts. Do you know exactly when this happened?'

Hettie shook her head.

'So it happened more than once?'

She nodded and stole a quick glance at Chloe.

'Don't worry,' Chloe told her. Then, realising how stupid that sounded, she added, 'I mean, it will sort itself out somehow.'

She gave the girl an encouraging smile but her mind was working. If the child's father was away that ruled out Uncle Matty. It was a relief. At his age and in his situation he was hardly the ideal husband for a girl as young as Hettie. At least a young man would be more willing to marry her and more capable of earning a living with which to support a family.

Something else occurred to her. She said, 'So Hettie's been with child for several months. Without knowing?'

He looked up from his writing. 'It can happen. It's not too unusual. The normal monthly cycle continues in some cases so there are no warning signs. Or if there are the woman prefers to ignore them in the hope they may be wrong about their suspicions.'

This didn't tell Chloe very much since she didn't know what the warning signs were and she made a mental note to ask Dorothy.

The doctor laid down his pen and looked at Chloe. 'So no one knows who's responsible.'

He tutted and Chloe felt that somehow she was considered at fault.

She protested, 'We can hardly wring it out of her!'

He inclined his head by way of acknowledgement and said, 'Well, come back when you know more or in a month's time, whichever is the sooner.'

And with a few reassuring platitudes, he showed them out.

'Mr Berry?' he announced and as Chloe and Hettie left

the waiting room the elderly man coughed his way across the room.

Binns helped them back into the dog cart and they drove back in silence. Chloe tried to put an arm round the girl's shoulders but Hettie shook it away.

She stared sullenly ahead, nursing her disquiet, saying nothing. Once back at Fairfields she hurried into the kitchen and slammed the door.

Chloe went upstairs to report to Jessica. She was pleased to see that her employer was once more sitting in her chair and had almost completed the jigsaw puzzle. Chloe made up her mind that tomorrow she would persuade Jessica to spend an hour or two downstairs on the sofa in the drawing room in preparation for the portrait sittings that would be necessary later. But for now Chloe spoke only of Hettie.

'Oh! That foolish child!' Jessica grumbled when she learned the bad news. 'You'd better send her to me first thing in the morning. I'm simply not up to it today. I've been thinking and I have a feeling it's Binns. Do you feel up to speaking with him about it? If he disclaims any knowledge we shall have to think again.'

Chloe groaned inwardly. 'Unless Hettie can bring herself to tell us his name.'

'It doesn't appear very likely. The question now is, what to do with her. She can hardly continue as our maid because the baby will take up all her time . . . And if she marries whoever it is she'll move out and we'll have to replace her.'

Chloe said, 'We ought to inform her parents in case she dares not tell them herself. It's their job to help her now, surely.'

'More trouble.' Jessica sighed heavily. 'The whole business is most vexing. Oh Hettie! *Hettie*! Really, I could box her silly little ears!'

And on that note, the matter was allowed to rest.

Four

By Tuesday morning Jessica was fuming with frustration. She sent for Bertha while Chloe was in the kitchen talking to Mrs Letts about Jessica's meals.

'Sit down!' Jessica began. 'The silly girl is driving me to distraction. She simply—'

'Miss Blake?' Bertha was astonished. 'I thought you approved of her.'

'Not Chloe. *Hettie*. She simply refuses to say who the father of this child is. I'm rapidly losing patience with her. I've sent Binns round to her parents with a letter telling them what has happened but I know they're going to blame us. Chloe hasn't had any more success than I have so now you must have a go at her. If I don't get to the bottom of things soon I shall give her her marching orders and that will be that.'

Bertha's mouth twisted distastefully at this prospect. 'I'll talk to her if I must, Mama, but she'll simply turn on the waterworks. She's in a fearful state. Mrs Letts said she let slip that she can't tell the father because he isn't here but she won't say where he is.' She sighed.

'Then it can't be Binns, because he is here.'

'Mrs Letts asked him outright and he swears he doesn't even like her. Says he rather fancies another young lady.'

'Good heavens! Rather sudden, isn't it? Still it's possible, I suppose. Who is she?'

'The daughter of someone called Stanley Moffat.' Losing interest in Hettie, Bertha said, 'Talking about Binns – I was coming to tell you, Mama, that Grandmother's silver salver is missing. Mrs Letts has looked everywhere and it was there a day or two ago.'

Jessica looked shocked. 'But that salver is worth a great deal of money.'

'Mrs Letts says she remembers Hettie polishing it a couple of days ago.' She gave a small shrug. 'I can't help wondering about Binns. It can't be Mrs Letts or Hettie.'

Jessica put a hand to her head. 'As if we haven't got enough to worry about!'

They both fell silent considering the various problems but at that moment Chloe came briskly into the room. Stepping into the silence she said, 'Fish chowder, Mrs Maitland. My sister's own recipe, given to her by the Reverend Parks' mother and . . . Is something wrong?'

'We don't quite know,' Bertha told her and explained about the missing salver. 'Nothing else seems to be missing.'

'Not that we're accusing anybody,' Jessica added quickly. 'Unless it's Binns. It's very worrying. It might turn up but again it might not and it's been in the family for years. Since the Queen's wedding, in fact. My father bought it for my mother to mark the occasion.'

Seizing the moment, Bertha brought up the next topic. 'Changing the subject, Mama, I was wondering if you could spare Chloe tomorrow. I would take her place, obviously, but we're planning a surprise for your birthday and it entails a trip to London.' She gave Chloe a meaningful look.

Jessica's face brightened. 'A surprise?'

Chloe chimed in promptly. 'Yes. It's a wonderful idea. Your son's, actually, and he needs someone to—' She smiled. 'But I can't tell you more without giving too much away. Bertha doesn't fancy the train journey and I offered to go instead. Please do say I may go.'

Bertha and Chloe waited.

Jessica's expression softened. 'Oliver's idea? Of course it would be. He's such a thoughtful boy. Then you must go, Chloe – if you're sure you can face the journey. Trains are noisome things but if you take sensible precautions you'll be well enough, I daresay. Don't get into a conversation with a man, Chloe. He may look harmless enough but some of the worst men are great charmers and you never know where conversation may lead. Change carriages if you find yourself alone with a man.'

'I'll remember.'

'And on no account put your head out of the window. I know someone who got a speck of grit in his eye from smoke from the engine. The smoke always blows backward, you see. It infected his eye and it never did right itself, poor man . . .' She shook her head at the memory. 'And take a small basket of food for the train and save just a little in case of breakdown. Ask Mrs Letts to prepare a small picnic for you. What she calls her "travelling baskets".' She smiled. 'And keep account of whatever you spend and we'll reimburse you.'

Bertha laughed. 'Anyone would think she was going to the moon, Mama!'

'The moon! Now you're being silly, Bertha.'

Bertha made her excuses and left and a few moments later Chloe also found an excuse to 'pop downstairs'. She went immediately in search of Uncle Matty.

He was sitting in the garden in a deckchair close to the terrace, glancing nervously towards the shrubbery from time to time. He was reading the *Racing News* and looked up at Chloe's approach.

'My favourite young lady!' He smiled through the usual cloud of cigar smoke and lowered the paper so that he could peer over it. 'Come to keep a silly old man company, have you?'

Despite his best efforts he looked guilty, Chloe thought. She resisted the urge to smile. Instead she folded her arms and regarded him sternly. 'You've taken it,' she announced. 'The silver salver. You've taken it and you have to put it back.'

He blinked several times as his colour deepened. 'Salver?

What's this about a salver? I don't know what you mean, young lady.'

'You *do* know. You've taken it to give to that dreadful Sid Jakes – to pay off your debt. And you needn't deny it because—'

'Deny it? Of course I deny it.' He threw down the crumpled newspaper with a good attempt at indignation. 'I don't know how you can even think such a thing. I don't need salvers to pay my debts. I've got money.'

'You've got money, have you? Then why didn't you pay Sid Jakes?' She glared at him. 'Why let him attack me and throw rocks through our window? They are going to pin the blame on poor Binns and I'm sure he didn't do it. He hardly ever sets foot in the house so he wouldn't have had the chance. And I don't think he's bright enough to know what to do with it if he *had* stolen it.'

It was his turn to glare. 'Well, that's a fine thing. To be accused of stealing by an uppity servant. How many times—'

'I'm not a servant. I'm a companion.'

'Whatever you are, you're uppity.' He glanced away. 'And you're quite wrong. Barking up the proverbial wrong tree. I know nothing about the salver and if you suggest to Jessica that I have it I . . . I shall deny it. You will look very bad.'

'And if it's found in your room?'

For a moment he said nothing, his expression resentful.

'I'm disappointed in you,' he told her at last. 'Very disappointed. I thought we were friends. I thought you understood.'

'I *do* understand and have the bruises to prove it!' Chloe waited for him to give up the pretence, swinging her foot against the daisies and carelessly regarding the rest of the grounds.

As it became obvious that she would continue to challenge him, Uncle Matty's courage failed him.

64

'Suppose I did take it,' he muttered. 'The damn thing's never used – pardon my language. It's not even pretty.'

'Of course it is. And it's a valuable item and it was sure to be missed. However did you expect to get away with it?'

'I was going to pawn the blessed thing and get it back later.'

Chloe tutted with exasperation. 'They think it's Binns,' she repeated. 'Would you really allow him to take the blame?'

He rolled his eyes. 'I'm not a very nice man,' he told her. 'Sometimes it's the lesser of two evils. Jessica would never sack him on a first offence. She'd give him a second chance. Just to please you I'll put the wretched thing back although you really don't understand what you're doing to me. I'm in serious trouble if I don't pay up. They're not nice people to deal with. I could get hurt. Seriously hurt.' He lowered his voice. 'I could get killed!' He gave another quick look into the far shadows as if to reassure himself that today at least he was safe.

Chloe sat down on the grass beside him. He was exaggerating, of course, but he might well be hurt by the wretched Jakes. Her own recent experience proved that. Seeing that he was genuinely frightened, she relented a little.

'Surely you have something of your own that you could sell.' She certainly didn't want to be responsible for him being injured but nor could she allow Binns to be blamed.

Uncle Matty shrugged. 'I've got a snuffbox but it won't fetch enough.'

'Give them that,' she advised, 'and promise the rest later. Buy some time. Something is better than nothing.'

'You'll get me shot!' he muttered. 'But who cares? Who's going to miss Uncle Matty? I'm expendable.' He reached down for his newspaper and began to smooth out the crumpled pages.

Now that she had succeeded, Chloe took the hint and left him in peace. At the door she glanced back. He looked old and vulnerable and she did hope she had done the right thing.

A few miles away, later that evening, George Brier stood at the sink in the kitchen of Myrtle Cottage and washed his hands. His mother, Ellen, was carrying dishes to the table. A bacon hock from last season's pig, a bowl of boiled potatoes and a jug of onion gravy. When they were both seated Ellen said grace and told her son to help himself. She was a widow and George was the only child who was still at home. Although she enjoyed his company she wanted to see him settled with a family of his own.

Watching him carve a few slices from the bacon she said, 'So how's her ladyship?'

George rolled his eyes. His mother was referring to Mrs Maitland.

'Going on fine,' he told her, hiding his exasperation. 'Bertha says the new companion's done her a lot of good. She's a sight more lively these days.'

'More's the pity! I'd as soon she slipped away in her sleep, that one. Then maybe Bertha would get around to marrying you.'

He laid two slices on her plate and started cutting more. 'She'll marry me when she's good and ready. Like I said, I'm not rushing her.'

'Well you should be. Time's passing and you'll be wanting a family . . .'

'That's enough, Ma. I've heard it all before.' Frowning, he helped her to potatoes and then served himself. 'Bertha says she'll ask again when the time's right. Best leave it at that.'

'More fool you, then, George Brier. She'll be a dried-up old maid afore you get her to the altar.'

'I said enough!' A slow flush spread into his face. 'And I'll thank you not to talk about Bertha that way.' The gravy boat remained poised above his plate. 'I thought you liked her.'

'I did until she started all this nonsense . . . Are you going to take some gravy or not?'

Thus prompted, he poured gravy over his potatoes and set the boat down in front of his mother.

Ellen refused to be silenced on one of her favourite subjects. 'I know why her ladyship won't agree to the wedding so don't think I don't. She thinks her daughter's too good for you. Bertha's got to stand up to her.'

'Nice bit of bacon.' George kept his gaze on the food in front of him.

'Bacon be blowed!' Ellen regarded him with exasperation. 'Don't you go changing the subject, George Brier. I'm right and you know it. What a heartache there'll be for the pair of you if she's too old to have children. What is she now – thirty-six?'

'Never you mind . . . The left-side wall's down now. Not that you're interested.'

Ellen, softening, laid down her knife and fork. 'Of course I'm interested, son. It's just that I can't abear to see you pining.'

'I'm not pining. I'm waiting and I'm saving. We'll have a nice little nest egg . . .'

With a sigh Ellen scooped up a mouthful of onion. 'You said they'd most likely ask us to tea one day. Not much chance so far.'

He looked up sharply. 'And you said you'd go to tea with her "when the cows come home"! Remember?'

She looked guilty. 'I must have been out of sorts that day. I didn't mean it.'

'And you said you'd ask her to take a bit of tea with us but you never did. Pot calling the kettle black.'

Ellen pointed an accusing knife. 'And *you* said we could have a new tablecloth and one of them plates on a stand for the cakes but we never did! Can't ask a girl like that to this place. Leastways not the way it is.' She mashed a potato into the gravy and spooned it up with a sigh of satisfaction. 'You give me the money for the tablecloth and—'

'Here!' He pulled some coins from his pocket, reached for her hand and pressed them into it. 'Now get what you want. I'm inviting her next Sunday and I don't want no arguments, Ma.'

Taken aback, Ellen hesitated. Talking about it was one thing. Actually inviting Bertha Maitland was another. She said, 'I'll have to clean the windows and polish up the copper kettle.'

He grinned at her. 'I've called your bluff, haven't I?'

'Bluff? I don't know what you mean, George Brier. I just wish your pa was alive to see this. Inviting Miss Maitland to sup with us. He'd be all of a tizzy.'

She crossed to the dresser and dropped the coins into a jam jar. Faced with an imminent visit from Bertha her heart fluttered anxiously but at least something might come of it. She'd been dropping hints about Polly Greening, the policeman's daughter, but George could be very stubborn – just like his father. Polly was suitable, she told herself. Young and biddable. A bit giggly but that's how young girls were. A child would soon settle her high spirits.

'Polly Greening's still not wed,' she ventured. 'Pretty little thing. But I daresay she's walking out.'

'She is pretty. Maybe she could be a bridesmaid!' George grinned, helping himself to more gravy. 'It's Bertha or nobody, Ma. Best get used to the idea.'

With another sigh, Ellen resigned herself to the inevitable. Bertha Maitland might well be a bit on the hoity-toity side but if she was the one her son wanted, amen to that. Ellen would work her fingers to the bone and the cottage would shine like a new pin. No one should ever say that his mother spoiled George's chances. She wanted him settled. She wanted him to be happy.

She sat down again, her mind already busy. 'We could have some cold cuts,' she suggested. 'And some of my chutney and . . . Oh George!' She put a hand to her heart. 'Maybe *I* could talk to her. Persuade her to try again with her ma.' She had a sudden vision of herself holding her first grandchild in her arms. 'And I'll bake one of my caraway cakes.'

'And some of your cheese scones.'

Now they were on familiar territory. Ellen could cook as well as the next and suddenly, concentrating her mind on the food, her anxiety left her. She smiled at her son and patted his arm. 'I suddenly feel very hopeful,' she told him. 'Very hopeful indeed!'

That night Chloe had been in bed about ten minutes when there was a knock at the door. She groaned softly. She had been thinking about Oliver and hated being interrupted. Sliding reluctantly from the bed she hurried to the door and opened it a few inches.

'Who is it?'

'It's me.'

Recognising Hettie's voice, Chloe opened the door. Hettie stood outside in her nightdress, her hair in curling rags. The candle she carried wavered in her hand and she looked very pale. Like a sad little ghost, Chloe thought with a rush of compassion.

'Come in,' she told the girl. 'You're not ill, are you?' She hoped Hettie wasn't suffering from something connected with her pregnancy because she, Chloe, would have no idea what to do.

Hettie stepped into the room and Chloe took the candle from her shaking hand. 'Sit on the end of the bed,' she advised and wrapped her in the counterpane. 'You look terrible,' she said tactlessly. 'I mean, you look pale.'

'I'm fine. I have to tell you, because you're going to London.'

'I'm not going for long. Just a day. Did you think I was leaving?'

'I can't tell them but I talked to Mrs Letts and she said I was to tell you because you're going to London.'

'Tell me what?'

'About who it is. The baby's father. So you could give him a message.'

Chloe stared at her, perplexed. 'The father comes from London? How on earth did you meet him?'

'I didn't. I mean, not in London. I met him here.'

'I give up!' said Chloe. 'I'm no good at riddles. Just tell me his name.'

'And you'll give him the message?'

'Certainly. If Mrs Maitland agrees and if you tell me where I can find this man . . .'

She stopped. Hettie's face had changed and she now regarded Chloe with apprehension. 'Oh no! You can't tell *her*! He made me swear. If she finds out she'll put a stop to it. That's what he said. And I'll get the sack and we'll never see each other again.' Her mouth trembled.

I'll get the sack . . . Chloe felt suddenly cold as an idea took hold in her mind. Fairfields and London . . . Could it be Oliver? No. Of course it couldn't. She felt disloyal even considering the possibility.

'Tell me his name,' she said sharply.

'It's Oliver.' Hettie averted her eyes, twiddling with the counterpane to hide her discomfiture. 'I mean Mr Maitland but I can call him Oliver.'

Chloe's hand flew to her mouth as if to prevent the escape of any words that might reveal the extent of her dismay. Illogically she wanted to lean forward and slap the girl but she knew that was unfair. Oliver and this slip of a girl! It sickened her even to think of them together. A deep sadness filled her as her illusions about Oliver were shattered. It was as though Hettie had stolen him from her. She swallowed hard, forcing down a mixture of jealousy and grief. So much for her secret imaginings, she thought with uncharacteristic bitterness. She had been so stupid. So blind.

Time passed as she wrestled with her emotions and she became aware that Hettie was staring at her.

'You'd better tell me,' she muttered.

Hettie said, 'He came to my room and he was ever so

70

kind and . . . and he said such nice things and promised me nothing would happen. And I do love him, Miss Blake. Really I do but I don't know what he'll say.'

Chloe felt shaken. If this was true then Oliver was entirely to blame. He had gone into her room and taken advantage of her innocence. How could she have misjudged him so completely? She closed her eyes. What would this news do to Jessica – and to Bertha? They would both be horrified. Chloe forced herself to concentrate. 'How long has this . . . this regrettable behaviour been going on?'

'Since before Christmas. They had a party one evening and Oliver had too much to drink. He had to go up to his bedroom to lie down and then Mrs Maitland said on my way to bed I was to call in and see if he needed anything. And Oliver said, "Only you, Hettie," and he made me sit on the edge of the bed and he was still a bit drunk and he started—' She glanced up at Chloe as though wondering whether she should continue.

Chloe was sure she ought to stop the account but it held a dreadful fascination for her. 'Go on,' she whispered.

'He started to touch my arms and my neck and he undid the buttons of my bodice and—'

'So he didn't come into your room. You said—' Chloe was clutching at straws and she knew it.

'He did! I said I should go because he had a funny look on his face so I ran back to my room and then a few minutes later he followed me. I'd just blown out my candle when I heard the door open and he sat on the bed and slid his hand inside my nightgown and . . . Well, I did say no at first but then it was so nice and he said such lovely things . . .'

Chloe was aware of a rush of furious envy, which she tried hard to ignore but it was difficult. In her imagination, such desirable things had happened to *her* but now she was having to listen to Hettie telling her that *she* had been the one Oliver wanted.

Chloe said, 'That was very unwise, Hettie.' She sounded

pompous, she knew, but couldn't help it. 'Didn't you know what might happen?'

'No, because he promised it wouldn't and I trusted him. If he marries me it will be all right, won't it? Mrs Letts says that you could tell him what's happened and then it's up to him to decide what's to be done. She says I might have to go away and have the baby and then maybe I could come back.'

'But what about the baby?'

Hettie's mouth drooped. 'It's up to Oliver – unless he pretends it wasn't him.' She looked at Chloe with large anxious eyes. 'He wouldn't do that, would he? Not Mr Maitland. He's a gentleman, isn't he.'

'Of course he is.' The answer came automatically but was it true? Chloe wondered. Was Oliver a gentleman – or a cad?

And what would happen to the child? Surely it would have to be adopted. Jessica would never allow her son to marry a servant – unless they went to London to live in the studio. There nobody knew of the girl's background.

She said, 'Does your mother know?'

Hettie shook her head vigorously. 'I wouldn't dare tell her. Not Ma. And my pa would wallop me if he knew. They'd take me away from Fairfields for sure – unless Mr Maitland marries me. Then they might not be angry.'

Chloe looked at her with compassion. The idea that Hettie and Oliver might be husband and wife was wishful thinking on the girl's part. If she was going to keep the baby there would presumably be some kind of financial settlement – but that would be regarded as a confession of guilt. If they found adoptive parents . . .

A new thought occurred to Chloe, making her sit up abruptly. 'Would you agree to have the baby adopted?'

Hettie shrugged slim shoulders. 'I don't know. I don't know what I think.'

'I mean, if we could find some truly nice people who desperately want a baby to love and would give the baby a nice home. People who haven't got any children because . . . because they can't have any.'

'Would you?' Hettie, wide-eyed, looked helplessly at Chloe. 'If you were in my shoes?'

Chloe hesitated. 'I'd think about it,' she said at last. 'I'd want whatever was best for the baby.'

'Then so would I.' Hettie smiled suddenly. 'So when you go to London will you tell Mr Maitland? And give him my love. He is a good man, isn't he?'

With an effort Chloe managed an encouraging smile. 'Yes,' she said. 'He's a good man.'

Tuesday the seventeenth of June. I have decided not to tell anyone else about Hettie's baby until Oliver knows. I hate being a carrier of bad news but Oliver will have to sort it out. I can't imagine he will marry Hettie but if he doesn't it means that he might well lose contact with his child. Also that his mother will never see her first grandchild, which is sad. However will it end?

When I asked Hettie about adoption I was thinking about Dorothy and Albert. How would it be, I wonder, if they were to adopt Oliver's baby? I have to think very carefully before I suggest such a thing but it might solve the problem. On the other hand it might go wrong in some way and then everyone will blame me. My shoulders are broad but I should hate to be responsible for anyone's unhappiness. I must wait and see.

The silver salver reappeared this afternoon. Everyone is determined to blame Binns and assume he has had second thoughts. I have said nothing about Uncle Matty. The salver is back and that is what matters. Perhaps the money from the snuffbox will satisfy Sid Jakes for the time being.

The next day Chloe was in the back garden collecting Jessica's sheets from the washing line when a woman approached her. She looked agitated and immediately Chloe guessed her identity.

73

'Can I help you?' she asked brightly.

'I have to speak with the mistress of the house. She wrote to me about my daughter. It's terrible. My husband's—'

'Are you Mrs Leeming?'

The woman nodded. 'My husband wouldn't come. He's too ashamed. I have to talk to my daughter. She can't stay here. I have to take her home with me.'

Chloe's smile had faded. 'There may be no need for that. At least not—'

'But my husband won't take no for an answer. You don't know him, Miss . . .'

'I'm Miss Blake, Mrs Maitland's companion.' Chloe, her arms full of sheets, led the way into the house. 'I'll see if Mrs Maitland is available,' she said.

As they went through the back door which led into the kitchen Hettie turned towards them. She was carrying a tray of crockery, which she dropped at the unexpected sight of her mother. For a moment the crash silenced them all and they stared at the broken cups, saucers and plates.

Hettie cried, 'Oh Lord!' She turned towards Mrs Letts. 'Ma made me do it!'

Her mother, white-faced, stepped forward and boxed her ears. Hettie burst into tears and Mrs Leeming began making wild recriminations.

'You're a stupid, wicked girl and your pa says . . . I just don't know how you could do this to us after all we've done for you . . . I shall never hold my head up again . . . Your pa's threatening blue murder . . . Oh Hettie!' She, too, began to cry and Chloe took her by the arm and sat her down at the kitchen table.

Mrs Letts said, 'I'll make a pot of tea.'

Mrs Leeming cried, 'Look at that mess, Hettie! You pick those bits up this minute, d'you hear me?'

Hettie cried, '*You* made me drop them!' and ran from the room.

'She's a wicked, *wicked* girl, to bring this shame on us,' her mother sobbed. 'My husband is in such a rage. He'll take his belt to her as likely as not. He's such a proud man and after our Lizzie . . . I just don't understand young people today. It's not as though we didn't warn her. Don't go getting yourself into scrapes, her pa told her. She's always been such a good girl and now look what's happened.'

She took the handkerchief that Chloe offered but went on sobbing. 'He's at home now waiting for us but he's a bit the worse for drink. You know what men are like.'

Chloe thought ruefully that she was finding out. She began to gather up the broken crockery and pile it on the tray.

Mrs Letts filled a mug with milky tea, added three sugars and pushed it towards Mrs Leeming. Then she took a bottle from the cupboard and added a tot of whisky. 'Drink that, my dear. It'll steady you.'

Chloe looked at the housekeeper. 'Should I tell Mrs Maitland that she's here?'

'Probably best – but say she'll be along to talk to her in a bit. Maybe ten minutes or so.'

Chloe hurried upstairs. Jessica, still in her dressing gown, looked up irritably. 'I've been ringing my bell. Where were you?'

'I was in the garden collecting your sheets.' She passed on the message from Hettie's mother, ignoring Jessica's protests. 'I'll remake the bed,' she said, 'but you'll want to be dressed and in your chair.'

'Will I?'

'More professional, don't you think?' Chloe added the information about Mr Leeming's temper and his threats.

Jessica frowned. 'I don't think we should let Hettie go home to that, do you? Maybe we could say she can't be spared for a day or two. Give the father a chance to calm down. If only we knew the name of the baby's father. Oh dear! This whole thing makes us look very remiss indeed.'

Guiltily Chloe turned away. She knew it was wrong to keep back Oliver's name but she had promised Hettie and she would feel even worse if she betrayed her.

Jessica walked slowly to the big swing mirror and gave

her reflection a careful scrutiny, tucking her hair into place and giving her cheeks a brisk pat to bring some colour into her pale face. Chloe had noticed that she now made short trips across the bedroom without realising what she was doing. Soon she would be unable to pretend she was still an invalid.

Ten minutes later the bed was restored and Jessica was dressed and ready to see her visitor. Chloe asked if she needed her to stay.

Jessica hesitated. 'Maybe not,' she decided with clear reluctance. 'I think I should be seen to deal with this alone. If it seems a good idea to include Hettie I'll ring for her. Maybe her mother can wring the truth from her. If only Oliver was here. He's such a calming influence. Such a support in times of trouble.' She sighed. 'But then he has to work. He has to make a living for himself.'

Greatly daring, Chloe said, 'You must be looking forward to the day he'll marry. Grandchildren and all the fun that goes with them.'

For a moment Jessica seemed about to agree but then she shook her head. 'I don't think about it. Bertha is the one. It's a tragedy in some ways. Miles Sandford has been waiting for years – such a sweet man! – but she won't even consider him.' Seeing Chloe's pretended surprise she said, 'Oh didn't you know? He's an old friend. Much older than Bertha, of course, but wealthy. He'd be ideal for her and I haven't given up on the match yet.' Her smile was conspiratorial. 'But I'm ready for Mrs Leeming now. Please go down and fetch her.'

Chloe did as she was asked and soon delivered a very nervous Mrs Leeming to Jessica's room. As she went downstairs she saw Bertha waiting for her in the hall below with a finger to her lips.

'I've been invited to take tea with George and his mother,' she told Chloe. 'I daren't tell Mama so I thought—'

'Why not?' said Chloe. Really, she thought, this woman is incredible. No spine at all. 'I think you should tell her.'

Taken aback, Bertha stammered. 'But why? I mean, what's it got to do with her? If I say—'

'Your mother has been telling me about Miles Sandford. Is that who you want?'

Bertha flushed to the roots of her hair. 'Miles? Of course not but—'

'Then you'll have to make a stand. The longer you leave it the harder it will be for you to tell her. Face her with two alternatives – that you remain a spinster or that you marry the man you love. Or perhaps you don't love him enough to risk your mother's displeasure.' She smiled suddenly. 'If George Brier wanted to marry me *nothing* would stand in my way.'

She gazed unwaveringly into Bertha's eyes.

Bertha sighed shakily. 'Mama can be so . . . so domineering. You have no idea.'

'This is how it's done,' Chloe told her, hiding her exasperation. 'First you *tell* your mother that you've accepted an invitation to tea with George Brier and his mother. You do not ask permission. She won't like it and she'll try to dissuade you. She'll be upset. Let her be.'

'Oh but Mama can be very unpleasant.'

'Let her be as unpleasant as she likes. Let her rant and rave and then quietly repeat that you have already accepted and that you are going. Be prepared for a nasty scene but tell yourself it's the price you have to pay. Don't lose *your* temper. Simply repeat from time to time that you have already accepted and that you're going. Short of tying you to the bed your mother can't stop you.' She could see that Bertha was wavering and went on. 'I could tell her for you but that wouldn't solve anything. You have to stand up for yourself – and you can do it. You've got more strength of spirit than you think.'

Before Bertha could answer this Chloe strode away down the hall. Whatever am I saying? she wondered. I've never had to fight for a man I love.

The truth was she had never met a man she wanted that much. It was a rather sobering thought.

77

Five

The following morning Chloe sat in the train carriage, her heart beating, her eyes sparkling with excitement. Her first ever train journey – and she was on her way to London, England's capital. The town in which Buckingham Palace was to be found and sometimes Queen Victoria herself. The Tower of London was also there and the River Thames and Marble Arch. She had also heard tell of 'the changing of the guard', which meant marching soldiers in red uniforms with black bearskins on their heads. She had seen pictures of them and thought them wonderfully inspiring.

Chloe clutched her lunch basket and smiled to herself as the train clattered and rocked along the rails, setting up a rhythm which she found soothing. At first she had avoided all eye contact but now she allowed her gaze to flit from one to another of her fellow passengers. Opposite her sat a small plump clergyman dutifully perusing a bible. To her left an elderly woman sat with a cat in a basket. Further left still a young woman rocked a baby which was crying fitfully and Chloe at once thought of Hettie and Oliver's child. To her right she saw a young couple discreetly holding hands and whispering to each other and she felt a pang of envy. Would she ever find a man who would look at her that way? A man she could love in return? Could she love any man enough to love, honour and *obey* him?

Obeying was something Chloe found difficult. Her mother had often despaired of her rebellious daughter, pleading with her to be more like Dorothy. Her schoolteachers had grumbled at her in vain and she still recalled the sting of Miss Took's cane when it came down on the back of her hand.

Her reminiscences ended abruptly as the train drew into the station and the next part of her journey began. She soon found herself in a queue for hansom cabs and waited impatiently until it was her turn to climb up into the upholstered seat behind the coachman.

'Thirty-four D, Bestwick Terrace,' she told him.

'Is that near the Embankment?' he asked.

'I have no idea,' she confessed. 'I thought you'd know.'

'We'll try there,' he told her and whipped up the horse, which set off at a spanking pace.

Chloe sank back in her seat as the cab wove its way through the traffic, which came at them from every side. She had never seen so many vehicles and the noise was incredible. Motor engines roared, horses neighed and drivers yelled at each other. Everyone seemed to be in a desperate hurry and Chloe crossed her fingers and hoped they would reach their destination without mishap.

She tried to remember the little speech she had planned but the smooth sentences had deserted her and she began to panic slightly. Whatever she said to Oliver must be dignified and in no way judgemental, she reminded herself. It was not up to her to be disapproving. She was merely bringing a message from Hettie – and, of course, asking Oliver about the portrait. She mustn't forget the original reason for this trip.

Eventually, as she was still struggling for suitable words and phrases, the horse clattered to a stop outside a row of tall but unimpressive terraced houses.

'Here you are, miss. Number thirty-four.'

Thanking him, Chloe was helped down and paid her fare. It seemed exorbitant but she was in no mood to argue. This was London and a far cry from the wilds of Sussex.

The house was five storeys, built of brick which was blackened by soot. The front door had once been painted

79

black but this was peeling off and the brass doorknob was badly in need of polishing.

She knocked three times and was rewarded by silence. For a moment her courage wavered. The street itself was gloomy, overshadowed by large trees, and the few people who walked the pavement threw suspicious glances in her direction. One man, an ugly ruffian, abruptly changed direction and headed straight towards her. Disliking the expression on his face, Chloe chose the least risky option and seized the door handle. To her relief the door opened and she hurried inside. Closing the door, she leaned back against it, listening to the approaching footsteps. Was the wretch going to come in after her? Afraid that the answer might be yes, Chloe started up the stairs and was relieved not to hear the street door open behind her.

A dim light filtered through a fanlight over the front door but this was soon exhausted. The stairs were bare wood and the walls were covered with a dark old-fashioned paper. There was a smell of damp and the whole place was thoroughly unwelcoming.

'Do you really live here, Oliver?' she muttered. Perhaps he was starving in a garret.

On the first landing she saw a door numbered 34A and she hurried on up the stairs becoming more depressed with each step.

'Ah! Here we are.' Faced with a green door, Chloe knocked and waited, a nervous smile on her face. When the door opened, Oliver stood before her. It took him a few seconds to realise who she was and then he frowned. 'Miss Blake? I hope nothing's wrong. It's not Mama is it?'

He looked dishevelled, Chloe thought in surprise, and he was wearing carpet slippers and a loose shirt which hung outside his trousers.

She said, 'No. Your mother is well. May I come in?'

He hesitated. 'It's not terribly convenient . . .' he began.

'It's rather important, Oliver.'

'Important?'

'*Very* important.'

'Come in then,' he said with obvious reluctance.

Chloe stepped into a room which could kindly be described as 'bohemian' although 'untidy and unclean' would be a more accurate description. Chloe wondered what Jessica would think of it.

Oliver snatched some clothes from a sofa and Chloe sat down. He nudged a pair of shoes under an armchair with his slippered foot.

'I wasn't expecting anyone . . .' he began. 'We're in . . . That is, I'm in a bit of a muddle at the moment. It's . . .'

He's searching for an excuse, thought Chloe, amused.

He said, 'The fact is, I've got an exhibition coming up shortly.' He waved his hand towards a large easel at the far end of the room – the area which presumably was his 'studio'. The painting, which was half finished, showed a partly nude woman relaxing on a sofa.

'It looks very good,' Chloe told him. It *was* good. She was impressed. 'May I see the others?'

'Which others?'

'You can't have an exhibition with only one painting.'

'Oh!' He frowned. 'The rest of them . . . um . . . They're already at the gallery.' His smile was unconvincing but Chloe let it pass.

Oliver took out his watch and frowned. 'Can I make you a quick cup of tea?' he asked.

A quick one? Why the hurry? Chloe wondered. 'That would be very welcome.' She smiled. 'I haven't finished my lunch yet. Would you mind if I eat while we talk?'

'One of Mrs Letts' famous travelling baskets?'

He grinned suddenly and Chloe felt her heart lurch. He *was* an attractive man and she was sorry she brought such devastating news.

'Go ahead,' he said. 'I might even find a biscuit.'

He disappeared through a small door into what Chloe imagined was a small kitchen or scullery. She wondered where the bedroom was and tried to imagine Hettie and a small child sharing this cramped accommodation. From the basket she retrieved an apple and took a bite as she surveyed the room. In the small window recess there was a rickety table and two chairs. Her eyes narrowed. He had said 'we' earlier before correcting himself. Did he share this flat? There were a couple of bookshelves on the wall, a large wicker trunk, an overstuffed armchair and an ancient ottoman. The same dank smell from the hallway pervaded the room but it was mingled with the smell of what might be his artists' paints.

Oliver returned with a cup of tea and sat down on a nearby chair. 'No biscuits, I'm afraid. So what brings you here, Miss Blake? If it's not Mama then is it—'

'It's Hettie,' Chloe told him. 'She's with child and . . . and she claims that you're the father. I'm so sorry.'

Seeing the colour drain from his face, she hastily looked away.

After a moment he said, 'And you believe this? Does Mama know of her . . . accusations?'

Taken aback by this reaction, Chloe outlined exactly what had happened so far. 'Nobody knows but Hettie and myself . . . that she's named you. Everyone knows that she's going to have a baby.'

He leaned back in the armchair and ran agitated fingers through his hair.

'This is quite impossible. Nothing could have happened . . .' He sat up sharply. 'It could be anyone! It could be Binns! It doesn't have to be me. I wasn't the only one, you know.'

'She says you were.' Chloe spoke gently.

Oliver jumped to his feet, strode to the window and stared out across the rooftops. 'It's out of the question. She'll have to go. I'll have to find someone. These things can be stopped. There are certain doctors . . . Oh God!'

'It's your own son you're talking about,' she reminded him, forgetting her resolve to say nothing disapproving. 'Or maybe your daughter.'

He thumped his fist against the window sill. 'Damn! That wretched girl!'

Chloe said, 'She's certainly very wretched at present. Very fearful that everyone is going to be against her. Except you, that is. She thinks you're going to marry her.'

'Well, she'll have to be told that she's wrong.' Oliver glanced at a small clock on the mantelpiece. 'You must go soon,' he told her. 'I have a . . . colleague due at two thirty or thereabouts.'

'But what exactly am I to say when I get back?' She regarded him with growing disappointment. 'Hettie will be insisting that you are responsible and your mother will find out. And Hettie's father will be demanding that you make an honest woman of her. And before I forget there's something else – a portrait. Bertha has suggested that you have your mother's portrait painted for her birthday and . . . What is it?'

He was staring at her in disbelief. 'A portrait of Mama? Are you mad? Who cares about a birthday at a time like this?'

'The question is, are you willing or not? The portrait, I mean.' Chloe spoke rather sharply. Oliver was now beginning to annoy her. She had believed him to be a very decent man and yet everything he said revealed a lack of compassion.

'Do what you like! I don't care.'

Chloe hardened her heart. 'So we can tell your mother about the portrait? I think she'll be—'

'Tell who you like!' He stared around him like a caged animal.

'And when will you be home again? Your mother is sure to ask me.'

'Soon. I don't know. I only know I can't and won't be pushed into marrying Hettie. She'll have to get rid of the child.' He slumped back into his chair and sighed heavily. 'God knows what . . . I'll have to think about it.' He looked at Chloe. 'You'll have to be on your way,' he said.

'But it's not two thirty yet.' Chloe finished her apple and glanced round for somewhere to put the core.

'Throw it into the fireplace. It will hardly be noticed.'

That was true. The small fireplace was full of scraps of paper, matchboxes, nutshells and miscellaneous unrecognisable scraps. Chloe leaned forward to do as Oliver suggested and immediately spotted a dress thrown over a chair beside the easel. Was this something one of Oliver's models wore? As she let her gaze wander her eyes narrowed. Surely that was a lady's buttoned boot protruding from beneath a fringed chenille throw that covered the table.

At that moment there were footsteps on the stairs and Oliver sprang to his feet. 'Damnation! This is quite impossible.' He covered his face with his hands as the door opened and a woman stepped into the room.

Chloe guessed her age at nearer forty than thirty. She was still pretty, with a mass of bright red hair and beautiful green eyes. Her cheeks and lips were unnaturally red and Chloe suspected make-up. She wore a red jacket over a gaudy skirt of red and black and carried a rolled red parasol. Red lace gloves completed the outfit. Dazzled, Chloe thought she looked as though she had stepped from a painting and made a vow to choose her own clothes with less caution in future.

The woman looked at Chloe and then raised her eyebrows. Chloe understood at once that she had not expected to find another woman with Oliver.

He threw Chloe an imploring look. 'Adele, this is my mother's new companion, Chloe Blake. She . . . That is, Bertha wants to arrange a portrait of my mother for her coming birthday. I've said I'll find them a suitable artist.' To Chloe he said, 'This is Adele. Mademoiselle Dupres. She . . . sometimes models for me.'

Adele said, 'More than sometimes, Ollie!' She nodded towards Chloe and said, 'Enchantée, mademoiselle.'

Chloe said, 'Pleased to meet you.' Was she French?

Adele threw down the parasol and began to pull off her

gloves. Then she turned back to Oliver. 'You do not ask 'ow it went, Ollie?'

Hearing an accent, Chloe decided she was definitely foreign. She regarded the newcomer with renewed interest as she sipped her tea. This was presumably the person Oliver had not wished her to meet. Perhaps now that they *had* met she would be allowed to stay with them a little longer.

Oliver looked distinctly flustered. 'Oh! Yes, of course. How did it go?'

Adele smiled. 'It was vairy good. I have won the part.' She swung round on her heel, throwing her arms into the air with an extravagant gesture of delight, and launched into a series of dance steps which she accomplished with great panache.

'Bravo!' Chloe clapped her hands.

Oliver turned to Chloe. 'Adele's a dancer, in case you haven't guessed. She's been for an audition.'

Adele laughed. 'Last week I am in the back row in an 'orrible little music hall but next month I shall dance at the Empire!'

'The Empire, Leicester Square?' Chloe was impressed. 'Good gracious!'

Adele nodded. 'And I will have a solo spot – how you say? – in the spotlight!'

Chloe watched her with undisguised admiration not untinged with envy. A dancer. *Very* bohemian.

'You'll be famous, Adele,' she told her. 'Perhaps we shall come and see you dance.'

Adele flashed a triumphant glance at Oliver, who tightened his lips.

'I don't think so, Miss Blake. Mama would hardly approve.'

Adele, obviously annoyed, looked at Chloe. 'I believe not everyone regards the Empire with such . . . such disdain. Not everyone prefers rotten old ballet.'

'Not that again, please, Adele!'

She tossed her head. 'You are so stuffy, Ollie!'

85

'Your favourite word! I'm stuffy. My family is stuffy.'

She pulled off her jacket and dropped it on to the floor.

He glanced at his watch again and then turned to Chloe. 'I really think . . .'

Chloe resigned herself to the fact that she was not welcome and stood up. She was, however, becoming suspicious of this relationship and was not ready to leave. 'So when shall I say you're coming home?'

'Ah . . . That's tricky.'

Adele smiled at Chloe. 'I would so like to meet Ollie's family.'

Chloe, trapped, said, 'I'm sure that can be arranged . . . one day. At least—'

Oliver's furious look silenced her.

Adele looked from one to the other. She was not only beautiful, thought Chloe, but very bold. An independent woman. And they obviously knew each other well. What exactly was going on between them? A fresh envy filled her.

'Poor Ollie. Everything is so tricky for him. All of life is tricky, isn't it, my sweet Oliver?'

With great deliberation, Oliver walked to the door and opened it. 'Miss Blake is leaving now,' he said through stiff lips. 'She has a train to catch.'

Chloe picked up her basket. 'We'll look forward to your visit,' she told him. With a polite smile to Adele she swept from the room, pretending not to see the cold look Oliver gave her as she passed. The door closed promptly behind her and she went down the stairs full of confusion.

Downstairs she found herself on the pavement in the same unfriendly street. There was no sign of a cab and Chloe blamed herself for not thinking of the return journey.

I'll just have to walk, she decided, and strode out briskly, wishing she had a brolly in case she was accosted. If necessary she would hit any would-be assailant with her lunch basket, she thought with a faint smile. Fortunately she soon reached a main road where she was able to hail another hansom cab and was soon on her way back to the station.

Half an hour later Chloe was on the Rye train, her composure restored, her mind buzzing with the excitement of the day's disclosures. Oliver was going to dispute his involvement in Hettie's condition because he had other irons in the fire. There was more to his relationship with Adele than he was prepared to admit. They might even be living together. Just fancy! Oliver Maitland sharing a garret with a French dancer from the Empire Music Hall. What on earth would his mother have to say about that?

As soon as Chloe reached Fairfields Jessica summoned her to the bedroom and Bertha joined them. As Chloe took off her jacket the questions were coming thick and fast.

'What's the studio like?'

'What was the train like? Would you feel able to travel by train again?

'How was Oliver? Did you see any of his paintings?'

'Did you meet any of his friends?'

Chloe did her best to answer them discreetly, describing his flat as 'small and bohemian as befits an artist'. She told them that he was preparing for an exhibition of his paintings – which she rather doubted – and then ventured on to the subject of his friends.

'I met his model,' she said. 'A beautiful woman. French and very—'

'*French*?' Jessica frowned. 'How very unfortunate. He knows his father didn't trust the French. He couldn't abide the language either and neither can I. I much prefer Italian.'

'She's very vivacious.'

Bertha asked, 'Did they seem very friendly – towards each other, I mean? Mama worries that London is a big place and . . .' She glanced at her mother. 'And Oliver might be lonely.'

Chloe managed to keep her face straight. 'Very friendly together. She obviously likes him.'

Jessica grunted. 'Women always do. Oliver's too attractive for his own good.' She looked thoughtful. 'His *model*,
did you say? You mean he paints *women*?'

'Certainly, and very well. Her name's Adele and she's a
dancer.'

Jessica brightened, clasping her hands. 'I've always
adored the ballet. When my husband was alive we used to
go to Covent Garden whenever we could. I always admired
their dedication, those dancers. The hours and hours they
train, you know, and they have to be very fit. But those
days are long gone.' She sighed. 'But do go on, child.'

Chloe decided not to mention the Empire Music Hall.
'Well, of course,' she said, 'the main purpose of my visit was
the surprise birthday present. Oliver's idea is most exciting.'
She gave Bertha an almost imperceptible wink.

'The surprise! Oh yes. Do tell us, Chloe.'

Chloe turned to Jessica. 'Oliver wants you to have your
portrait painted as a birthday present from him and Bertha.
If you are willing, he—'

Bertha cried, 'It's a splendid idea, Mama! Do say you
agree.'

For a moment Jessica hesitated but then nodded. 'I think
that would be very nice,' she told them. 'A portrait.' Colour
touched her cheeks and her eyes glistened. 'That's so like
Oliver. He's such a dear boy. Fancy thinking of that. It's
a splendid idea.'

Bertha said, 'That's settled then. How very exciting.'

Chloe smiled. 'He's going to find someone to do the
portrait but you will have to be up and dressed for the
sittings. You can't be painted in bed.'

Jessica blinked. 'Good gracious. You're right, child.'

Bertha smiled. 'That won't be too difficult, will it Mama.
You already spend a considerable time out of your bed,
thanks to Chloe. I think we must bring you downstairs
and find a suitable background for the portrait. And maybe
something new to wear?'

Jessica nodded with a show of reluctance. 'It will take

every scrap of strength I have,' she told them, 'but I won't disappoint Oliver. Or you, Bertha,' she added hastily. 'And yes – a new gown might be the answer. Something in a soft green, perhaps, with cream lace at the throat . . .'

Bertha winked at Chloe. The ruse had succeeded.

Thursday and Friday passed without incident, for which Chloe was pleased. She had no wish to deal with further trouble involving Uncle Matty, and Oliver did not put in an appearance at Fairfields. Bertha continued to oversee the new wrought-iron screen and gates but had not yet plucked up enough courage to confront her mother with the invitation to tea.

During Chloe's trip to London Hettie's father had appeared at the door and a stormy scene had followed. Bertha had been shouted at and insulted and Hettie had been dragged away from Fairfields for a family conference from which she had not returned.

'He's obviously a very uncouth person,' Jessica told Chloe with distaste. 'He's threatening to take a shotgun, find the father and "send the pair of them up the aisle"! Have you ever heard such a thing? The man is out of his mind.'

In preparation for the sittings, Chloe daily urged Jessica to spend even longer out of bed and helped her to walk around the bedroom. The self-styled invalid no longer clutched at the furniture or leaned on Chloe for support as she walked and on Saturday morning it was decided that she was ready to spend an hour or so in the drawing room.

Chloe helped her down the stairs and on to the sofa. Uncle Matty had been persuaded to sit with her and chat for a while and when he withdrew Chloe brought down Jessica's sewing.

As Chloe tucked her into bed again Jessica patted her arm.

'I enjoyed myself, Chloe,' she said. 'I'm tired but that's to be expected. Bertha is right – it's thanks to you I'm making such wonderful progress. Don't think I don't appreciate all you do for us.'

Sunday came and the sky darkened with every indication that a summer storm was on the way. Rather appropriate, thought Chloe, for it was today that Bertha would be spending the afternoon with the Briers.

At five to one the entire family gathered at the table for the midday meal.

Uncle Matty beamed at Jessica. 'This is a wonderful day,' he told her. 'We've missed seeing you at table. Welcome back.'

Jessica, startled by his enthusiasm, smiled nervously. 'I shan't be down every day,' she warned. 'It does require an effort, you know.'

Bertha said, 'But it shows how much stronger you are, Mama.'

Mrs Letts came in with a tray and set two tureens on the table. 'I don't know when Hettie's coming back,' she said to nobody in particular. 'It's not just that I'm run off my feet – I worry about the girl. That father of hers is a mean devil. She's better off here than at home.'

Everyone looked at Jessica.

She said, 'I'll send Binns over this afternoon to bring her back.'

Bertha gave Chloe a quick glance, which reminded her of the invitation to tea with the Briers. If Binns was away on an errand, Bertha would have no means of transport. So why didn't she ask for it? Chloe decided to force Bertha to speak for herself.

'I think you need the dog cart, don't you Bertha?'

Bertha's face flushed. 'I was hoping . . . that is . . . that I could have Binns for . . .' She gave Chloe a frantic look.

Chloe turned to Jessica. 'Bertha has been invited out to tea with the Briers. It really is time they spent some time on the plans for the gates, which are going to look marvellous.'

Uncle Matty said, 'The gates? Ah yes! Meant to mention

90

them to you, Jessie. He's made a good job of the demolition. All cleared away shipshape and Bristol fashion! Can't wait to see the screen or whatever it's called.'

'It's a screen with gates.' Bertha spoke breathlessly. 'I showed you the plans, Mama, a few weeks ago.'

'Did you, Bertha? I don't remember.' Jessica picked daintily at her roast beef. 'Where's the gravy? Mrs Letts is always so slow with the gravy. She knows I hate dry beef.'

Chloe rolled her eyes at Bertha and said, 'What time will you need the dog cart? I can always walk across the fields to the Leemings' cottage to fetch Hettie. I'm sure Mr Leeming's bark is worse than his bite.'

Jessica looked doubtful. 'There's going to be a storm, Chloe. You'll probably get caught in it and I don't want you laid up in bed with a chill.'

Mrs Letts hurried in with the gravy boat.

Chloe smiled at Bertha. 'I'll go straight after lunch. I love walking through the fields and I need some exercise.'

Faced with Chloe's determination Jessica changed her mind. 'Perhaps we'll give Hettie another day or two. I don't want to antagonise her parents.'

Bertha's colour was returning to normal. 'I'll need to leave here at three o'clock.'

Jessica paid this announcement no attention and it seemed the matter was settled.

Uncle Matty filled his mouth with potato, chewed with obvious pleasure and swallowed noisily. 'So who is the baby's father? Do we know?'

Chloe spluttered as a piece of carrot went down the wrong way.

Jessica said, 'You should eat more slowly, Chloe. As for Hettie, if she doesn't tell us soon I shall think quite seriously about—' She stopped abruptly and turned to stare at Bertha. 'The Briers? But isn't that . . . You mean you're going to tea with the blacksmith?'

Every eye was on Bertha. Chloe held her breath. This

is your chance, she told Bertha silently. Don't let her override you.

'Yes, Mama. Tea is at four thirty. I'm looking forward to meeting Mrs Briers.'

'The blacksmith and his mother? Have you taken leave of your senses?'

'No, Mama. I'm sure I shall enjoy myself.'

It dawned slowly on Uncle Matty that all was not well. He frowned. 'Why shouldn't Bertha go out to tea? She doesn't get out enough, if you ask me.'

'I'm not asking you, Matty.' Jessica turned back to her daughter. 'You know what I think of the man.'

'And you know how I feel about him.' Bertha was now very pale.

Uncle Matty stared at Bertha. 'How *do* you feel about him?'

Jessica said, 'She thinks she's in love with him. I've told her he is not suitable. Miles Sandford is being very patient, but he won't wait forever.'

Uncle Matty snorted. 'That old windbag!'

Bertha said, 'I will never marry Miles and I've told him so several times. If he can't accept "no" he'll have a long wait!'

'You're being stubborn, Bertha. I simply can't bear the idea of my daughter marrying beneath herself.'

'Why not?' Chloe could keep quiet no longer. 'No one raises an eyebrow when a man marries beneath him. When a wealthy man marries an actress nothing is said.'

Matty said, 'Ah! The stage-door johnnies! I wouldn't have said no to an actress in my younger days. I actually proposed to one once but she turned me down flat. Damned near broke my heart. There's a lot to be said for—'

'Matty!' Jessica snapped. 'We don't want to hear about your blighted hopes.'

'Or mine, apparently!'

They all stared at Bertha.

'I think I am old enough to choose my own husband. If I'm ever to marry . . .' Her voice shook.

Chloe said, 'I agree with Bertha. Why shouldn't a woman have the same chance of happiness as a man?'

For this impertinence Chloe was given the benefit of one of Jessica's icy looks. 'Thank you, Chloe. This is *family* business.'

Chloe ignored the snub. 'George Brier is no ordinary blacksmith. He's a very skilled craftsman. An artist in his field. He's going to be famous one day.'

Uncle Matty blinked in surprise. 'Going to be famous? Is he really? I'll be damned.'

'Please mind your language, Matty.'

Unabashed, Matty looked at Bertha with interest. 'Are you in love with him, Bertha?'

Uncle Matty is intrigued, thought Chloe, and not at all disapproving. Another ally, perhaps.

Bertha nodded. 'Yes I am. And I'm going to tea with them, Mama, and you can't stop me. I'll walk all the way if I have to.'

'Well really, Bertha! I never expected a daughter of mine to be so . . . so disrespectful. I just hope you'll change your mind and save yourself a lot of heartache. The man's not worth it.'

'How can you say that, Mama?' Bertha glared at her. 'You don't know anything about him. You don't want to know because you're not interested. And that's because I'm not Oliver. You care more about him than you do me.'

Chloe agonised for her but decided she must let Bertha fight her own fight. If this was the moment, Bertha must seize it. Reluctantly Chloe remained silent.

Jessica appeared too surprised to answer and Bertha pressed home her advantage. Standing up and pushing back her chair, she said, 'It's my life, Mama. If I'm making a mistake it will be me that suffers.'

Chuckling, Uncle Matty reached out with his fork and

speared another potato. 'There's no answer to that, Jessie my dear.'

'Oh do be quiet, Matty,' snapped Jessica, clutching her table napkin. 'You know nothing about such matters. You're just a meddling old fool! If you had an ounce of sense you'd have found a wife for yourself. But no! You have to spend your days at Fairfields annoying the rest of us and interfering. My only daughter is not going to throw herself away on a blacksmith and that's final.'

Bertha stood behind her chair, clutching it for support. 'I don't need your permission, Mama. I'm old enough to make my own decisions. And as a matter of fact I've made one already.' She drew herself up a little straighter. 'I *shall* marry George, with or without your approval.'

'God give me patience!' If Jessica was surprised she hid it well. 'Sit down, Bertha, and finish your meal. You're being melodramatic.'

Bertha hesitated. Don't obey her, thought Chloe. All eyes were on Bertha, who tightened her lips and then turned and walked out of the room. No one spoke. Jessica gave an exaggerated sigh and shook her head in despair.

Uncle Matty tutted. 'Now look what you've done. You've upset the poor girl.'

'Upset *her*?' Jessica clutched her heart. 'Bertha has upset *me* – but that doesn't seem to worry you. Do you want to see her married to a blacksmith? Living in a cottage with a brood of children?'

Uncle Matty was loading his fork with cabbage and potato. 'If she doesn't wed soon she won't have *any* children.'

Jessica gave him a poisonous look. 'I shouldn't really expect you to understand. You've never thought about anyone but yourself – and you've dropped a piece of cabbage down your jacket.'

He glanced down, scraped up the offending morsel and put it in his mouth. It was deliberate provocation and Chloe held her breath.

Jessica groaned. 'You're a disgusting old man!' She closed her eyes.

How, Chloe wondered, could anyone get the better of someone like Uncle Matty?

Jessica opened her eyes. 'That's it! I won't stay here a moment longer. I made an effort to rejoin the family and this is the thanks I get.' She turned to Chloe. 'Help me upstairs. I'm going back to bed.'

Ten minutes later, with Jessica safely installed in bed, Chloe went in search of Bertha. She found her in the summer house, still shaking with shock.

'Here!' Chloe held out a small glass of sherry. 'I'm sure you need something. You were wonderful in there. Really, I was full of admiration.'

'But Mama is furious.' Bertha tossed the sherry down in two large gulps.

Chloe shrugged. 'It won't do her any harm to face up to life's hurly-burly. We all have to do it.' She grinned. 'She has retired, thoroughly mortified, but did you notice something? She hasn't said you can't have Binns. So you can go out to tea. That's what you wanted, isn't it?'

Bertha nodded uncertainly. 'But Mama can't bear upsets. It's bad for her.'

'Leave your mother to me,' Chloe told her. 'That's what I'm here for.'

The following day was Monday, Chloe's day off, and by ten thirty she was cosily ensconced in Dorothy's kitchen drinking home-made barley water. Dorothy was leaning across the table listening eagerly to her sister's account of the events at Fairfields concerning Bertha and George Briers. Chloe told her everything, secure in the knowledge that nothing would be passed on.

'Not even to Albert,' she warned. 'This must be in the strictest confidence.'

'Cross my heart.' Dorothy looked at her curiously. 'Why do you say that? Is there something else?'

Chloe nodded. 'This is strictly between me and you. It's about Oliver and a housemaid.'

She then explained what had happened between them. 'So my guess is that Oliver won't marry her.'

Dorothy's kindly face darkened. 'Oh that poor girl! But it just shows you. That might have been you, Chloe. I did warn you.'

'But it isn't me.' Chloe hesitated. What she had to suggest might sound outrageous to her sister.

Dorothy brightened. 'Perhaps Albert will be asked to officiate at the christening. Could you mention us, do you think? It's not a large fee but every little bit helps.'

Chloe leaned forward and took hold of her sister's hand. 'If Hettie has to have the child adopted . . . Well, I wondered . . .' It was much harder than she had anticipated. 'It crossed my mind that you and Albert . . .'

Dorothy's eyes had widened. 'Adopt a child? Is that what you mean? Oh Chloe.' She withdrew her hand and fiddled with her apron. 'I don't know. I've thought about adoption, of course, but I couldn't bring myself to say anything to Albert. It would make him think I've given up hope. I really don't know what to say.'

Chloe sat back. 'It was an idea, that's all. It might not come to that. Hettie might keep the baby or her mother might want to bring it up. Or Oliver *might* do the decent thing by her.'

'But he's already denying that it's his.'

'Yes, but Hettie's in love with him. I don't think she's been with any other man. I wouldn't like to see the baby farmed off to someone uncaring.'

'Because it will be *Oliver*'s child?'

Chloe shrugged. 'I suppose so. I admit I do like him a little but from what I now know I see that he's hardly trustworthy.' She finished her barley water. 'Will you at least think about it? And only tell Albert if you think you like the idea. And please don't set your heart on it. It all depends on whether or not the baby is to be adopted. We won't know anything definite until Oliver comes home and the truth comes out. And even then, we shouldn't try and persuade Hettie to do anything she doesn't want to do. She's the mother and ideally the baby should stay with her.'

Dorothy regarded her earnestly. '*I* could adopt a child,' she said, 'but men are funny about things like that.'

Unable to argue with her sister and feeling that she had said enough, Chloe changed the subject and told her about Uncle Matty, Sid Jakes and the broken window.

Dorothy frowned. 'Sid Jakes? He's been trouble before. Apparently he caught a poacher with a couple of hares and gave him a thorough beating before handing him over to the police. Rather nasty. Poor Lennie's got two broken ribs but he was in the wrong so the constable says there's nothing to be done.'

'Can't Jakes be charged with brutality or something? The wretch is dangerous.'

'They say there's no charge they can bring against Jakes because he was doing his job as a gamekeeper and the fellow was resisting capture.'

'But it surely wasn't necessary to use such force.'

Dorothy helped herself to another biscuit. 'Albert went to see the chap's mother and was very concerned. Lennie's as poor as a church mouse and Albert says he was driven to it. He's getting a basket of food together for them. I'm making a cake, Edie Watts is giving them a jar of honey and Mrs Deekes is giving a leg of salted pork. She's a generous soul.'

'Isn't she the woman that keeps three pigs? And one escaped and was halfway to Rye before they caught up with it?'

'Yes.' Dorothy smiled at the memory. 'She makes a bit of money out of them. They also keep rabbits. If the housekeeper at Fairfields wants some rabbit that's free of shot . . .'

'I'll tell her.' Chloe sighed. 'Did I tell you a silver salver had disappeared? I accused Uncle Matty and it mysteriously reappeared.'

Dorothy tutted. 'The whole family is jinxed!' she declared. 'Nothing but misfortune. I should feel most unsafe there. Too many mysteries for my liking. Should you stay on there, Chloe, do you think?'

Chloe laughed. 'I'm not in any danger,' she said.

'But that wretch pulled your hair and pushed you over.'

'It was a show of temper. Bluster. Men like that are all talk.'

'What do you know about men like that? Or any men? Nothing.'

Chloe knew this to be true but she said, 'I'm learning fast,' and changed the subject. They talked about Albert's indigestion and Dorothy's new recipe for marrow jam, the Sunday school outing and Albert's mother, who had written to say she had been stung by a bee.

Dorothy said, 'This must sound very dull compared with Fairfields but I'm beginning to worry about you, Chloe. I'm sure it's possible to have too much excitement.'

Before Chloe could answer, Albert came in and welcomed Chloe with a brotherly kiss. She was always pleased to see her brother-in-law but the womanly confidences inevitably came to an abrupt end when he appeared.

When she left at the end of the day Dorothy hugged her. 'Do be careful,' she insisted. 'I know you're enjoying your job but I'm not entirely happy about you being there. To me Fairfields sound like a slumbering volcano and I'd hate you to be around if it erupts!'

When Chloe returned to Fairfields she was ambushed by Bertha, who positively bubbled with excitement. She led Chloe to the summer house and sat her down without preamble to tell her about the previous day's visit.

'George's mother is so sweet,' she told Chloe. 'I liked her at once and I think she liked me. She was very deferential at first but I tried my hardest to put her at ease and I think I did overcome her shyness by the time I had to leave. She even thought of Binns waiting outside in the dog cart and sent for him when the storm broke. She gave him a slice of caraway cake and a mug of home-brewed ale. Binns thinks they're a wonderful family.' She stopped to smile and added a deep sigh of satisfaction. 'George's mother wants us to marry. Isn't that wonderful? Naturally she didn't say so in as many words but I could tell by her tone and the way she looked at me. She has such a cheerful attitude. So unlike Mama.' Bertha frowned briefly but then the joy broke through again. 'We had the very simplest fare but I was so happy to be with them it all tasted delicious. They have an ancient cat and a few pigeons in an old dovecot.'

Chloe said, 'What happened when you came home? Has your mother caused any difficulties?'

'None at all!' Bertha shook her head emphatically. 'I went up to see her but she pretended to be asleep. Uncle Matty said she's been very subdued and he thinks I did the right thing to stand up for myself. Oh! And there's been a message from Oliver. He's coming down tomorrow. And Hettie came back without prompting. Her father's coming up tomorrow to speak to Mama but if Oliver's here he can deal with it.'

Chloe said, 'That's probably for the best,' and wished she could have prepared the family for the revelations that were to come.

Six

Tuesday morning arrived with heavy clouds that blew in fast from the west. After a restless night Chloe was up early and washed and dressed before Jessica woke at ten to eight.

'I haven't slept a wink,' she told Chloe as she made her way slowly towards the blue and white washbasin. Chloe lifted the hot-water jug and poured carefully into the cold water that was already there.

'We have to think carefully about your clothes today. I think you need to look imposing,' Chloe told her. 'You have to impress Hettie's father so that he's totally overawed and doesn't start to throw his weight about. He's got a temper, apparently.'

She crossed to the wardrobe and rummaged along the rail. 'Here we are. A dark green skirt and a rather severe cream blouse.'

'I'm dreading it,' Jessica confided. 'I do hate scenes. I was brought up to believe that loss of control is in very poor taste.'

Chloe remained silent. In her opinion there was no way the family could avoid a scene. It was as inevitable as Christmas.

Jessica was installed in the drawing room by nine thirty and Bertha was hiding herself in the garden looking busy with a watering can.

Chloe was watching the drive for Oliver's arrival. He had obviously caught an early train, because he appeared just before ten o'clock looking harassed and pale.

As well you might!, Chloe thought as she came face to face with him on the doorstep. He could not be feeling worse than Hettie.

As soon as he saw Chloe he caught her by the arm and pulled her out on to the steps, where they would not be overheard.

'What have you told them?' he demanded. 'How much do they know about Adele?'

'Only that she sometimes models for you when you paint and is a dancer. Your mother has decided that she's a ballerina and I didn't disillusion her.'

He twisted his mouth. 'She'll be disillusioned soon enough! Oh hell! What a damned mess. Pardon my language but I feel like throwing myself under a train.' He stared gloomily across the lawn.

Chloe said, 'That wouldn't help anybody.'

'I'm no use to anyone. More of a burden.'

'Now you're feeling sorry for yourself and that's not going to help either. Hettie's father is coming up later and we'll all need to keep our heads. He's a difficult character at the best of times and now that he's got a legitimate grievance he's going to be very difficult.'

'Do you know if—' He broke off as Bertha appeared beside them.

Bertha looked suspiciously from Oliver to Chloe. 'What are you two whispering about? Secrets?'

Oliver said, 'Oh for heaven's sake grow up, Bertha! We're just talking.'

She reddened slightly. 'Well, you'd better "just talk" to Mama. She's working herself up into a frenzy and Uncle Matty is making her worse.'

'He would!' Forgetting Chloe, Oliver stalked inside and Bertha followed.

Halfway along the passage she turned back to Chloe. 'Why's Oliver so bad-tempered? Do you know something I don't?'

'Oliver wants to tell you in his own way.'

'That sounds ominous.'

In the drawing room they found Uncle Matty smoking a cigar and Jessica waving her hands in an ineffectual attempt to disperse the smoke. Seeing Oliver, Jessica's face brightened.

'Oliver, my dear boy!' she cried, holding out her arms.

He kissed her dutifully and then said, 'I've something to tell you and it won't be easy for any of us but I want to get it over with.' He glanced at Chloe. 'For family ears only, please.'

Chloe turned towards the door but Bertha put out a hand to stop her. 'I'd like Chloe to stay,' she said. 'She's almost family.'

Jessica stared at her. 'Almost family? What are you talking about?'

Uncle Matty blew a smoke ring and watched it float towards the ceiling. He said, 'She's not a servant, if that's what you're suggesting.'

Chloe said, 'Please! Don't argue over me. I'm going.'

Bertha looked at her brother. 'A detached viewpoint might be useful if we're to deal with Mr Leeming . . . He's going to blame us for not keeping an eye on her.'

Oliver said harshly, 'It's much worse than that. Oh, let her stay then. Please . . . Sit down, Chloe.'

They regarded him nervously.

Bertha cried, 'Oh Oliver! You're not ill, are you? I couldn't bear that.'

'I'm not ill. It might have been easier if I *were* ill. A few pills from the doc would make it all better.' He caught his mother's expression. 'I promise you, Mama, I am *not* ill.'

Bertha clutched Chloe's hand.

Oliver sighed heavily. 'You all know Hettie's with child. I'm probably the father. I don't think Hettie's the type to lie and she says I was the only one. I wish I could think otherwise but—'

'Wait!' cried Jessica. 'I'm a little lost, Oliver. You're not saying you are the father of . . . You can't mean that, can you?' Wide-eyed she stared at him then, as he didn't reply, her eyes turned towards Uncle Matty. 'He's not saying what I think he's saying, is he?'

Uncle Matty shrugged plump shoulders. 'I'm sorry, old thing, but that's exactly what he does mean.'

Jessica gave a little scream of horror. 'No! Not Oliver and that dreadful girl!'

Bertha said, 'She's not dreadful, Mama. She's very unfortunate but she's not dreadful.' She glanced at her brother with distaste. 'It's Oliver who's dreadful.'

'Thank you, Bertha, for that vote of confidence!' He glared at her. 'You're not making this easy for me.'

'Why should it be easy? You get a servant into trouble and want things easy. Listen to yourself, Oliver.'

Chloe said quickly, 'Shall we hear the rest of it and then we can decide how to deal with it?'

Jessica said, 'Yes, let's listen to Oliver. I'm sure it's all been a big misunderstanding.' She regarded him hopefully.

Once again they all turned towards Oliver.

He cleared his throat nervously. 'It started as a moment's foolishness after a party last year. I was on my way to bed and I'd drunk too much wine. I was feeling a bit light-headed. As I passed Hettie I stumbled and fell against her. Then I kissed her and said, "Happy Christmas, Hettie." That was all I meant to do.' He ran his fingers through his hair distractedly and drew a deep breath. 'I suspect she might also have had something to drink – maybe mulled wine. Mrs Letts usually makes some for the staff. Anyway, one thing led to another and before I knew it I was in her bedroom . . . That was that. It was nobody's fault.'

'It was *your* fault,' said Bertha. 'You're old enough to know better.'

Jessica began to cry softly and Bertha moved to kneel beside her.

Oliver went on. 'I went back to London and forgot all about the incident but the next time I—'

'Incident?' cried Bertha furiously. 'It was a *seduction*, Oliver, not an incident.'

Uncle Matty wagged a finger at her. 'Now, now. Hear the lad out.'

Jessica cried, 'Hear him out? Oh God! Haven't we heard enough?'

Oliver closed his eyes and Chloe began to feel sorry for him.

He said, 'After that, whenever I came home Hettie gave me a lot of encouragement. Said she was in love with me. It was so easy. Fatally easy. It became a bit of a habit.'

Jessica blew her nose and straightened her back. 'No son of mine is going to marry a servant,' she declared. 'Hettie must go.'

Bertha cried, 'Go? Go where? How can you give her a reference . . . and how can she get work without one? She's Oliver's responsibility now.'

Uncle Matty leaned back in his chair and surveyed the ceiling in search of inspiration. 'Hettie's not a bad-looking girl,' he said at last. 'Young, full of energy. She could make a good enough wife.'

'Nonsense,' snapped Jessica. 'She's not at all suitable. A common girl like that? And think of her family. Do you seriously think—'

Bertha interrupted. 'Oliver obviously thought she was good enough to have his child. My nephew or niece and your grandchild.'

It was clear from Jessica's face that this angle had never occurred to her. 'My grandchild?' she whispered. 'Oh no! That's quite unbearable.'

Bertha said, 'I'm not exactly pleased by the prospect.'

They all looked at Oliver, who turned away from the accusing faces and crossed to the window.

Uncle Matty pursed his lips. 'But Bertha's got a point there. Another member of the Maitland clan!' He roared with laughter then, seeing the faces regarding him stonily, turned it into a cough. 'Look here, Ollie old lad,' he said.

'There's a quick way out of this. Give old Leeming a fistful of fivers and tell him to pack her off to one of her aunts. She has the child, it's adopted and bob's your uncle.'

Bertha said, 'She may not have an aunt.'

'Everyone's got aunts.'

Chloe said, 'And that's the last you see of Oliver's child. Gone forever.'

Jessica's gaze lingered on a photograph of Bertha and Oliver as children. Taken on the beach at Porthleven, Bertha carried a small parasol and Oliver was filling a bucket with water for a nearby sandcastle. She turned to look at her son. 'Do you love her at all, Oliver?' she asked softly. 'Could you love her?'

'No Mama, I don't love her. If you must know, I love Adele. I've loved her for years but—'

'The dancer?' Jessica stared at him as though at a stranger. She put a hand to her head. 'The ballet dancer?'

'She's not a ballet dancer, Mama. She dances at the Empire Music Hall, Leicester Square.'

'What? That scandalous place? Why, the Empire is a byword for—' Jessica bit back the word but they all knew it. *Immorality*. A bawdy music hall where elegant women of the night might be found touting for customers among the wealthy male patrons.

Again Uncle Matty's laugh boomed out and Chloe longed to throttle him. He seemed to have no sensitivity. Couldn't he see how difficult this was for them?

'The good old Empire. Used to spend a lot of my time there when I was a military man. We all did.'

He winked at Chloe but Bertha caught the look and said, 'If you can't be serious for heaven's sake go away. This isn't funny.' She turned back to Oliver. 'If you love this Adele woman why didn't you marry her? Why do this . . . terrible thing to Hettie?'

He turned to face them. 'Because Adele won't marry me. She says she loves me but wants to be free to make her way as a dancer.'

'But she doesn't object to sharing your home!' Bertha said. 'She sounds rather selfish to me.'

'Actually, I live in *her* flat.'

Jessica rallied. 'If she won't marry you, she doesn't love you enough! What's the matter with the woman? Apart from the fact that she's French, of course.'

Chloe had lost interest in Adele and decided to bring the conversation nearer to home. 'Maybe we could find someone locally – a decent, good-hearted couple – who would bring the child up as their own. Then Oliver could see the child occasionally. You all could.'

Oliver threw up his hands in a gesture of despair. 'I don't know what to say. Can't you understand? I want to make everything right but I can't. I can't see how to do the right thing – unless I marry Hettie. That means living a lie, because I'll always love Adele. I've lived in hope for years that she'll change her mind and say yes.'

Jessica said, 'Perhaps I should speak to her.'

Oliver rolled his eyes. 'No, Mama! Please don't!'

'Well really! I am simply trying to help. Being in love with a dancer seems to have ruined your manners, Oliver.'

Uncle Matty sat up suddenly and pointed his cigar in Oliver's direction. 'Does this dancer know about Hettie's child?'

Oliver looked horrified. 'Of course not. She's hardly likely to marry me if she finds out how stupid I've been. Whatever I do, nothing will be any good. This has ruined my life.'

Shocked, they all sat in silence, coming to terms with his tragedy. Chloe also thought about Hettie and *her* tragedy. Finally she decided to break the tension.

'Should we have a tray of tea?' she suggested.

'Oh yes, child.' Jessica gave her a tremulous smile. 'Ring for Het— . . . for Mrs Letts.'

'Hettie might come,' Chloe reminded them. 'I'll go to the kitchen and fetch it.'

Glad to escape the sight of so many stricken faces she hurried from the room. She sat in the kitchen while Mrs Letts laid the tea tray with a lace cloth, silver jug and sugar bowl and the second-best china. Chloe felt like advising against any fuss. A tot of whisky would probably be of more use in the circumstances but no one could persuade Jessica that alcohol was the answer. It would be tea or nothing.

Hettie said, 'When's Mr Maitland coming?'

'He's already here,' Chloe told her and saw Hettie's face light up.

Hettie turned to Mrs Letts. 'He's here!'

'What's that to you?'

'It'll be all right now. You'll see.'

Mrs Letts' eyes narrowed. Hettie realised her mistake but it was too late.

The housekeeper turned to Chloe. 'It's not . . . Is she saying that Mr Maitland . . . ?' Open-mouthed, she saw Chloe nod. 'God Almighty!' she whispered and sat down. She stared at Hettie. 'Well, now you've gone and done it!'

Hettie's response was to burst into tears, pull open the back door and flee into the garden.

Chloe said, 'It's a terrible mess.'

Mrs Letts fanned her face with her apron. 'I'm all of a sweat,' she muttered. 'That's a shock, that is. I can't believe it.'

The kettle whistled but Mrs Letts ignored it. Chloe was spooning tea into the pot when the front doorbell rang. They looked at each other in horror.

Chloe said, 'That might be Mr Leeming. Give me time to take the tray in and then open the door. Oh, I'd better take another cup and saucer although I doubt if tea is his tipple.'

Five minutes later Mr Leeming had finally been persuaded to sit down although he refused the tea. A shapeless man, he sprawled in the chair with his legs outstretched and his arms folded across his chest. He wore what probably passed as his Sunday suit but his collarless shirt was unbuttoned and his hair needed a wash. He seemed rather to enjoy their dismay as he glared at each in turn.

To Uncle Matty he said, 'Seen you down at the local, haven't I?'

Uncle Matty, sipping his tea, said, 'Not to my knowledge, old chap.'

Without further preamble Oliver confessed that he had fathered Hettie's child. For a moment Mr Leeming was too surprised to speak but then his expression changed.

'You!' he exclaimed. 'You and our Hettie?' A broad smile spread over his face. 'By all that's holy, she's picked herself a winner.'

'Hardly.' Jessica's gaze was frosty. 'There is no way, Mr Leeming, that Oliver is going to marry your daughter. We are here to explore the alternatives.'

Oliver said, 'Naturally I shall make some provision for her.'

Mr Leeming's face had darkened. 'Not marry her? You damned well *will* marry her. You'll make an honest woman of her, that's what you'll do. No man messes with my daughter and gets away with it.'

Chloe leaned towards Jessica and asked her in a low voice if she should remain.

Jessica whispered, 'Safety in numbers!' and Chloe nodded.

Relieved, Chloe sat back. She had felt obliged to ask although her disappointment at being excluded would have been immense. There was an awful fascination in seeing the drama through, especially when she herself was not involved. But beyond the fascination, she did feel that she had something to offer. A detached view, free from the emotional entanglements.

Jessica said, 'An unhappy marriage is hardly a solution, Mr Leeming.'

He turned to her. 'Yeah, well, most marriages are unhappy if you did but know it. Ours hasn't been the best but at least I done the right thing by my missus. You got to be respectable and a kid born the wrong side of the blanket is not respectable. My daughter needs a husband.'

Bertha said, 'She might want to have the baby adopted. Have you thought of that?'

'Her ma's thought about it but Hettie wasn't keen. Mind you, that was before we knew he was the father.' He jerked a thumb in Oliver's direction. 'Bit different now. He can look after her very nicely. Better than we could've hoped.'

Chloe could see fear in the eyes of each member of the Maitland family. She said, 'Hettie might be willing to consider adoption if—'

Oliver said, 'She should be in here. We should be asking her directly.'

Chloe said, 'She was in the garden last time I saw her. Shall I—'

But Bertha, looking strained and ill at ease, had risen. 'I'll find her,' she said and left the room before anyone could object.

Mr Leeming still had his eyes on Oliver. 'You talking money, are you? Like, settling a little sum on her for the kid if she goes quietly?'

'I wouldn't put it quite like that.'

'Course you wouldn't but that's what it would be, wouldn't it. No trouble for you or yours.' He shrugged.

Jessica said, 'Another cup of tea for anyone? I'll ring for Mrs Letts.'

There were several takers and the moment Mrs Letts withdrew with the tray Bertha arrived, pushing Hettie in front of her.

'Come in Hettie,' said Jessica. 'Sit there.' She pointed and, after a quick glance at her father, Hettie obeyed. She was red-eyed and her cheeks were blotchy. Oliver didn't look at her and she gazed studiously at her clasped hands.

Mr Leeming cleared his throat. 'Well, my girl,' he began. 'You've landed yourself in a bit of a pickle but the kid's pa is going to see you right – or I'll want to know why.'

She nodded. 'I do love him,' she said, 'and he loves me so—'

Bertha said, 'He doesn't love you, Hettie. I'm afraid he doesn't.'

Hettie looked at Oliver. 'You tell them,' she said.

Chloe's heart contracted at the trust shining in Hettie's eyes. She *did* love him and she thought he felt the same.

Oliver looked at her. 'I can't marry you, Hettie. There's someone else. In London. But as your father says I'll see you right. I'm truly sorry for what's happened.'

White-faced, she stared at him and her eyes grew dark. 'But you said nothing would happen if—'

'I know. I was wrong.'

'What d'you mean "someone else"?' Mr Leeming had suddenly caught up with the conversation. 'First I've heard of it. You mean you was just playing around with my daughter and all the time you was . . . Who is this someone else?'

'A woman in London.'

Jessica gave Oliver a warning glance. 'It's none of your business, Mr Leeming.'

Mrs Letts came in with more tea and set it down with an anxious look at her mistress. 'Did you want biscuits?' she whispered.

Jessica stared at her. 'Biscuits?'

'To go with the tea?'

'Oh for heaven's sake!'

Mrs Letts left them.

Mr Leeming's voice rose. 'So what's with this someone? You married, is that it?'

'Certainly not.'

'Living in sin?'

Oliver hesitated. 'I live with her, yes.'

Jessica gasped and Bertha said, 'Oliver! There's no need to tell him everything. He has no right to ask.'

Hettie said, 'Aren't you going to marry me, then? Not ever?'

Suddenly Chloe wished herself anywhere but in the midst of it. The raw emotion in the room was painful to bear. She stood up.

Bertha said urgently, 'Don't go. We need you.'

Chloe said, 'Perhaps we should all go away and think things over and—'

Jessica said, 'No! I can't go through this again. We have to settle it.' She looked at Hettie. 'Do you want to keep the baby, Hettie, if my son isn't going to marry you? If so he will give you some money. Or you could have the baby adopted.'

Tears ran down Hettie's cheeks. 'I won't give it up,' she sobbed. 'It's Oliver's baby and mine and I want to keep it.'

Mr Leeming stood up and faced Oliver. 'That's it then. I'll get off home. I'll expect a letter from you in the morning saying what you're willing to pay. And make it generous. Hettie, you're coming home with me.'

'No!' she cried. To Jessica she said, 'Please let me stay on. I won't be any trouble, I swear it.'

Bertha, seeing the girl's apprehension, said, 'She could stay, couldn't she, Mama? For a few weeks.'

But Mr Leeming had grabbed his daughter by the hand.

'Oliver!' cried Hettie but was pulled, protesting, to the door.

Chloe looked at Oliver but he was sitting with his head in his hands. Bertha was comforting her mother. Uncle Matty, apparently unperturbed, nodded his head.

'Let her go,' he advised. 'It's for the best. The girl has to talk with her mother.' He heaved himself from the chair and lumbered out of the room.

Bertha said, 'Mama wants to go back to bed.'

Oliver said, 'I'll give you a hand.'

But Jessica shook her head. 'No thank you, Oliver. You've done quite enough already.' She looked at Chloe, who moved to take her right arm then helped her back to her room.

Chloe went next door into her own room and shut the door thankfully behind her. As she passed the large swing mirror she noticed with surprise that she was crying.

Just before midnight Hettie's mother slipped from the bed, wrapped a shawl around her shoulders and crept into her daughter's room. For a moment she studied Hettie as she slept. In the candlelight she looked peaceful enough but the bruise on her face was visible. Tomorrow she'd have a black eye. The evening had been one long row and had ended in tears, threats and worse. She had never seen her husband so angry and she'd failed to keep father and daughter apart.

Reluctantly Betsy shook her. 'Het! Wake up.'

There was no response and Betsy tried to imagine her daughter lying with Oliver Maitland. Her little girl and a man like that. She felt a twinge of envy as she imagined soft hands roaming her daughter's body. Her own husband was rough and careless but no worse than most men, she supposed. Love with a gentleman must be wonderful – unless it ends in sorrow.

She shook Hettie again until she opened her eyes. 'We have to talk,' she said softly.

'But Pa . . .?'

'He's sleeping it off. Snoring fit to wake the dead. He didn't mean half of what he said so you mustn't mind him, Het. He's so ashamed. 'Tis hard on a man like your pa.'

'He hit me and I hate him!' Hettie sat up, her lips quivering. 'He said Oliver's selfish but he isn't. Oliver isn't bad. He's wonderful and I want to keep the baby.'

'What you want and what you get are two different things!' Betsy sat down on the edge of the bed. 'I've been thinking. Suppose we could find you a nice husband who didn't mind about the baby. Some men are good like that. Would you marry someone else? The money you get from Oliver Maitland would set you up a treat and—'

Hettie rubbed her eyes. 'I want to marry Oliver.'

'I know, ducks, but did he ever promise you?'

'Not exactly but . . . he said he loved me.'

'Was he drunk?'

Hettie sighed. 'A bit. Not so much. Not falling down or anything. Just merry. Happy.' Her eyes filled with tears. 'I couldn't say no to him because I loved him.'

'Did he give you any money?'

'No! I didn't want to be *paid*.'

Betsy stared round the familiar room in search of inspiration. A small shabby table on which sat a rag doll and an ancient teddy bear with one eye. A chest of drawers, a wooden chair and a handmade cotton rug. For a moment she tried to imagine the home her daughter might have had if Oliver Maitland had stood by her . . .

'There you are then, Het. His sort don't marry your sort. You've got yourself in a right mess and you'll have to make the best of a bad job . . . Maybe Lizzie would take the baby.'

Hettie sat up. '*Lizzie*? Have my baby? No, she can't!'

'But she's got one already and she's still feeding him. She could feed another one and then the baby will have—'

'No! *No*! She can't have Oliver's baby. I want my baby to have a father and Lizzie's never going to get that Sam of hers to the altar. Anyway, I don't want Sam to be my baby's pa.' Hettie regarded her mother with a sullen expression. 'Why can't I marry Oliver? It's not fair.'

Her mother sighed heavily. 'He's told you. He's in love with this other woman. Face facts. Your baby's a mistake . . .' She brightened. 'What about Frank Shaw? He's a nice enough lad and he might wed you. He's got a job, too.'

'He's got crinkly hair.'

'Beggars can't be choosers, ducks.'

'And it's not much of a job, mucking out stables.'

'But the Shaws are a nice enough family. They'd see you right.'

'Frank used to dip my pigtails in the inkwells! I hate him. Anyway, he's walking out with that Jenny Fell from Winchelsea.'

'That skinny little miss?' Betsy tossed her head. 'She's got no more sense than a turnip, that one! You'd be a real catch for Frank Shaw.'

'He's got that funny laugh. I don't want young 'uns with a funny laugh.'

Betsy was running out of patience but she persevered. 'He looks very nice in his Sunday suit. Remember him at that funeral, when his uncle died? Real spick and span he was. You think about it. You could do a lot worse.' She stood up. 'Now I'm off back to bed but remember – don't go upsetting your pa tomorrow. He's got his pride and you've hurt him pretty bad and if you don't watch your tongue you'll get another wallop.'

She went back to bed feeling marginally better. Hettie was biddable. They'd talk her round. In the morning she'd have a quiet word with Frank's mother. If there was enough money from Oliver Maitland it might just do the trick.

The next morning Oliver asked to have his breakfast in his room but Chloe was not to be deterred. She finished her own breakfast then hurried up to knock on his door.

'Who is it?'

Without answering, Chloe went in. Oliver, still in his nightshirt, was sitting at a small table by the window. A bowl of porridge remained untouched. He opened his mouth to complain about the intrusion but Chloe put a finger to her lips.

'I only have a minute,' she warned. 'Your mother will miss me. It's about the baby. I have a sister Dorothy—'

'The vicar's wife?'

'Yes. She . . . That is, they have been unable to have a child of their own. They might be willing to adopt your child. I was—'

'Hettie's child?'

Chloe saw that he was red-eyed and very pale. So he was suffering too. She let the contradiction pass and continued.

'They would be wonderful parents and you would see the child from time to time – if you wished. And if they were willing.'

He swivelled in his chair to face her, pulling the nightshirt down over his knees. A little late for modesty, thought Chloe.

114

'Hettie might not agree,' he said.

'But on the other hand she might. I could go to my sister this afternoon before the Leemings make other arrangements.'

'Hm. Mama might be happy with that. I wonder . . .' He studied her thoughtfully. 'You seem to be taking a lot on to your own shoulders. Is this idea for my benefit or that of your sister?'

Chloe glanced down, wondering how best to answer. 'A little of both?' she admitted.

The silence that followed lengthened uncomfortably. Chloe thought how far they had come since she first arrived for her interview. Then Oliver had seemed a being apart, a man very much in control with her future in his hands. Now he was in trouble and she was attempting to help him. During the past few weeks he had fallen in her eyes and she now saw him very clearly as just another person desperately trying to find a way through the maze that was life. She couldn't despise or blame him. He had his problems and she had hers.

At the thought of the father she could scarcely remember her eyes darkened. After leaving them he had written only once to tell them he was in America. California, apparently, was a wonderful place. He was working as a clerk on the railway and he enclosed some money. He promised more but they never heard from him again. Now he would be in his late forties and somehow Chloe meant to find him and talk to him before he died.

'I wish I'd never set eyes on the wretched girl.'

Chloe wrenched her thoughts back to the present.

Oliver went on. 'If Adele ever finds out . . .'

'You won't tell her then? That would be the honest thing to do.' Immediately she wished the words unsaid. They made her sound righteous but she was putting herself in Adele's place. If Adele ever agreed to marry Oliver it would be hard to deal with the existence of a child by another woman.

'Of course not,' he told her. 'I live in hope. If she did

find out she would never forgive me. I would lose her forever.'

'So what's your answer about Dorothy? I have to get back to your mother.'

He hesitated. 'Sound your sister out and tell me what she says. If you need an excuse to take the dog cart say I've sent you with an urgent letter for the post. I've written to Adele to say Mama is unwell and my return to London must be delayed so you won't actually be lying.'

Chloe's visit to her sister was brief and to the point. Dorothy had finally persuaded her husband to agree to adopt the child if the chance arose but only on the assumption that the child would never know the identity of the real parents. Chloe thought this a shame but it was not her decision to make. It also worried her slightly that Albert had been at all unwilling but she told herself that when they saw the baby love would grow and Albert would never regret it. She drove home in a cheerful mood, pleased with the news she had to impart.

As soon as she reached Fairfields, however, she suspected that something was wrong. Bertha was nowhere to be seen although the blacksmith was busy about his work on the new screen. Inside the house there was no sign of anyone and, growing increasingly alarmed, Chloe hurried up the stairs in search of Jessica. Before she reached her bedroom she heard voices from Uncle Matty's room and Mrs Letts came out carrying a slop pail.

'Oh Miss Blake, thank goodness you're back,' she cried, setting down the pail. 'It's poor Mr Orme. He's been set upon. Beaten something cruel. Miss Bertha's been washing the wounds.'

Before Chloe could reply Bertha came to the door.

'Thank goodness you're back,' she exclaimed as Mrs Letts took up the pail and made her way carefully down the stairs. 'Uncle Matty was strolling in the garden not a stone's throw from the house when a man ran from the shrubbery and leaped upon him. He was carrying a heavy walking stick and rained down blows on his head and shoulders.' She stopped to catch her breath and then went on. 'I heard Uncle Matty shouting for help and hurried out. I was screaming for Oliver but the brute saw me coming and ran off. Poor Uncle Matty. We half carried him inside. He was badly shocked and in such dreadful pain he could scarcely walk.'

She caught hold of Chloe's arm and dragged her into the room. Uncle Matty lay on his bed with a towel round his head. His eyes were closed and his mouth hung open. Oliver stood beside him looking helpless. There was blood on the pillow.

Oliver looked up. 'Mama's gone to her room. She fainted when she saw Uncle Matty and I thought it best not to involve her further. I've sent Binns for the doctor but he's taking his time.'

Chloe moved to stand beside him. Uncle Matty opened his eyes and groaned.

'I'm so sorry,' she told Uncle Matty. 'This is terrible. We must notify the police. Did you see who it was?'

'Not a chance,' he muttered thickly. 'He came up from behind me before I could take a gander at him. Ruddy thug.'

Bertha said, 'I don't know what the world's coming to. We have a queen who's the envy of the world, an empire to be proud of and yet this can happen to God-fearing people in their own home! It's a disgrace. The government's too lenient by far.'

Oliver looked concerned. Lowering his voice he said, 'He's taken a nasty bash on the side of his head and says his hearing's a bit ropey. And his right shoulder's painful. He can't lift his arm. We'll have to pray there's no permanent damage.' He turned towards the window. 'Where on earth is the doctor?'

He made no reference to Chloe's absence or the reason for her journey but presumably he would want to know what had transpired, she thought. But her first duty was to Mrs Maitland so she made her excuses and left the room.

Jessica was sitting by the window with a shawl round her shoulders.

'I can't stop shivering,' she complained. 'Why should anyone pick on a helpless old man? It's beyond belief. It's a wonder he isn't dead. Ask Mrs Letts to bring me some hot milk and a couple of biscuits. And then come back and stay with me, child. I need company.'

An hour or so later the doctor arrived and said Uncle Matty would make a full recovery but it would take a week or so and he must rest. There were no bones broken but the ribs were badly bruised and the muscles in his shoulder would take time to heal properly.

Just before retiring Chloe went to see Uncle Matty in his bedroom, making a small glass of sherry the excuse for her visit. With his untidy bed and his bandages he looked almost comic. Like an overgrown baby, she thought. All he needed was an ivory rattle and the picture would be complete.

She said, 'Are you feeling better?'

'Feeling better? Damned if I am!' He groaned. 'I'm feeling closer to my maker than ever before in my life! Help me up and let me get to that whisky!'

'It's sherry from the kitchen. The doctor said no alcohol but a mouthful won't hurt you.'

'A tumbler of Highland malt would do me more good.'

Somewhat self-consciously Chloe straightened his pillows. 'You know why I'm here,' she said. 'You have to tell the police about your attacker – and you could throw in the broken window for good measure.'

He downed the sherry. 'It's your fault,' he told her indignantly. 'You made me give back that salver. The snuffbox was worth much less. I knew it wouldn't satisfy him and now look what's happened.'

Chloe was silent. She had thought the same thing herself but had tried not to feel guilty about her part in the incident.

'It's hardly fair to blame me,' she protested. 'It was you who ran up the debt.'

'Now you're making excuses,' he told her. 'You nearly had me killed. I hope you realise that.' He peered at her over his spectacles. 'This man means business. He'll kill me as soon as look at me if I don't pay up.'

Chloe said, 'If you won't tell the police then I will. Something has to be—'

He clutched his chest dramatically. 'You've just signed my death warrant,' he whispered. 'I've told you, if they think I've reported them they'll be after me in earnest.' He drew an invisible knife across his throat. 'Please, Miss Blake. I know you think you're helping but I wish you wouldn't interfere. Believe me, it's better that way.'

'But don't you think—'

'Of course I think and I know exactly what I'm going to do.' He was slipping sideways and tried to move, grunting with pain. 'I'm going to borrow some money from young Ollie. He can't be short of the odd few guineas. And you can deliver it for me, the way you did before.' He closed his eyes. 'Now go away and let me suffer in peace.'

Chloe went.

Sunday the twenty-ninth of June. I spoke to Oliver this evening and urged him to make his peace with poor Hettie. I told him about Dorothy and Albert and he thinks as I do that they would make excellent parents. If he can persuade Hettie to agree, the problem is solved and I shall feel satisfied that I have been of some help.

Oliver is suffering so, poor man. Adele is adamant that she will never marry him and he drifts on from year to year with hopes that are never realised. I suppose she believes that one day she will become a lead dancer and be famous. And why not? I ask myself. But Oliver meanwhile pines for her and wastes his life. What can anyone do in the circumstances? I suggested that Adele might one day have a child but he laughed. 'She would probably strangle it at birth!'

Seven

B inns leaned against the back door, a mug of sweet tea in his hand. He watched Mrs Letts as she dried the crockery from breakfast and stacked it on the kitchen table. Red-faced and perspiring, she was asking for an end to the humid weather.

Binns said, 'A good storm. That's what we need. That last one fizzled out. A really good storm clears the air. My pa reckons it helps the vegetables grow but don't ask me why.'

She tossed the cloth on to the overhead airer and began putting away the crockery. 'Thursday already. I don't know where the week's gone and that's the truth. I woke up this morning with a bad headache and no Hettie so I have to do everything. I thought she was supposed to be coming back but she hasn't turned up.' She pursed her lips disapprovingly and glanced at Binns. 'It's all right for the likes of you, guzzling tea while the rest of us—'

'So is it true about Hettie? In the family way, is she?' He grinned slyly. 'Been a bit naughty, has she?'

'Never you mind. But yes, she has, silly little thing. But I blame you men.'

He looked affronted. 'Don't look at me, Mrs Letts. I never touched her. Not that I wouldn't have had a go if she'd given me the wink.'

Mrs Letts glared at him. 'Had a go!' she repeated. 'Now that's what I mean about you men. To you it's a bit of fun. You never think about the consequences. Poor silly girl. What's going to happen now? I'm sure I don't know.'

'Who was it then? He going to marry her?'

Mrs Letts hesitated. 'Nothing's settled and it's none of your business if it was. She'd make a fair enough mother but will she get the chance? God only knows. Says she won't part with the baby but who knows? She might not get much choice.'

'No shotgun wedding then?'

'It's no laughing matter, Binns. You drink up and get yourself off. Find something useful to do.'

'If she needs a husband I might think about it.'

She stared at him, appalled. 'You?'

'Why not? I'm as good as any, aren't I?'

Mrs Letts thought about Master Oliver's child being brought up by Binns and shuddered inwardly. He was amiable enough but a mite simple. Imagining the brothers and sisters the child would have, she shook her head.

'But why?' he persisted. 'If I was to ask her—'

'No!' she snapped. 'You keep out of it, Binns. She's got enough to worry about without you making things even more complicated.' Seeing from his expression that she had offended him, she added, 'But it was a kind thought.'

She reached out for the mug, which he surrendered reluctantly.

'Best get down to the veg then,' he conceded. 'What d'you want today? There's some nice onions and the last of the spring cabbage.'

'That'll do,' she told him and watched him go with another shake of the head.

For a moment she wondered if she should tell anyone about his offer but decided against it. She wouldn't want to inflict Binns on her worst enemy. Let the family sort it out, she thought. She'd got her hands full keeping them all fed.

Chloe was on the landing on the way down to lunch when Oliver reached out from his bedroom and caught her by the arm. He pulled her into the room and closed the door.

'Listen,' he told her urgently. 'I've been down to the Leemings' place. I got Hettie on her own and said what you'd suggested, about your sister and the baby.' He rolled his eyes. 'She wasn't very happy about it. Very *unhappy*, actually. Nothing against your sister but she won't consider anyone but me. She wants to marry me. She says it's our baby and we should be the ones to bring it up.'

Chloe frowned. 'She must know that's not going to happen.'

'She does but you know Hettie. She probably thinks that if she holds out long enough I'll give in and say yes. It seems her mother's trying to fix her up with a chap called Frank Shaw. She had a word with the chap's mother and explained about the money I would give her. She thought the idea of a dowry might do the trick. Frank said he'd think it over but Hettie was adamant she wouldn't have him. Me or nobody. She worked herself into a frenzy. Tears and tantrums. It's ridiculous.'

'She loves you,' Chloe reminded him. 'You know what that's like. You love Adele.'

'My baby's going to want his real pa ,' Oliver mimicked. 'Hettie said it over and over again. Like a damned chant! Sorry . . . Oh Lord! I'm no good to anyone,' he said heavily. 'It's just a nightmare and I can't see an end to it . . . But we'd better get downstairs or Mama will be asking awkward questions. And she doesn't know where I've been so don't let the cat out of the bag.'

During the meal Chloe was very quiet. She was wrestling with Hettie's problem. It came to her suddenly that perhaps if Hettie met with Dorothy and Albert . . . She sighed. Oliver was right. There seemed no end to the problems.

After the meal, while Jessica returned to bed for her afternoon rest, Chloe decided to have a final word with Hettie. Maybe woman to woman . . . ? It was worth a try.

Without telling anyone else she set off for the Leemings' cottage. The day was humid but she hardly noticed as she hurried through the long grass and down the lane.

Mrs Leeming came to the door, wiping her hands on her apron. Chloe could smell soap and a child wailed in the background.

'Hettie?' Mrs Leeming shook her head. 'I thought she'd maybe gone to Fairfields. Haven't seen her for the best part of an hour. Left me to wash the kitchen floor, she has, when I've got that much to do.' Her eyes narrowed. 'Master Oliver's sneaked up here. Thought I didn't know. But Het wouldn't tell me what was said. She can be real tight-lipped, that one, when she's a mind to be.' She regarded Chloe hopefully.

'Well, it was nothing in particular,' Chloe told her. 'Do you have any idea where she might have gone?'

'Afraid not. Like I said, I didn't see the going of her. If you was to promise her her job back . . .'

'She can come back anytime. We thought maybe you were keeping her away. Well, I won't trouble you.'

Back in the lane Chloe was reluctant to give up her search. But where could Hettie be? Somewhere quiet, presumably. Somewhere she could think without the intrusion of other people. Maybe looking for her was not a good idea. Left to herself, Hettie might come to see the wisdom of passing the child to Dorothy and Albert.

In a more hopeful mood Chloe returned to Fairfields and the afternoon passed peacefully enough. It was nearly eight o'clock when Mr Leeming arrived on the doorstep. He looked less belligerent than when they had last seen him and he brought the disturbing news that Hettie was missing.

'We've had no sight of her for hours,' he told Bertha. 'The wife's beside herself with worry and there's bad weather on the way. I'm minded to get down to the police station to see if there's been an accident but thought I'd check here first.'

'We haven't seen her,' Bertha replied. 'Has she ever done this before?'

'Never had no need to.' His meaning was plain.

'Then you'd best notify the police,' Bertha agreed. 'If they decide on a search let us know. I'm sure my brother would—'

'We won't be needing *his* help!' His jaw clenched. 'He's done quite enough already.'

He turned away and strode off and Bertha relayed the bad news to the rest of the household. Throughout the evening they read and Oliver and Jessica played chess. From time to time Mrs Letts put her head round the door to enquire after Hettie but there was no reassuring news. At nine o'clock, when Jessica retired to bed, the threatened storm had broken and the rain poured down. In between flashes of lightning and rumbling thunder Chloe saw lanterns flickering across the dark fields and knew with a frisson of alarm that a search was in progress for the missing girl. Where on earth could she be in this weather? she wondered, and as time passed her apprehension grew.

They had all retired to bed when, a few moments after midnight, the doorbell rang. Chloe was the first to reach the door.

The policeman looked thoroughly dejected. His uniform was sodden and rainwater dripped from his helmet.

'It's about your maid,' he began. 'May I come in?'

'Of course.'

As he entered Bertha reached the bottom of the stairs and Mrs Letts was peering over the top of the banisters.

Bertha looked at the policeman. 'It's not . . .' she began, clutching her shawl to her chest. 'Is it about Hettie Leeming?'

He nodded. He was about thirty, tall, with a thin face and dark eyes. 'We found her in the wood. Poor little—'

'Oh thank goodness!' cried Chloe.

'I'm afraid it's not good news. I'm afraid she's dead.'

'Dead? Oh no! Not Hettie!'

Bertha clutched the banisters for support, her face ashen.

The policeman said, 'I'm sorry, ma'am, but that's about the size of it. She wasn't dead when we found her, mind, and we got her to the doctor's house. He did what he could but . . .' Tucking his helmet under his arm, he ran wet fingers through his hair.

Chloe and Bertha stared at him in shocked silence while Mrs Letts came slowly down the stairs.

Chloe said, 'But how? I mean, what did she die of?' She thought of Sid Jakes with horror. Had he killed her?

'We pieced the evidence the best we could. There were marks in the mud. Seems she slipped over, rolled down a

124

steep bank and hit her head on a tree. That's where we found her. At the bottom of the tree. Unconscious, poor soul, but at least she was still breathing.'

Mrs Letts reached the bottom of the stairs. 'Then what went wrong? Why couldn't he save her?'

He turned to her. 'The doctor did everything he could for her. I'm sorry to say she died half an hour later. Severe damage to her skull, the doctor says. She must have gone an awful purler down that slope. Everything against her, poor lass, raining the way it was . . .'

Mrs Letts said, 'I'd best make some tea.' She made her way slowly towards the kitchen and Chloe saw her dab her eyes with her handkerchief.

Chloe said dully, 'So the baby's dead, too.'

He brightened marginally. 'No ma'am. The baby was still alive so the doctor did one of those operations they do . . . to get the baby out.'

Bertha stared at him. 'But it wasn't due to be born yet. Is it going to survive?'

'They don't think so but the doctor said he had to try. Didn't want it on his conscience, I suppose. He said it's touch and go. Little girl. Very tiny. Like a doll.' He shrugged unhappily. 'She did regain consciousness for a few moments but then it was all over.'

There was a stricken silence. Chloe felt dizzy with shock. She kept seeing Hettie lying senseless in the wood, the unborn child still moving within her.

Bertha looked at the constable. 'You look as though you could do with a hot drink. Take off your tunic and we'll dry it for you.'

He shook his head. 'It's past drying out, thank you, ma'am, but I'd love a mug of tea before I get back. Got a report to write up.'

In sombre mood they all huddled together in the kitchen while Bertha went to find Oliver and bring him down. The constable repeated his terrible news and Oliver closed his eyes. Then he turned and went out without a word.

Bertha said, 'Let him go. He's going to need time. He's going to blame himself.'

So he should, thought Chloe sadly. He was mostly to blame but he couldn't have expected it to end this way. Poor Hettie. Chloe thought about the last time she had seen her, when her father tried to drag her away from Oliver. She thought of her in happier times, flitting round the house, dustpan and brush in her hands, or bustling into Jessica's bedroom with the breakfast tray. Usually with that cheerful smile on her face. If only . . .

Choked, Chloe tried to think about the child. Would it survive at this stage? Would Oliver want to see his daughter? Would he want to hold Hettie's baby in his arms or would that be too painful for him? The guilt must be crushing him. But suppose he delayed and the little girl died?

As though he had read her thoughts, Oliver reappeared in the doorway.

'Where is the child, constable? I want to see her.'

All heads turned towards him and the constable rose to his feet. 'I'm not sure that's a good idea, sir. The parents are pretty upset and they blame you. If you want my advice—'

'I don't.' His eyes were dark with shock and his face was drawn into a painful caricature of his former self.

Chloe's immediate thought was that he might be the next to crack under the strain.

Oliver said, 'Is the baby at the doctor's house or at the Leemings' place? I want to see her. Don't waste time, constable. Just tell me.'

'She's at the doctor's house but . . . but she might already be . . . That is, she didn't have much of a chance.'

Oliver looked at Chloe. 'You're coming with me. If it's possible we'll take the child to your sister.'

Bertha said, 'Wait! What are you talking about? Chloe's sister?'

He said, 'There's no time. I'll tell you later – and break it gently to Mama.'

Bertha cried, 'Oh no! You must tell her yourself. First thing in the morning.'

For a moment they glowered at one another. Then Oliver said, 'Just as you wish.' He turned to Chloe. 'Fetch your coat while I get down to the stables.'

He hurried out again. The constable shrugged and, taking out his notebook, made a note of this new development.

Upstairs Chloe scarcely had time to wonder why she was obeying Oliver. She pulled on her coat and a felt hat. It was a wild night and she had no desire to be out in it but she couldn't deny that she wanted to see Oliver's child with all her heart.

As they bowled along, heads down against the rain, she worried about Dorothy's reaction. Turning up after midnight with a baby that had little chance of survival was hardly a kind thing to do to them.

Oliver shouted at the horse and slapped it with the reins. 'Get up, damn you!' he urged.

Chloe stole a look at his face and decided to say nothing. This was not the time to voice her doubts. She crossed her fingers and hoped that they would not find the Leemings at the doctor's house. If they decided to bring up the child Oliver might well lose touch with her. If the child was dead . . . She shook her head. Don't think that way, she told herself, and don't get too involved.

They were in luck. As the doctor's wife showed them into the house she explained that the baby girl was still alive. They found her wrapped in a blanket and sleeping peacefully. The doctor told them that the Leemings had gone home, talking vaguely about Hettie's sister Lizzie, who might or might not want to care for the child. It would all depend on Oliver and his generosity, apparently.

'With Hettie gone the child is your responsibility,' the doctor told Oliver tiredly.

Chloe and Oliver stood beside the deep drawer that served as a makeshift cot and stared down at the tiny child. Even in sleep the baby had a resigned look, thought Chloe, as though she somehow knew that her life had not begun well. There was a droop to the small mouth and the tiny hands clenched defensively.

The doctor's wife said, 'Poor little thing!' and gave Oliver a look which spoke volumes – and none of it charitable.

He stared down at his daughter, his unwanted child, with an expression which Chloe found hard to interpret. Was it possible, she wondered, that he could see the child and not be moved? She stood silently beside him, willing herself to remain neutral.

At last Oliver said, 'I'm sure your sister and her husband will be good to her.' He explained his decision to take the child to the rectory.

The doctor's wife could not bear his detachment. 'Aren't you even going to hold her?' she cried. 'Or kiss her? She's your flesh and blood! Don't you want to know her name? Her mother's last words almost.'

Her husband said, 'Hush, dear! Don't take on so. You'll only upset yourself.'

'I won't hush,' she told him. 'It's not natural. She's born of a dead mother and a father who cannot even touch her!' Tears ran down her face and, turning, she hurried to the door.

Oliver said, 'I can't. I daren't. I don't want—'

The doctor's wife cried, 'Hettie named her Olivia, after her father.'

She went out and they heard her making her way up the stairs. Oliver appeared stunned by her anger.

Chloe was fighting back her own tears. 'May I?' she asked.

Oliver nodded and she bent down and scooped the sleeping child from the drawer without waking her. She held her close, rocking her slightly.

'Will she be warm enough outside?' she asked and the doctor found another blanket for extra protection.

Oliver thanked the doctor for all he had done and was handed a bottle of milk which his wife had prepared. Together Chloe and Oliver walked to the dog cart and settled themselves for the rest of the journey.

They drove through the night in silence and Chloe was aware of a feeling of unreality as the wheels hissed on the wet road. The rain had stopped but there were clouds which from time to time obscured the moon and then a velvety darkness enveloped them. Occasionally a bird swooped over them and the screech of a hunting owl broke the eerie silence. When they finally pulled up outside the rectory the church clock was striking one.

Albert answered their knock and for a moment he stared without comprehension at the trio on his doorstep. Then he opened the door and called hoarsely up the stairs to Dorothy. For a few moments all was confusion and doubt as Chloe explained the circumstances leading to the child's early appearance. Then Dorothy's compassion swept her apprehension away. Her delight was infectious and before long the baby was being hugged and kissed, albeit gently so as not to wake her up. Dorothy laid her in the wooden cot that had been made in expectation of her own child and tucked her in with hands that trembled.

'Sleep well, little one,' she whispered.

Chloe was touched by her sister's obvious joy and took note that Albert also appeared to be pleased. He was not an emotional man but his cheeks were flushed and she could sense his excitement. Please God let this be the right thing, she begged. Surely if good came out of the tragedy there was something to be learned for all of them.

Her only regret was Oliver's reaction. She had expected that the sight of his child would stir him but he appeared unmoved. Perhaps he was thinking of Adele, she thought. Perhaps to Oliver, loving this child would seem a betrayal to the woman he really loved. And maybe he was right.

She sighed and caught Oliver's eye.

'We should be going,' he said.

He sounded so matter of fact that both Dorothy and Albert stared at him.

Dorothy said, 'We'll take great care of her.'

'Maybe you'll call in tomorrow,' Albert said to Oliver.

'Maybe . . . Possibly not. I have to go back to London.'

At the door Dorothy caught Chloe's sleeve. 'She's so very small,' she said anxiously. 'Will the doctor call, do you think? I feel sure he should keep an eye on her. So very tiny . . . and so frail. If anything happens to her . . .'

Chloe saw a spark of panic in her sister's eyes. 'The doctor said he would call and I'm sure the Maitlands will make suitable arrangements to see you through the next few weeks.' She leaned forward and hugged her. 'You'll be a wonderful mother,' she whispered and was aware of a frisson of envy. A baby had never been part of Chloe's plan but Oliver's child had stirred unexpected emotions.

The return journey passed in a long silence. Oliver appeared deep in thought and Chloe was reluctant to intrude. She wondered what he was thinking about – poor Hettie whose young life had come to such an abrupt end or Adele who might now never marry him. Or perhaps the innocent child who lay sleeping in a cot in Icklesham.

In the darkness Chloe struggled without success to make sense of her chaotic thoughts and she was relieved when the journey came to an end and she found herself at last alone in her bedroom. Wearily she tugged off her clothes and pulled on her nightgown. Then she knelt beside the bed and prayed.

'Please God take poor Hettie into your loving care,' she whispered. She frowned. Where had He been when Hettie was alone and afraid in the woods or when she made that fatal step on muddy leaves and fell to her death? Why couldn't He have saved her? Chloe had been brought up to believe in a powerful, loving Father. 'So why did you let her die?' she demanded.

There was no answer so she went on. 'Please forgive Oliver his sins and help him in his hour of need – and *please* show him how to love his daughter.' She thought of Hettie's last words. She had named her child Olivia in a desperate attempt to keep the link between father and daughter. 'Please let Olivia live,' Chloe begged, 'and give her a happy life. Amen.'

She climbed into bed but was too tired to sleep. She thought about Oliver and pitied him with all her heart. He had a lot of decisions to make but there was time for all that.

'Tomorrow is another day,' she promised herself and was soon asleep.

Breakfast next morning was a sober affair. For a long time nobody spoke and they avoided each other's eyes. None of them had much appetite but Chloe struggled with a plateful of porridge while Bertha nibbled toast. Oliver stared at a full plate of egg and bacon and didn't eat any of it.

At last Bertha said, 'A penny for them, Oliver.'

Chloe said, 'Don't press him, Bertha.'

Bertha tossed her head. 'He's my brother. I'll say what I like to him. He must have something to say.' She glared at him. 'Sulking won't help you now.'

He glanced at her. 'Just eat your toast!'

Chloe, embarrassed, said nothing.

Bertha said, 'You have to tell Mama what's happened, Oliver.'

He frowned. 'It would come better from you. Woman to woman. That sort of thing.'

She raised her eyebrows. 'I see. Now that you want something from me you can be polite. Even flattering.' She smiled thinly. 'You'll have to do something for me in return then. You'll have to back me up over George Brier. I mean to marry him and I want Mama's blessing.'

He didn't even lift his head. 'You must be mad. You should marry Miles.'

Chloe pushed away her dish and reached for her tea-cup.

'Miles? Honestly, Oliver. You know he's a pompous bore. You know he's pathetic but you wouldn't mind me marrying him because the Sandfords have money!' She turned to Chloe, who was pouring fresh tea. 'That's the way Oliver thinks. He has no pride. He's sharing a flat with this poor

French woman and is probably living rent free. Oliver trades with charm, not money.'

Oliver looked at her coldly. 'If you had a little more charm you wouldn't be so bitter and—'

Bertha leaned across the table and slapped his face.

Chloe stood up. 'I've had enough of this,' she told them. 'We're in the middle of a family crisis and all you two do is bicker. I thought better of the pair of you!' She turned to go.

Bertha said, 'I'm sorry. Don't go. Don't you and Dorothy bicker?'

'Hardly ever.'

Oliver looked shamefaced. 'We're behaving very badly. I apologise. We never have united in times of trouble. Do sit down. We need your common sense.'

As Chloe obeyed Oliver rubbed his eyes. He looked desperately tired and had probably been awake most of the night.

He said, 'Look, I have to get back to Adele. She hates it when I disappear down here but if the baby is going to stay with your sister, Chloe, even temporarily, I should meet with them again or maybe write to them. That might be easier for all of us. I'm willing to settle a proper amount on the child but I can't face telling Mother. She's going to take it very hard when she knows what's happened and Bertha can deal with her better than I can.'

He and Chloe both looked at Bertha.

'Only if Oliver goes up to her first and explains why he thinks I should marry George. And makes it convincing.' She looked at him. 'Mama will listen to you.'

'Give me one good reason why you should marry him.'

Chloe groaned. 'Because she *loves* him, Oliver. That's a very good reason. And George isn't a pompous bore. That's another good reason. He loves her and he's a superb craftsman and can support her reasonably well. How many reasons do you want?'

The two women stared at Oliver, who gave an exaggerated sigh. 'If I must,' he conceded.

They waited. He didn't move.

Bertha said, 'Well go on!'

'I'm going, I'm going!' He left the room.

Bertha looked at Chloe and smiled faintly. 'Poor charming Oliver. Let's see how effective he can be.'

When Chloe merely shrugged Bertha reddened. 'There we go again. Sorry. No doubt you take Oliver's side and think badly of me.'

Chloe thought it tactful not to answer.

Bertha glanced down at her hands. 'I've promised George. He was so happy. He was positively beaming.' She smiled at the memory. 'I shall run away with him if I have to – to Gretna Green. Do you think I'm foolish?'

'No. I don't think your mother does either but I think she worries about how you will live. She wouldn't want you to suffer hardships. You haven't been brought up to it. Will you live with his mother?'

'No. We shall find a cottage. But he is willing to move into Fairfields so that I can care for Mama if that becomes necessary. I think she would miss me, especially as Oliver is so dreadfully unreliable and is mostly away in London.'

'She has your Uncle Matty.'

Bertha tossed her head. 'Who is about as reliable as Oliver. And totally useless. Look at the state he's in. He can't even look after himself, let alone Mama.' She sighed. 'I know I cannot go too far away but George is confident he can find enough work locally. Until the important commissions come in. Even then he can work here in his smithy and will only need to travel when he reaches the stage where he instals the pieces.' She brightened. 'He thinks he has a commission from The Bishop's Palace in Maidstone. It only has to be confirmed.'

'That's wonderful.'

'We shall never be poor. I wish Mama would stop fussing about me. I'm not made of glass and if we ever were to be poor I could manage . . .' She blushed suddenly. 'And there are the grandchildren to think about. They will help to keep her cheerful.' The smile faded as quickly as it had come.

'Though Oliver has given her a grandchild already and that isn't making her happy.' She glanced nervously upwards. 'I wonder how she's taking it. There's no knowing how she will react . . . And then there's Uncle Matty. He'll have to be told but the news won't upset him at all. It will be water on a duck's back as far as he's concerned. I sometimes envy him. The only time he gets upset is when he is involved personally.'

'Like the beating.'

'Exactly. I'd love to know what inspired that. He's full of secrets, you know, and none of them very savoury. I think he gambles but I've never been able to prove it. Not that I want to. I'd rather remain in blissful ignorance.'

'Would you like me to tell him about poor Hettie and the baby?'

Bertha nodded. 'Tell him he's a great-uncle,' she suggested. 'Or a half-great-uncle. That will make him laugh.'

Chloe went upstairs feeling inexplicably cheerful. Could it be that this astonishing family would survive all its problems? People were so interesting, she thought. Fascinating. At least life at Fairfields was never dull.

While the rest of the family was at breakfast Matty had opened his eyes and was trying to recall the details of his dream. Something about a carrion crow . . . or was it an eagle? A bird of prey hovering over him . . . a buzzard, perhaps. His brow felt damp with sweat and he lifted his hand to wipe the perspiration from his forehead. No prize for understanding that dream, he thought, and sighed deeply. His head ached and when he tried to turn in the bed his limbs complained.

He groaned. 'Damn Jakes!' he muttered. 'A mad bull on legs! Someone should put him out of his misery.' He could think of plenty of ways it could be done and if only he was fitter he'd willingly volunteer for the job.

Slowly the events of the last few days filtered through his aches and pains and he remembered Hettie and Oliver and someone called Adele. Lucky old Ollie! Found himself a French tart. He started to laugh but stopped abruptly as the movement made his ribs hurt. Perhaps Miss Blake was right and he should inform the police about Jakes – before it was too late. But Jakes would spill the proverbial beans and his own illegal betting would become public knowledge and then Jessica would probably throw him out. What a miserable woman she was. She had threatened him with eviction on more than one occasion when his drinking had become excessive. Women. They could be the very devil. Thank God he had never married.

Mind you, Miss Blake was going to make someone a good wife one of these days. 'But not Ollie!' he muttered. He had seen the way she looked at him and had guessed that she found him attractive. But Ollie would never make a good husband. He was too selfish by far and too weak. He had always been the same. A timid boy, easily led. He had an easy charm but relied on his good looks to see him through. And, to give him his due, he had obviously made an impression on Adele. No doubt this French woman was wondering where he was and why he hadn't returned to London. Presumably Oliver would keep the child a secret from her but that would simply lay up trouble for the future. Truth will out. That's what they say.

He closed his eyes as a fresh problem began to trouble him.

'Ooh!' he muttered.

He desperately needed to use the chamber pot but that meant an agonising climb out of bed and he had been delaying the moment. Damn Sid Jakes and his trusty club. If he didn't pay up the rest of the money it would probably be a knife in the ribs next time! Groaning aloud at the unfairness of life, he pushed back the bedclothes and crawled out to meet the new day. It might be an improvement on yesterday but he wasn't too hopeful.

As he climbed carefully back into bed there was a knock on the door.

'Uncle Matty? Are you awake? It's Chloe . . .'

Eight

An hour later a resolute figure pushed through the crowds at Charing Cross Station and bought a ticket to Rye.

'Will there be a bus to carry me from Rye to Icklesham?' she demanded as she reached for the change.

Hearing the accent, the railway clerk narrowed his eyes. French, he decided.

Adele ignored his reaction. 'A bus to – how you say? – bus to connect?'

'As like as not,' he replied, giving her the suspicious look he reserved for all foreigners.

She gave him a withering look. 'You do not know this for sure?'

'Not my job to know, is it,' he told her with undisguised triumph. 'I know about tickets. That's my job. Connections are somebody else's job.'

She regarded him with growing despair. Was all the world against her? How she despised officious little men. She said, 'If there is no bus—'

The man behind her touched her arm. 'Hurry it up, miss. You're not the only person that wants a ticket.'

Adele turned to face him. His face was pinched and he hadn't shaved. He carried a bulging sack and a greasy cap covered most of his straggly hair.

Adele turned back to the ticket office window. 'But I need to know—' She began, a tell-tale tremor in her voice.

The man behind her dug her in the ribs with his elbow. 'You've got your ticket so hop it.'

Adele gave in. Snatching up the ticket, she turned sharply on her heel. She must not cry. Blinking furiously, she hurried to the nearest platform and asked the ticket collector where she could find the train for Rye. Behind her irritation a deep fear was growing.

'Twenty-five minutes, miss,' he told her and pointed to the correct platform. His friendly smile warmed her a little.

Once on the platform she sat down on one of the seats to await the train and to wonder afresh whether she was doing the right thing. Oliver had never lied to her before but recently she had thought him distracted and unwilling to talk to her. Intuition told her that there was something troubling him and it also told her that a woman was involved. Was it the woman who had been in the apartment? Miss Blake. The companion to his mother was young and pretty enough to catch Oliver's eye.

A child ran past pursued by a young, fresh-faced nanny while the mother strolled along behind them. Adele watched as the child was caught and returned to the mother, who said, 'You must not run away from Eloise, Frankie. I don't want to tell you again.'

The boy stuck out his tongue in the direction of the nanny and his mother caught hold of his arm and shook him. Children. Who needed them? Who'd be a mother? she thought, and remembered Oliver's rosy vision of family life. Her rejection of this vision had been such a disappointment for him.

She tried to concentrate. She was going to Oliver's home to confront him and it was about time. For too long she had allowed him to lead his double life in which she was the skeleton in his cupboard that must be hidden away from the family. Loving him as she did, she had shared her home and her life with him but he had been ashamed of her. How could that be true love?

With a screech of brakes and a rush of steam a train pulled in two platforms away and she watched as the doors were opened and passengers spilled from the carriages. Porters rushed to assist them with their luggage, weaving their trolleys with great dexterity in and out of the hurrying feet.

She had vowed to herself that she would never marry Oliver while he treated her this way but that didn't mean she didn't want to be his wife. She adored him and always would but she had her pride and she wanted recognition. Meanwhile Oliver had a home and a family – and maybe another woman. Suppose he was already married? The idea, as always, made her sick with terror. She had lain awake all night and the night before that, waiting for him to come back to her. She had waited in vain. Suddenly she had known the time had come. Life was passing her by and she would not spend another year in this uncertain state.

Staring down the line she saw the smoke from her train as it rounded the bend and drew near to the platform. Swallowing hard, she stood up. If there was no connecting bus she would walk all the way in her new buttoned boots. She was going to find Oliver and she was determined to learn the truth.

Jessica sent for Chloe as soon as her prolonged conversation with Bertha had ended. The moment Chloe saw her she felt a frisson of alarm. Her employer was very pale and had sunk back against the pillows, clutching a bottle of sal volatile. The shock of Hettie's death had obviously affected her deeply. She seemed shrunken and helpless.

'Chloe! Come in and shut the door.' The voice quavered.

Chloe did as she was told and then advanced briskly towards Jessica. Before she could say anything Chloe smiled. 'Nothing's as bad as it seems,' she announced. 'That's what my mother used to say.'

'Your mother and her sayings!' Her voice was weak and her breathing was shallow. 'But I'm afraid it is, Chloe. In fact it's much worse. How much do you know of this appalling mess?'

Chloe pulled up a chair and sat down beside the bed. Then she took Jessica's limp hand in her own. 'I know

Hettie's dead and her child is alive and being cared for by my sister and—'

'And Bertha is determined to marry her blacksmith. Even Oliver seems reconciled to the idea of a blacksmith in the family. Goodness only knows what the mother is like . . . And then there's this dreadful French woman!' She closed her eyes. 'Children are nothing but a worry!' She sighed deeply.

'Adele isn't at all dreadful,' Chloe protested. 'I liked her. I feel very sorry for her. Oliver has treated her very unkindly by betraying her with Hettie.'

She waited for the outburst, which was not slow in coming. 'You take her side against that of my son?' A spot of colour burned suddenly in Jessica's cheeks.

At least she looks a little less frail now, thought Chloe. She said, 'Adele trusted him and he betrayed her with a servant. Isn't that what happened?'

Jessica eyed her balefully for a moment but then abruptly the defiance left her. 'Poor Oliver. He was always easily led.'

Chloe let her get away with that. 'My sister may be willing to adopt the baby if that's what Oliver wants. He has to make the decision. She and Albert would be kind parents.' As Jessica still looked doubtful she added, 'Or perhaps Hettie's sister would agree to bring up the child.' She left unstated the choice – between a respectable vicar and his wife and the unmarried sister who already had a child out of wedlock.

The silence grew between them until it was broken by Jessica.

'What is the baby like? '

'Very small. She may not survive. We have to be prepared for that to happen.'

'I wonder . . . Would that be for the best?'

'Do you want Oliver's child to die?'

'I don't know . . . I can't cope . . . Oh Chloe! All this is going to make me ill!'

139

'Bertha has sent for the doctor. He'll give you something to calm your nerves.'

'The baby – does she take after Oliver?'

Chloe nodded. In fact the child had looked to her like any other child – a wrinkled face, button nose and rosebud mouth – but it was important that Jessica accepted her. 'Olivia is a good name for her. She is so like Oliver, especially around the forehead and eyes. You must see her somehow before . . . That is, in case she doesn't survive.'

Jessica sighed. 'And there's poor, lovesick Bertha. My daughter can't see the wood for the trees. Totally smitten with this wretched blacksmith. I don't think he's a suitable match and I never shall but what can I do? She was always so biddable. I don't know what's happened to her.' Her face crumpled. 'What on earth has gotten into my children? Why can't they behave properly like other people's children? Where did I go wrong?'

Chloe picked her words carefully. 'But at least Bertha's willing to stay near you. To live nearby in case you ever need her.'

'I shan't need her. I've got you. If she marries that man she can live where she likes. I shan't care.'

Chloe took a deep breath. She had been dreading this moment. 'I won't be with you indefinitely,' she said cautiously. 'There was never that understanding. I haven't promised to be here forever.'

Jessica stared at her. 'Won't be here? Then where on earth *will* you be? And why wasn't I told?'

'I have to . . . to go abroad at some stage. I didn't think it necessary to go into explanations and Oliver didn't ask me how long I could stay. I have to find my father.' Seeing the expression on Jessica's face she rushed on. 'I don't remember him and we have no likeness of him. He left my mother with his two little girls but she never forgot him.'

'Oh Chloe!' Jessica's expression had softened. 'That was a terrible thing to do. Where did he go? Why?'

'He went to America to make his fortune. He believed there was still gold in California and intended to come home a rich man.'

'And he didn't?'

'No. We never saw him again. It broke my mother's heart and I made up my mind that one day I'd find him and . . . and challenge him. I want to know why he didn't come back to us. Or why he didn't send for us to join him. I suspect he found another woman.'

Jessica frowned. 'Maybe he fell on hard times and was too ashamed to tell you.'

'That's possible although he did send one letter containing money. But my mother deserved to know. Anything is better than feeling you have been rejected or forgotten!' She swallowed hard, aware that she was perilously close to tears.

'Oh my dear child!' Jessica regarded her with alarm. 'What a dreadful thing to happen. I had no idea.'

Chloe blinked hard. 'So you see, it's not just the Maitland family that has problems.'

Jessica nodded. 'Have you told the others?'

'Only you. I don't want everyone to know.'

Jessica seemed to be recovering. Chloe thought the colour was coming back to her face.

'Listen to me, child. You really can't go traipsing off to America on a wild goose chase. It's much too dangerous. From all one hears, it's not at all like England. Morals are very lax there.'

Chloe hid a smile. They could hardly be lower than Oliver's, she thought.

'I'm not planning to go just yet,' she told Jessica. 'It will be months and months before I have saved up enough money for the sea journey.' She smiled briskly, afraid she had already said too much. 'In the meantime, I'm wondering whether Oliver should go and see his daughter again before he goes back to London. What do you think?'

Jessica regarded her through narrowed eyes. 'I think,

Chloe, that you are a very determined young woman. A very strong woman.'

'My mother was very strong. She had to be.'

Jessica nodded. 'As for Oliver, I agree. He should visit the child. Go and talk to him, Chloe. Don't take no for an answer. Tell him I insist. Where would he have been if his father had turned his back on him at birth? The more I think about it, the more disillusioned I become.' She sighed. 'You could go with him to your sister's. It might make things easier. Then if he must go back to London to this wretched Adele he can hire someone to take him on to Rye. That way Binns can bring you back to Fairfields. And Chloe . . .' Her eyes filled with tears. 'Give the little darling a kiss from me. I shall want to see her for myself as soon as I'm well enough.' As Chloe still hesitated she waved her away. 'Well, hurry up, child. Find Binns and tell him to get the horse ready.'

The young Olivia was sleeping when they arrived, lying in a basket under the shade of a small cherry tree. Albert was in church so Dorothy led the way, pale-faced and chattering with anxiety. Together the three of them watched the sleeping baby, who was cocooned in a shawl which Chloe knew had been handed down through their own family.

Chloe resisted the urge to pick up the child and forced herself to say and do nothing. She felt that Oliver should have had this moment to himself but he had been unwilling to make the small pilgrimage alone and had jumped at the chance to take Chloe along.

Now he said, 'How is she doing?'

Dorothy smiled nervously. 'She's been very good although she woke several times in the night. She's so small and she doesn't take much milk before she falls asleep. She's lovely . . . but of course we may not keep her . . . Nothing's decided yet, is it.'

'Isn't it?'

Chloe watched Oliver's face for tell-tale traces of emotion but his expression revealed nothing. She wondered suddenly

142

if her own father had watched her and Dorothy as they slept. What sort of father had he been for those first few years? Dorothy had known him for longer and Chloe had always envied Dorothy her sharper memories. Later, Chloe had tried to ask her mother about him but the subject had always brought a tearful reaction and she had learned to avoid the subject. Only once, seeing the tears in Chloe's eyes, had her mother given an answer designed to comfort her. 'Of course he loved you. You're his daughter.' Chloe had clung to that small crumb of comfort all her life.

Dorothy said, 'I expect you'd like to hold her. You needn't worry about waking her.'

'No. I think not,' Oliver replied.

Instead he knelt on the grass, leaned down and kissed the small downy head. When he straightened up there was a glint of tears in his eyes. Chloe felt a surge of despair as she looked at him. Was he really going to walk away from his daughter? Was he thinking only of himself and Adele? When the child grew up she would ask the questions Chloe herself had asked. At least Dorothy should be able to tell Olivia that Oliver had held her in his arms.

Lifting the sleeping child from the basket, Chloe dumped her into Oliver's arms. Ignoring his protests she said, 'Love her a little, Oliver!'

Then she took Dorothy by the arm and moved away with her. Dorothy looked at her, startled.

Chloe choked back tears. 'He has to at least hold her!' she cried fiercely. 'There has to be something for Olivia to remember. Something we can tell her about.'

Her sister put an arm round her. 'I know,' she said softly.

'He's so unkind!'

Dorothy held her close. 'He's thoughtless, that's all. He doesn't understand.'

'He's a grown man.' Chloe's voice was hard. She pulled back from her sister's embrace, struggling for composure. 'I can't believe that I ever admired him. When I first came here I thought he was the sanest member of the family but every day I discover something else that I don't like about him.'

Dorothy shrugged. 'He's only human. We can't always feel as we should. Poor Albert—' She stopped abruptly. 'He may be afraid to love her.'

Chloe turned to look at Oliver. He had turned away from them and was rocking the baby gently in his arms. 'I hope you didn't mind Hettie naming her. It should have been you and Albert but—'

Dorothy broke in. 'No, no! Certainly not . . . Nothing's definite yet. We're caring for her for a few days, that's all, while we wait to see what will happen. Oliver might decide to keep her.'

'With Adele? I can't believe that will happen. But I suppose Hettie's mother might want her. Oh dear! It's all such a muddle. How can it ever work out for the best?'

Dorothy smiled faintly. 'The best is never perfect. That's what Albert says. We have to be prepared to make compromises . . . and be ready to face disappointment.'

'Like having an absent father, you mean?' Chloe fell silent but then suddenly remembered her conversation with Jessica. 'I've told Mrs Maitland about my plans. She knows now that I'm not staying there indefinitely.'

Dorothy's shocked eyes met her own. 'You're not . . . Chloe, you can't mean that . . .' She closed her eyes in anguish then slowly opened them. 'Tell me you're not still planning to go to America. Please!'

'But of course I am. I'm going to find Papa and ask—'

'But suppose he's dead? Or remarried? He might not want to see you.'

'Remarried? That would be bigamy!'

'He's a widower since Mama died.'

'How could he possibly know that if he hasn't been in touch?'

Before Dorothy could answer they were interrupted by Oliver. He had replaced the baby in the basket and now seemed poised for flight.

144

'I have a train to catch in Rye,' he told them. 'I have arranged to travel in with the carrier. If I don't get back to London soon Adele will be frantic with worry.'

Chloe said, 'Adele, Adele! Is that all you think about?'

He stared at her. 'But Adele is so insecure. If I am away too long—'

'But the baby?' Chloe was bristling with indignation. 'You haven't said one word about her! Don't you like her?'

'The child is . . . is very acceptable.'

'Acceptable?'

Dorothy touched Chloe's arm. 'Please, Chloe! This doesn't help anyone.'

Chloe ignored her. 'You should *love* her, Oliver. She's your daughter.'

He glanced from Chloe to the makeshift cradle. 'She reminds me of my grandmother on my father's side. The same broad forehead and neat little chin.' He caught Chloe's glance and said hastily, 'It's no good, Chloe. I know how strongly you feel about the child but I have to marry Adele and she would never want to bring up Hettie's child. She would—'

'*Your* child, Oliver! You should ask Adele. If she loves you enough she might consider it.'

'I wouldn't ask it of her.' He pulled an envelope from his pocket and handed it to Dorothy. 'A little money for her upkeep – until we have decided whether it will become a permanent arrangement.'

Dorothy took it reluctantly. 'I'm sorry you haven't seen my husband. Perhaps another time?'

'Certainly. Now I must find the carrier or I shall miss the train.'

They followed him back through the house, trailing after him in confusion. Outside the carrier waited, his cart full of boxes and packages destined for the guardroom of the London train. Only when the cart had disappeared from view did the two sisters look at each other. Neither put into words the fact that they were no nearer to knowing what was going to happen.

Chloe drew a long breath. 'He could see how well and happy the baby is with you,' she said.

Dorothy swallowed hard and for the first time Chloe had the suspicion that something was wrong. 'Dorothy, what is it?'

'Albert . . .' she began. 'I couldn't tell you while Oliver was here . . . He's finding it difficult to imagine the child as ours.' She put a hand over her mouth to hold in her fears. 'But there's time, isn't there, Chloe? He can change his mind.'

Chloe put an arm round her shoulder. 'Plenty of time,' she agreed. 'Men are different. Their emotions are slower.'

Dorothy gave a shaky laugh. 'Suddenly you're an expert on men?'

Chloe smiled. 'I'm learning fast,' she told her. 'You do when you're around the Maitland family! Don't fret, Dottie. I can see all three of you in a few months' time, as happy as sandboys. That's a promise.'

Dorothy brightened a little. 'Me and Albert and Olivia?'

'Exactly!'

'You always were a schemer, Chloe.'

Chloe rolled her eyes expressively. 'I'll take that as a compliment!' she laughed.

Chloe was very quiet on the way back, replying in mono-syllables to Binns' attempts at conversation. She wanted to sort out her emotions and convince herself that she had not overstepped the mark where Oliver was concerned. Dorothy's words had stung her more than she would have liked to believe. 'Schemer' could be interpreted as interfering or meddling or 'poking her nose in where it wasn't wanted'. Guiltily she wondered if that were true. Perhaps she was taking too close an interest in the affairs of the Maitland family. She was merely their paid employee and had no right to try and influence them.

Biting her lip in vexation, she considered her behaviour

with hindsight and was mortified. She *had* gone too far and, on further reflection, Oliver might well come to realise that fact. But she had her reasons and they had seemed valid at the time. What she really wanted was for her sister and Albert to bring up the child with Oliver in the background as a benevolent 'uncle figure' who might at some later stage reveal his true relationship with his daughter – if Dorothy and Albert gave their approval. But would that be best for the child? Or for Dorothy? Suppose it proved disastrous in some way that she couldn't foresee? She would blame herself.

'And rightly so!' she muttered. Her 'scheming' might come back to haunt her.

Binns glanced sideways at her. 'What's 'at you say?'

'Nothing. Sorry. Just thinking aloud.'

Pretending not to notice his sulky expression, she was still busy with her thoughts when they reached Fairfields. To Chloe's surprise the blacksmith waved his cap to slow them down.

To Chloe he said, 'Miss Bertha says to warn you that Adele has arrived and will you take over as we've things to discuss.'

'Adele?' Chloe's thoughts spun off in a new direction as she nodded. She told Binns to drive on and drop her at the front door.

As soon as she rang the bell she knew it would be Bertha who would open it. With Hettie dead, Mrs Letts was full of complaints and the family was stepping warily around her.

Bertha clutched her arm, obviously distraught.

'You'll have to calm her down,' she told Chloe. 'She's convinced that there's another woman and she thinks it's you! I've been fending her off for nearly an hour and I can't take any more. Plus Mama keeps ringing her wretched bell and calling down to know what's happening.'

Chloe was pulling off her gloves and jacket and now she tossed them on to the hall stand. 'You go up to your mother and tell her Adele's here. I'll—'

'Tell her? Not me! She'll have a heart attack!'

147

'We'll have to risk it, Bertha. And then . . .' She thought hastily. 'Then tell her I'll be up as soon as I can. And George says you and he have things to discuss.'

Bertha coloured slightly. 'I said I'd get back down to him but I couldn't leave Adele.'

Chloe glanced at herself in the hallstand mirror and patted her hair. 'I'm not going to lie to her, Bertha. She doesn't deserve that. What exactly have you told her?'

'I pretended not to know anything. I know it was cowardly but I don't see why Oliver can't tell her. It's all his fault so he should stand up and be counted. When she pressed me I said I didn't think it my place to discuss such a personal matter and she should wait and talk to Oliver.'

'When is she going back to London, did she say?'

'I didn't ask. She also wants to speak to Mama and we know that's out of the question. She can't leave soon enough for me.'

'Go tell your mother who's here and say I will be up shortly – then go down to George.'

Bertha's haunted look vanished. 'You're an angel, Chloe!' she cried and hurried upstairs before Chloe could change her mind.

Feeling distinctly out of her depth, Chloe took a deep breath and tried to prepare herself. She didn't know how she would deal with Adele but she did know that she didn't want to deceive her.

As soon as she entered the room Adele rose to her feet and Chloe saw with a pang of compassion that she had been crying. The green eyes were tear-stained and damp strands of her red hair clung to her face.

Before Chloe could speak Adele cried, 'It is you! I know it. You looked at each other – I saw it in your eyes.'

Chloe held up a warning hand. 'It is not me, Adele. Please sit down and we can—'

Adele remained standing, her hands clasped tightly around a handkerchief. 'Don't lie to me.' Her eyes flashed angrily as she swallowed. 'I noticed nothing wrong until you joined

148

the family and ever since . . . Oliver – he will not talk to me. He lies to me. He's hiding something. I will not leave this house without the truth.' Trembling, she took a step towards Chloe who, somewhat alarmed by the desperate expression in the green eyes, almost stepped back. Maintaining her ground, Chloe sat down with as much composure as she could manage. She stared fixedly at the carpet until Adele, her anger collapsing, sank into the seat opposite.

For a moment neither spoke. Then Adele said, 'I'm sorry. Please tell me what you know.'

Chloe said, 'Oliver should be the one to tell you but he is on the way back to London. He was worried that you'd be alarmed by his absence.'

'Always I worry.' Wide-eyed, Adele regarded Chloe. 'So who is this woman if it isn't you? His sister says she knows nothing. Except that her brother keeps secrets. That I know for myself.'

'Look, mademoiselle, Oliver—'

'Call me Adele. Unless the idea of a first name is too bohemian for this family. This is what Oliver tells me. That no one will have respect for me because I am a dancer and show my ankles and . . . and flaunt myself on the stage!'

Chloe couldn't answer that. Instead she said, 'Oliver finds himself in a lot of trouble. He didn't intend it. He was . . . weak.' She had almost said 'misled' but changed it at the last minute.

'And it is *not* you? You swear this?'

'I do. I work here as a companion to Mrs Maitland.'

'How do I live with Oliver if I cannot trust him? Every time he goes out I think, "Will he come back?" For me there is no one else but Oliver. I would like to go back to Paris but he will not come because I will not marry him. And you know why this is?' She tossed her head as a note of defiance crept into her voice. 'Because he will not let me meet his family. Oliver is ashamed of me. He lives with me, eats with me and shares my bed but I am his sad little secret. And for why? Because I want to dance and I will not give this up.' Imperceptibly she had straightened her back and now glared at Chloe. 'Dancing is in my soul and I will not let him take this from me.'

Chloe said, 'If I tell you what has happened Oliver will be very angry with me.'

'If you do not, *I* shall be angry. I shall make what Oliver fears most – what you call a scene. I shall shout at his mother and tell her what a son she has who will not stand up for the woman he loves!'

Chloe smiled. 'Bravo! A brave little speech. And because I approve I shall tell you the truth.'

A third voice said, 'That won't be necessary.'

Chloe swung round to find Jessica in the doorway. Somehow she had come down the stairs without help. She was leaning on a walking stick and supporting herself against the door jamb.

Adele sprang to her feet, aghast.

Chloe said, 'Mrs Maitland, this is Adele Dupres.'

'I guessed as much,' Jessica snapped. 'When someone comes to the house and no one answers my bell I know I am being kept in the dark yet again. My health is frail but that doesn't mean my mind is affected.' Chloe went forward to help her but Jessica brushed away her efforts. 'I can manage, child.'

As soon as she had sat down she motioned to Adele to do likewise.

Chloe said, 'Shall I leave you together?'

'Certainly not. Sit down and make yourself useful. That's what I pay you for.' Jessica turned her steely gaze on Adele, who appeared mesmerised by the appearance of Oliver's mother.

Chloe wondered what she had expected. The formidable tone was hardly to be expected from a frail invalid and no doubt that was the way Oliver had described her.

For a moment nobody spoke. Then Adele rallied. 'Madame, I have come here because—'

'I'll do the talking, thank you.' Jessica fussed with her skirt then arranged her hands carefully in her lap. 'You have come here to discover the truth about Oliver and you shall have it. I warn you, it isn't pretty. He is my son but I am not proud of him and you would do best to find another man who might make you happy.'

'But I am in love with your son, madame, and—'

Jessica sighed. 'I am so tired of hearing about love,' she said. 'Love can come and go and frequently does. Common decency is much more valuable in a husband. Young women today have no sense.' She stiffened.

Bracing herself for the telling of her bad news, thought Chloe, admiring the older woman's composure at such a difficult time.

'Adele, you are right to doubt my son's affection. He has behaved very foolishly with Hettie, one of the servants, and . . .' Ignoring Adele's shocked gasp she continued. 'And now has a baby daughter. It has been a terrible blow to all of us and I understand how you must feel.'

Adele sank back in her chair, her face ashen. Chloe's heart ached for her. Perhaps, in spite of all the signs to the contrary, she had hoped for better news than this.

'A . . . a *child*!' she stammered. 'Oh no!'

'Yes,' said Jessica. 'But there's more to it. The mother felt betrayed when Oliver refused to acknowledge the child. She ran away in distress in the middle of a storm and had an accident. Poor Hettie is now dead. Only the baby is still with us.' She gave an elegant shrug. 'So you can see how hard this is for us to deal with. A love child, a dead mother and her grieving parents – and all because Oliver did not behave as a gentleman should.' Her voice had now taken on a hint of defiance. 'Oliver has disappointed us. He has brought shame to the family and has betrayed both you and the baby's mother. A charming fellow – and I raised him!'

Chloe, hearing the faint tremor in her voice, felt obliged to protest. 'You cannot blame yourself. These things happen.'

'But I do blame myself,' Jessica insisted with some bitterness. 'I have allowed him to become selfish. He only needs to start drinking and gambling and we shall have another Matty on our hands!' She turned back to Adele, who was crying silently, her face partly hidden in her hands. 'Someone should give you some advice and it will have to be me. Look at me, Adele! You must forget Oliver and go back to France where you belong. You can dance in Paris and maybe you will meet someone more suitable and have a happy life. It's never too late to put the past behind you.'

She turned back to Chloe. 'This poor woman must eat. Tell Mrs Letts to lay another place for supper. She must stay the night and Binns can take her to catch an early train in the morning.'

Adele wiped her eyes. 'I can't stay here. I can put up at the nearest inn. But first I would like to see Oliver's child.'

'No!' cried Chloe. 'That won't be possible. She is being cared for by . . . by friends. It's out of the question.' She looked to Jessica for support.

Jessica took her time. 'I can't see what good it would do,' she said at last. 'Seeing the child Oliver has had by another woman would not be easy and might make the situation worse. It might break your heart, Adele. It would certainly break mine were I in your shoes. Chloe is right. Unless Oliver himself wishes it . . .'

Adele shook her head. 'It's true. I was wrong. I don't know why I asked. I'm so confused and unhappy.' Tears flowed afresh and Chloe moved to stand beside her.

Patting her shoulder she said, 'You mustn't think of this family as the enemy, Adele. Even Oliver loves you in his own way.'

'I don't think so. Not any more.' She raised her head. 'Perhaps it is good he is not here. He can take time in London to think what he has done to me. To understand how he has killed our love. How he has ended our life together.' She gulped in air and dabbed again at her tears. 'I expect you think I am stupid.'

'Not at all,' said Chloe. 'It isn't stupid to trust someone you love.'

Jessica said, 'Unless that person is my son. Oh, how I wish

I could send him to bed with no supper the way I did when he was a boy. Not that it has taught him anything. I fear that Oliver—'

She broke off as the door opened and Uncle Matty came into the room in a cloud of cigar smoke. In his right hand he carried a walking stick and leaned heavily on it as he walked. He stopped abruptly when he saw Adele.

'My dear young lady . . .' he began, his eyes shining.

Jessica said, 'Not now, Matty. We have things to talk about.'

Undeterred, he put the cigar in his mouth, walked forward and held out his free hand. Adele took it nervously and he shook it with enthusiasm.

'Call me Uncle Matty,' he told her. 'I'm Oliver's half-uncle. Or step-uncle. We can never quite decide. Either way I'm a silly old buffer but quite harmless. Bit like the family pet. Excuse the walking stick but I'm still recovering from an encounter with the local bully.'

Jessica said, 'This is Adele, a . . . a friend of Oliver's.'

'Charmed, my dear!' He kissed her hand before releasing it. 'So you're Oliver's French secret, are you? And very nice, too. I wouldn't want to share you if I were Oliver.' He beamed at her. 'Seems you've just missed him. In the dog house by all accounts but that's where we men spend most of our lives!' His rich laugh rang out.

Chloe wondered how much of this was an act to hide his initial confusion and how much was genuine ignorance of the situation. A quick glance at Jessica showed that her lips were tightly pressed together – never a good sign.

Jessica said, 'For heaven's sake, Matty, take yourself off! I thought you were too bruised and battered to leave your bed.'

'A lightning recovery. I was bored, Jessie.'

She stiffened at the name. 'You can see this is not a good time for pleasantries, Matty. Mademoiselle has no time to waste on trivialities. We have serious matters—'

'They can wait, Jessica,' he told her. 'I'm sure the young

lady would appreciate a nice peaceful tour of the garden.' He smiled at her and rolled his eyes.

After a moment's hesitation Adele said, 'The garden? That would be nice – if Mrs Maitland—'

'Oh very well. Take a stroll if you wish.'

Matty grinned. 'Then allow me. One moment.'

With a gallant gesture, Uncle Matty laid down his cigar, crooked his arm and smiled at Adele. She stood up, slipped her arm through his and allowed herself to be escorted through the French windows and out on to the terrace.

Chloe and Jessica exchanged exasperated glances.

Chloe said, 'Glad to escape, I suppose. She must be under a great strain, poor woman.'

Jessica nodded. 'She doesn't look like a dancer. Quite pleasant, in fact. No one would guess. It's a shame she couldn't have taken up singing.'

Chloe's mouth twitched. 'Like Marie Lloyd, you mean?'

'No, that's *not* what I mean and well you know it.'

Chloe said, 'I don't think she should stay at an inn on her own.'

'Certainly she can't. She must stay here. Let Oliver stew in London for a few hours wondering where she is. Serves him right. He's caused enough grief to others.'

After a moment Chloe smiled. 'I wonder what Uncle Matty is telling her?'

'Nothing suitable, that's for sure. But at least Matty looks a little more cheerful than of late and he *has* left his bed. Hiding away in his room and never going out . . . I have a nasty feeling he's in debt again. He really is impossible. One of these days he'll get what he laughingly calls his "just desserts"!' She sighed. 'I think I'll go back to my room for a few hours but I'll come down for supper. Give Mademoiselle Dupres the room next to yours, well away from Matty! I don't know what it is about the men in this family but the sight of a pretty girl goes straight to their heads like wine!'

Nine

Two days passed. Adele returned to London and Chloe was left to wonder what would happen between her and Oliver when she eventually confronted him.

A letter arrived one night, delivered by hand and addressed to Uncle Matty, who took it to his room immediately and refused to disclose the contents. Chloe thought he looked pale and distracted after he had read it but all her attempts to discover the cause went unrewarded.

Only Bertha seemed happy and that was because, with or without her mother's approval, she was going to marry George Brier. She confided in Chloe that the banns would be called for the first time on Sunday the third of August in the church at Icklesham, where the Reverend Albert Parks would officiate at the wedding.

But first there was a sad event to be attended. Hettie was to be buried on Saturday and Bertha had asked Hettie's parents if the Maitland family might be allowed to pay for the funeral. After an initial objection on the part of her father, they agreed and the funeral, too, would take place in Albert's church. Bertha was sent to Rye to buy a length of white silk and this was transformed by a local dressmaker into a simple gown to clothe Hettie's body. Jessica ordered an elegant oak coffin which was lined with oyster satin.

'Nothing is too good for the poor child,' Jessica insisted. 'This family has treated her shabbily and the least we can do is send her to her maker with all possible ceremony. I'm sure the Leemings would be hard put to give her a decent burial and I want them to be able to remember her with pride.'

Still Oliver stayed in London but his mother was determined he should be at the funeral and had sent a letter to that effect.

Chloe had her doubts. 'Do you think the Leemings will want him to be present?' she asked. 'They blame him, quite rightly, for her death. Indirectly it was his fault. Seeing him might do more harm than good.'

'I'm more interested in Oliver's conscience.' Jessica's tone was very determined. 'He has to take responsibility for his actions. If they have unkind things to say to him then he must listen and learn. I'm thoroughly ashamed of him and I won't have him skulking in London when the mother of his child is laid to rest. And it won't hurt him to pay another visit to his daughter – if your sister is willing.'

During these preparations Chloe found time to approach Uncle Matty on the matter of the mysterious letter. On the day before the funeral, she found him in his bedroom, still in his nightshirt at quarter to eleven in the morning.

'You may well ask!' he told her. 'It wasn't nice at all. They're threatening to come for me – but I've heard it all before. I can call their bluff. I just stay put, out of sight, and what can they do?'

Chloe frowned. 'But what about the funeral? Aren't you coming to that?'

'What? Sit around in the church? I'd be a sitting duck! No. I'm not coming. I shall fake a sick stomach and cry off at the last moment – and don't you dare betray me!'

'I wouldn't,' Chloe assured him, 'but your sister won't be very happy.'

Matty rolled his eyes. 'Jessica's the least of my worries, believe you me. I did wonder whether Oliver would put me up in his London flat – for a day or two until the heat dies down. It's not his flat, I know, but I think Adele took a bit of a shine to me.' He smiled. 'I did rather lay on the charm.'

'We noticed!'

'But then if Oliver's got to be down here for the funeral it wouldn't be right for me to stay with Adele.' He sounded wistful. 'If she's still there, of course. She might have gone back to Paris. I'll have a word with Ollie at the funeral. Maybe I could travel back to London with him. They're hardly going to attack me if I'm with someone else.'

Chloe felt a rush of concern for him. 'Attack you? It's not that bad, surely?'

He shrugged. 'Couldn't be much worse but I'll survive. I've spent my life surviving. One disaster after another. I was arrested once. I bet Jessie didn't tell you that.' He gave a wry grin. 'I was accused of being drunk and disorderly. I was thrown out of a public house and tried to get back in again. They called the police and I spent a night in the cell.'

'And were you drunk and disorderly?'

'More than likely – but I don't remember any of it. Poor old Jessie had to bail me out and she has never forgiven me. Our side of the family was never much good. My father was what you might call a chancer. Used his undoubted charm to relieve elderly ladies of their money – by marrying them! My poor mother was glad to see the back of him. Poor old Cecil. He drank himself to death and nobody missed him. Mother married Henry Spurling and was finally happy. Jessie's never known the seedy side of life and never will.'

Alarmed by Uncle Matty's account, Chloe decided against adding to Jessica's troubles. She told herself that when the funeral was over she would have a word with Oliver. As the man of the family he should have a serious talk with Uncle Matty about the error of his ways. Not that she expected him to change at this late stage in his life but she was reluctant to do nothing – although the word 'schemer' still bothered her from time to time.

If any real harm came to Uncle Matty she would feel that somehow she had allowed it to happen. She was beginning to feel that travelling to America in search of her father would be simple compared with the complexities of the Maitland family.

That evening Dorothy laid the baby in her basket and went

quietly downstairs. Outwardly calm, she was inwardly in turmoil.

Albert glanced up from the table. 'A nice piece of pie,' he said. 'One of your best.'

'Thank you, dear.' It was one of the many aspects of her husband's character that she liked best – the ability to show his appreciation of her home-making talents. She had never been as clever as Chloe or as confident but she did enjoy being a housewife. She loved cleaning and polishing and preparing the meals. She even enjoyed the many economies that were needed to live on Albert's small stipend.

She sat down on the other side of the table and tried not to look as desperate as she felt.

'Dearest, I have to ask . . . That is, I need to know if there is anything wrong. I think there is. I can feel it.' Without waiting for his answer she rushed on. 'It's about Olivia, isn't it?'

A small muscle twitched in his cheek and what little hope she had withered. But would Albert be able to tell her the truth? He was a very private man in spite of his chosen vocation and speaking about his innermost thoughts was difficult for him. He began to stammer a pretence.

'I don't know what you mean, dear.'

'Albert, I can tell you're unhappy and I think it's because of the baby.' In his eyes she saw the truth and was filled with a deep misery. 'Tell me!' she cried. 'I promise to understand.'

He shook his head then abruptly covered his face with his hands.

She said gently, 'Are you sorry we said we'd care for her? If so I blame myself for persuading you. I knew you were doubtful about the idea.'

'It's so unchristian,' he mumbled. 'I shouldn't feel this way. I'm a man of God!'

Dorothy swallowed, fighting back her fear. 'Is it the child?'

'No, no!' He looked up. 'The child is very sweet and

entirely innocent. Poor Hettie should have lived to see her grow up.'

'Then is it the circumstances of her birth?'

'No! It's me that's at fault. It's something within me and I'm trying to conquer it . . . I need time.'

'Is it that you don't want us to keep her?' Dorothy wanted to close her eyes to shut out the sight of her husband's anguish. Instead she forced herself to look at him. 'If so you must say so and we'll let her go. I'll talk to Chloe.'

He leaned forward, resting on his forearms. For a while he couldn't speak and then, with an effort, he said, 'I feel that once we adopt Olivia we may never have a child of our own. I know it's totally illogical, superstitious even, but that's how I feel. I have this terrible conviction, deep down, that we are spoiling our chances. That God will think we *have* a child and not bless us with another.' He withdrew, hunched in shame. 'I don't want to feel like this – it goes against everything I've been taught – but I do. I've prayed long and hard but the feeling remains.'

Dorothy nodded, unable to speak. Her disappointment was like a physical blow. If they gave up Olivia and *didn't* have a child of their own they would regret it for the rest of their lives but there was no way she could force Albert to see that. He had agreed to care for the child to please her but she could not expect him to continue. He had tried for her sake and it would be unfair to place such a burden on his shoulders.

'Can we continue for a week or so?' she asked as calmly as she could. 'Should we wait until after the funeral before we tell them?'

She could see the relief in his eyes and tried to set her own feelings aside.

'A few weeks. A month,' he agreed eagerly. 'Just as long as we know she will never be ours. As long as she will go back to the Maitlands or the Leemings . . .' His face crumpled. 'Oh Dottie! This is so cruel of me. I know how much it means to you.'

She reached for his hands and held them tightly. 'You mean more to me than anyone in the world, Albert. We'll say nothing to anyone at the moment but it will be perfectly understood between us. You may be right – who knows? And we must trust in God. He'll listen to our prayers. Of course he will.' She moved round the table to kiss him. 'Now I'm glad we had that little talk. You look happier and that's what matters to me.'

As she began to clear the table she blinked furiously to keep the tears at bay. She would write to Chloe and explain. Upstairs, looking down at the sleeping child, she knew that parting with Olivia would be one of the hardest things she had ever done.

Saturday dawned bright and clear and from ten o'clock onwards friends and members of Hettie's family could be seen trooping across the fields towards Fairfields, where Hettie lay in splendour in her open coffin in the morning room. Bertha had insisted that this way everyone would know who the father of her child was and Hettie's memory and Olivia would be respected.

Jessica had fought against this idea but Bertha had finally persuaded her to agree.

'It gives the Leemings something to cling to. Something to be proud of,' she told her mother. 'It suggests that it was not a quick scuffle behind a haystack but a serious affair of the heart. No one else need know that Oliver had rejected the idea of marriage. Her death was an accident. Who knows what might have happened?'

'I don't know,' Jessica demurred. 'I think the less said the better for all of us.'

'But we're paying for the funeral. People will already be gossiping. It will be all over the village by now. Far better we are open about it rather than letting them guess. Do you want us to be vilified in the village as cruel and unfeeling?'

This sobering thought had weakened Jessica's objection and the room was duly prepared. Darkened by closed shutters, it was lit with seventeen candles – one for each year of Hettie's short life. A bowl of roses stood at either end of the coffin in which Hettie lay in her white gown.

One by one they came to say their last goodbyes and to whisper to each other about how beautiful she looked.

'So peaceful!' whispered Betsy as she clung to her husband's arm. Lizzie, slightly resentful of the fuss being made of her sister, clutched her child to her and gazed in an awed silence.

Dorothy stayed at home with the baby and there was no sign that Oliver was going to put in an appearance.

The horse carriage arrived, decked in black plumes, and the coffin was closed and lifted on to it. The little procession of horse-driven carts followed at a sedate pace and eventually arrived at the church, where Albert waited for them. Inside the church there were more flowers and the small choir rose from their pews as the cortège moved down the aisle.

To Chloe's surprise, Uncle Matty had decided to join them.

'Safety in numbers!' he muttered as he edged along the row to sit beside her.

Jessica was also there, looking pale but unusually elegant in black.

They had just begun the first hymn when there was a slight disturbance at the back of the church and every head turned.

Oliver had arrived. He looked flushed and disconcerted as he faced the mourners but, undeterred, he walked alone down the aisle towards the altar. As he passed Chloe she saw the three long-stemmed lilies which he carried and her throat was suddenly tight. Mr Leeming muttered something but was angrily hushed by his wife. Whispered comments died as Oliver walked slowly towards Hettie's coffin. He laid the lilies on the polished oak lid and bent his head in prayer as the congregation began the second verse of the hymn. At last Albert stepped forward, rested a hand

161

gently on Oliver's arm and led him away to sit alone in the front row.

Chloe glanced at Jessica and saw that she was crying softly but, although the voices wavered a little, the singing continued to the last verse. As they knelt to pray Chloe marvelled at Oliver's courage and revised her opinion of him yet again.

At the close of the service the mourners followed the coffin into the churchyard and listened as the final words were spoken. As the coffin was gently lowered into the grave a blackbird perched on a nearby headstone and began to sing a final blessing.

I was dreading the funeral but it passed very well considering. Oliver came, which no one had expected, least of all me. He behaved with great dignity and respect and the service passed without any unpleasantness. I was fearful about the meal but even that was bearable. Lizzie seemed to be in a bad humour and said very little but Mr Leeming drank a few mugs of ale and became rather unsuitably merry, much to his wife's disgust. Oliver quickly disappeared upstairs and didn't reappear but I couldn't blame him. Jessica was also tired and made her excuses early on. It was Uncle Matty who rose to the occasion. Totally unabashed, he made it his job to talk to everyone, putting them at their ease and pressing them to more food and drink. I can't imagine what the Leemings made of him. People constantly surprise me. Poor Hettie. I wonder if she was looking down at us. I shall never forget her. Now that it's too late, I wish we had thought to bring Olivia to the church. It would have been a last meeting with her mother.

The following day Jessica complained of tiredness and decided to stay in bed for the morning and get up in the afternoon if she felt stronger.

Bertha and Chloe met over breakfast and Chloe knew at once that something else had happened.

'I have to show you this,' Bertha told her with a nervous glance towards the door. 'I did something rather dreadful and sneaked around Uncle Matty's bedroom. I'd gone in there to collect his washing from the linen bag and began to take a look round.' She held out a crumpled note. 'No wonder he doesn't go out anymore. He's in serious trouble and I don't know how to help him – except to go to the police.'

She busied herself with her toast while Chloe read the untidy scrawl: *'Yore going to get wots coming to you . . .'*

Chloe sat down slowly and Bertha looked up.

'This sounds ominous,' Chloe agreed. 'Have you talked to him about it?'

'How can I, without admitting that I've been spying on him? I asked him if everything was all right, saying I thought he looked very worried lately. He said, "Nothing I can't deal with." I think I should tell Oliver but he's so depressed lately.' She shrugged helplessly. 'I daren't tell Mama but I'm beginning to think Uncle Matty is in some kind of danger.'

Chloe, equally alarmed by the note, decided to confide in Bertha. She said, 'You know he's had gambling debts?'

'It doesn't surprise me. His past is a very shady affair. Twice he went abroad. The first time he borrowed some money from a friend of Father's, who threatened to take him to court. Father gave him the money and he skipped to France with it and went racing at Deauville. He was convinced he could double the money, pay off the debt and repay Father. Of course he lost it all. Next thing, weeks later, we had a card from him. He was in Switzerland, cadging lodgings from an old school friend.'

Chloe said, 'How does he sleep at night!'

'He has no sense of shame. He was supposed to be getting married once, years ago. At the last minute he hurried off to Italy and left the poor woman in the lurch. Her family was furious and threatened to sue him for breach of promise . . .' She blinked suddenly. 'You don't think the note is from them?' She picked it up and studied it. 'Oh no! Of course not. Not after all this time. Anyway, it's too poorly written. The woman he was going to marry came from a very respectable family. I was only a child then and I'd been promised a white dress with rosebud embroidery. It had to be cancelled and I hated him for that.' She smiled. 'Mama says it would have been the making of him but I think the woman escaped a rather dreadful fate!'

Briefly Chloe told her about Uncle Matty's recent brush with Sid Jakes.

'That settles it!' Bertha exclaimed. 'I'm going to tell Oliver as soon as he comes down. Mama always treats him with kid gloves but that time is past. He might as well see what happens when people step off the straight and narrow. He'll end up like Uncle Matty if he isn't careful.'

They lingered over breakfast but Oliver didn't join them so Bertha set off upstairs to beard him in his den. Chloe went upstairs to see to Jessica and it was some time before she met up with Bertha again. She was looking distinctly unhappy.

'Oliver was in a very awkward mood,' she grumbled. 'I really wonder why I bother with the ungrateful wretch. So wrapped up in his own problems.' She frowned slightly. 'Actually, he looks quite ill but he wouldn't talk to me. He says don't interfere in Uncle Matty's affairs. According to Oliver, Uncle Matty is old enough to look after himself and we are two foolish, meddling women!'

Chloe raised her eyebrows but bit back a sharp comment. 'So we don't involve the police?'

'No.' She tossed her head. '"On your head be it!" I told him and washed my hands of the whole business. I've got my own future to think about. Tomorrow George and his mother are coming round and we are going to tell Mama formally that the banns are being called. I think if his mother is with us she will be better behaved but I did wonder whether you would put in a good word for us before he arrives. To soften the blow.'

Chloe smiled. 'I'll do what I can. I do believe she is warming to the idea. Or perhaps resigning herself would be nearer the truth.'

When she went upstairs ten minutes later Chloe paused outside Oliver's door. Bertha's comment lingered in her mind. *Actually, he looks quite ill.* Was he ill? Should he be ignored? Impulsively she tapped on his door. Receiving no reply she knocked. After a moment or two he called, 'Who is it?'

'Me. Chloe. Are you all right?'

Another pause and then he opened the door. 'No I'm not all right but it's none of your business.'

Bertha was right. Oliver's hair was tousled and he had obviously not washed. His face was drawn and his eyes looked huge.

'You'd better come in. I can see I'm going to get no peace.'

Chloe ignored the snub and went in. The room had a stale smell and looked untidy and neglected. The windows were tightly shut and Chloe had to resist the urge to throw them open and let in some fresh air.

He said, 'I suppose you want to know about Adele.'

'No. I wanted to—'

'She's left me. Thrown up her new job and gone back to Paris to her family. I shall never see her again. Never. I know it.' He sat on the edge of the unmade bed, his face in his hands. 'I can't even blame her. The fault's all mine. I was such a fool. Hettie was nothing to me. Just a . . . a plaything. And Adele's right. I was ashamed of her. Oh God! I should have married her when I had the chance and to hell with my family.' He glanced up, his face anguished. 'I've ruined my life!'

'And hers, probably!'

Chloe at once regretted the unkind words but she was disappointed in him. Oliver was still worrying about himself. Yet his distress was genuine and she wished she could help but what could she do? Unless . . .

165

'You could go after Adele,' she suggested. 'Find her and insist on marrying her. Convince her, Oliver.'

'And how do we accommodate Hettie's child? Simply pretend she doesn't exist? You probably meant well, Chloe, but you don't understand these things. You should never have told her about the baby.'

'Olivia is happy with my sister. She's in good hands.'

For the moment, she thought.

Oliver jumped to his feet and crossed to the fireplace. Catching sight of himself in the mirror he groaned. 'Lord what a state I'm in!' He ran his fingers through his hair with no noticeable improvement.

Chloe wanted to shake him. 'So is no one living in the flat?'

He reached out to a small table and dangled a key ring in front of her. 'She threw them at me. So either I let it go or I have to pay for it myself. And that means selling a great many pictures.' He tossed the keys on to the mantelpiece.

'So perhaps Uncle Matty could stay there for a few weeks – until this trouble blows over.'

Oliver's eyes narrowed. 'He could . . . if he's prepared to pay the rent. The way I feel right now I never want to set foot in it again! Everything will remind me of Adele and my own stupidity. Hell and damnation! If only I had seen where all this would lead . . . If only I could turn back the clock and do things differently.'

'At least if Uncle Matty moved in it would give you some time to decide what's the best thing to do.' In spite of all that had happened, Chloe could not bear to see him so crushed. 'Make a new start, Oliver. Throw yourself into your painting and become famous! Who knows?'

'I might throw myself into the Thames! That would make more sense.' He sighed. 'Look, no offence, Chloe, but I need to be alone. I'll speak to Uncle Matty about the flat.' He looked thoughtful. 'We might even come to an arrangement. Pay half each and see how we get along together.'

Chloe left him, pleased that he was at least thinking

positively. Throwing himself into the river had sounded distinctly defeatist. As she went in to see to Jessica she sighed. How to prepare her for the visit from George and Bertha?

Jessica was lying propped against the pillows with a book in her hands. Chloe went straight to the wardrobe and began to rifle through the garments displayed on their hangers. She brought out a violet silk skirt and a cream blouse.

'You always look very nice in these,' she told Jessica. 'Very elegant yet somehow in command. I'll press them for you.'

Jessica stared at her without comprehension. 'Are we expecting visitors?'

Chloe feigned surprise at the question. 'But of course. Tomorrow Bertha's young man is coming to talk about the wedding – and his mother is coming to meet you. They're calling the banns any day now.'

'The banns?' Her mouth fell open in surprise. '*The banns*? I don't think . . .' Confused, she put a hand to her head. 'Wedding banns? I've heard nothing of this!'

Chloe gave the skirt a good shake. 'I'm not surprised if you've forgotten, with all that's happened lately. Sometimes I don't know if I'm coming or going!' She laughed. 'This skirt hardly ever crumples. It's wonderful.'

'It's quality, that's why! But . . . wedding banns? Are you sure?'

'I thought I was sure. Why don't you ask Bertha yourself? She'll be up later. I must say that I'm glad they've been sensible. When I first came here there were murmurings about Gretna Green! What a scandal, I thought.'

Jessica cried, 'Gretna Green? You mean . . . *elope*?'

Chloe smiled. 'I thought she was joking but she wasn't – but then you agreed to the match so all is well.' She carried the blouse to the window and inspected it carefully. 'Fresh as a daisy.' She carried it back and draped it over the back of the chair. 'A wedding will be something to lift all our spirits after poor Hettie's death but there'll be so

167

much to think about. A photographer, Bertha's gown, the guest list.'

An expression of panic appeared on Jessica's face as she sat up. 'So soon? It's impossible! Bertha must be mad! The catering, the flowers . . . Oh no! It's out of the question!' Her eyes widened. 'A *hurried* wedding? People will think the worst!'

Chloe paused to consider this. 'I think you're right,' she said. 'Why not suggest that they delay it by a week or two. I'm sure my brother-in-law would agree to delay the banns if it made things easier for you.' She smiled. 'I'm so pleased Bertha has chosen a local man. If she'd married into the army, for instance, she might have been posted abroad and you would have missed her terribly.'

She had gone too far. She knew it even before the words were out of her mouth. Jessica was wagging a knowing forefinger and trying to keep a straight face. 'Don't think I don't see through you, child. I can read you like a book. Bertha has sent you ahead to talk to me.'

'Mrs Maitland!' Chloe grinned. 'How could you even *think* such a thing?'

Jessica rolled her eyes. 'I don't blame George Brier but he comes from different stock. Different standards. Different expectations from life. I wonder if he is . . . as sensitive as one might hope. You're a romantic and you take Bertha's side but in your heart you must wonder as I do.' She sighed. 'But a wedding *would* be pleasant. At least one of my children will be happy. Poor Oliver. I've done everything I could for that boy and here he is, in the middle years and still unsettled. Perhaps he should have married Hettie.'

Chloe said nothing.

Jessica closed her book and slid out of bed. 'We shall have to delay the sittings for my portrait until after the wedding. It will be something to look forward to after all the excitement.' She felt for her slippers and pushed her feet into them. 'I can see I'm going to have no more rest today. Tell Mrs Letts to bring up my hot water . . .

168

And that's another thing – we shall have to find a new girl to take Hettie's place. Oh!' Her face crumpled. 'That poor girl. Now and again I manage to forget and then it all comes crowding back. Her sweet face will haunt me for the rest of my days.'

Later that afternoon Chloe made her way to the stables in search of Binns and found him watching the farrier.

'Afternoon, missus.' The words came through a mouthful of horseshoe nails. The farrier, a thickset man with a bushy beard, had the horse's foreleg between his knees and was hammering nails into a new horseshoe.

Binns said, 'Master Oliver said I was to get it seen to pronto. Neddy dropped a shoe yesterday and ain't much use without it.'

Chloe said, 'We shall need the dog cart later on. Miss Maitland wants to see the vicar in Icklesham about her wedding and—'

A large grin lit his face. 'Getting married, is she? Well, no prizes for guessing who to!' He tapped the side of his nose.

The farrier released the horse's leg and glanced at Chloe. 'If she's marrying George Brier she'll not regret it. A right decent man, he is. And going far. Wonderful what he can do with a bit of iron, a fire and a hammer. Won't please my eldest girl, though. Fancied him for years, she has. But he had eyes for no one but Miss Bertha.' He straightened up and gave Chloe a sly look. 'Pleased is she? The mistress?'

Chloe smiled. 'Mrs Maitland is delighted.'

She had just returned to the house when Mrs Letts appeared with a letter.

'For you – brought by hand. And the window cleaner didn't come this morning. Probably his rheumatics. He's a bit old for that job. Up and down ladders all day with a gammy hip.'

Chloe looked at the handwriting. 'It's from my sister. News about the baby, I expect.'

Ignoring Mrs Letts' hopeful expression she hurried upstairs to her room in search of solitude. Smiling, she opened the letter and immediately her expression changed to one of dismay.

Dear Chloe,

I know this letter will come as a big disappointment but I have to tell you now that we definitely can't keep little Olivia. Not that she isn't the sweetest child imaginable and very good. She takes her bottle better and sleeps better. She is growing so fast and the doctor is delighted with her progress.

I know you will understand if I explain that poor Albert has found it impossible to accept and truly love another man's child. It is breaking my heart but I won't try to persuade him against his will. Of course we will care for her until the Maitlands make other plans. Please don't blame Albert. He has prayed hard but still feels the same about it. Maybe it is God's will. Who knows? You can imagine how I feel. I must put Albert first but it will be hard to part with Olivia.

Could you talk to Oliver Maitland? It might be easier coming from you. I cannot trust myself not to break down and cry . . .

Chloe closed her eyes and uttered a small groan. Her best-laid plans!

Knowing how much this would upset Dorothy she at once blamed herself for the original suggestion although she knew in her heart that she had meant only the best for everyone. It might have worked and could have proved a feasible solution. But it didn't.

With a heartfelt sigh she refolded the letter. She would have to seek out Oliver but not until later. Before she talked to him she would need to have something positive to say. In his present state of mind she was reluctant to add another burden.

170

Perhaps she should tell Jessica . . . But no – that was Oliver's task.

'Leave well enough alone, Chloe!' she muttered. 'You are a sight too eager to interfere.'

She wondered whether or not to visit Dorothy but again decided to let the dust settle. An unwelcome suspicion was growing that the more she tried to help, the more complicated everything became. For a moment she stood stock-still, appalled at the idea.

'But sometimes the onlooker sees most of the game,' she whispered, seeking reassurance. A little comforted by this, she slipped the letter into her pocket and decided to sleep on it.

Ten

The moment Chloe opened her eyes next morning her mind was filled with the familiar litany of troubles. Bertha's controversial betrothal, Uncle Matty's debts, Oliver's lost love and the unwanted child. Rubbing the sleep from her eyes she struggled out of bed. Pulling back the curtains she saw a clear blue sky but the wind was from the west and might bring the odd shower.

'Where have the past few weeks gone?' she muttered.

She had just finished washing and was towelling her arms dry when there was a knock on the door. Mrs Letts stood outside, wringing her hands.

'Miss Blake, it's the old gentleman. Mr Matty.'

'Oh no! Not again.' Visions of Uncle Matty lying unconscious leapt into her mind. 'Where is he? He's not hurt?' As she rushed to pull on her clothes, her heart thumped in her chest.

'He's not *anywhere*. He's gone to London. Binns has just come to the back door looking very sorry for himself. Seems he—'

'I'll come down at once. Go back down, Mrs Letts, and keep Binns there. I'll rouse Master Oliver.'

Mrs Letts hesitated. 'I doubt you will, miss. He and Mr Matty were a bit tipsy last night. I heard them staggering off to bed. You won't get much sense out of Master Oliver just yet.' She lowered her voice. 'Best let him sleep it off and no more said, eh?'

Chloe nodded. Bertha's words came back to her. Was Oliver going to take after Uncle Matty? She ran a comb through her hair, pulled it back into a tidy chignon and pinned it into place. Then she hurried down to the kitchen, where Binns was seated at the big table, warming his hands round a mug of tea.

Chloe sat down beside him. 'So Uncle Matty has gone.'

He nodded. 'I was to be outside the front steps at ten to four this morning. Took him into Rye to catch the milk train to London. And he only just caught it then. Had to run the last hundred yards!' He grinned at the memory and then his face darkened. 'My ma had to get me up that early! She wasn't too pleased, I can tell you, but he gave me a shilling so I mustn't grumble.'

'Did he say when he was coming back?'

'Nope.'

'Did he take any luggage?'

'Just a small carpet bag. Proper moonlight flit, it was. 'Cept it wasn't moonlight. Wasn't even dark. Not properly, being summer an' all that.'

Chloe stood up. 'I expect he arranged it with Oliver. I'll talk to him later – unless Bertha wants to deal with it.'

Mrs Letts beamed. 'I should reckon she's got better things to think about, what with the wedding. I was beginning to think she'd never wed, poor woman. Just shows, if you wait long enough . . .'

Binns stared pointedly into his empty mug but Mrs Letts ignored the hint.

She said, 'Since you're up bright and early you can let the hens out and bring in the eggs. The mistress wants scrambled eggs this morning and I'm almost out.'

He got up with a certain heaviness, as though the early morning rise had been too much for him. 'See what I can do,' he offered and let himself out into the brisk morning.

'So, Mr Orme's gone. One less for breakfast,' said Mrs Letts. 'And then we'll see what the good Lord has in store for us today.' Shaking her head, she poured herself a second mug of tea and looked enquiringly at Chloe.

'I think the blacksmith and his mother are calling. Probably around eleven, for tea and biscuits.'

'Are they now? Wonders will never cease! Still, never a dull moment in this house. But at least it passes the time.'

At ten to eleven George Brier and his mother were on their way to Fairfields in the pony trap. George was whistling tunelessly and his mother was staring grimly ahead, her hands clasped tightly in her lap.

Ellen said, 'I'm not going to curtsey and that's that!'

'Curtsey?' He laughed. 'Nobody's asking you to curtsey. They're not royalty, Ma.'

'They live in a big house and they put on airs and graces.'

'They do not, so stop working yourself up. They've been brought up differently, that's all. You grumbled that you'd never met Bertha's mother and now you're complaining because we're going for a cup of tea.' His glance was affectionate. 'It's not easy for us but it's not for them either. Just take it steady, Ma.'

'But what shall I call her?'

'Mrs Maitland. She'll call you Mrs Brier.'

She clutched her purse, her knuckles almost white. 'I never reckoned this was a good idea. I've got things to do back home. I think—'

'We're here, Ma, so stop fussing.'

As they swept into the drive he said, 'See my gates?'

Her mouth fell open in surprise. 'George, they're beautiful! Marvellous!'

He grinned. 'I'm marvellous and you're marvellous – so smile and try to enjoy yourself.'

In the drawing room ten minutes later Ellen was seated opposite Jessica and Bertha sat beside George on the sofa.

Ellen said, 'There's a nice little cottage just along the lane from us. I reckon they could get that at a fair rent. The farmer who owns it—'

Jessica smiled sweetly. 'Oh there's no need for that, Mrs

174

Brier. Fairfields has plenty of spare rooms. They could have three rooms at the far end of the house. No point in wasting money on rent.'

Bertha and George exchanged a quick glance and Bertha said, 'We've already discussed where we will live, Mama. George has found a roomy cottage in Icklesham that we can rent for a few years. Longer if necessary. It's in good repair and there's a good-sized garden.'

Ellen said, 'You do need a garden for the vegetables and chickens. And we keep a few rabbits. It all helps, you know. George is a dab hand with green things. He grows the most wonderful carrots.'

Jessica looked unimpressed. 'My daughter is used to space,' she murmured.

Bertha said, 'It has a front parlour, large kitchen, three bedrooms. Later on, if either you, Mama, or Mrs Brier needs help we'll make new plans.'

Jessica said, 'Help?'

Bertha nodded. 'Due to ill health, perhaps.'

Silence greeted this announcement. The two mothers looked at each other. Ellen, seeing that Mrs Maitland already looked rather helpless, drew herself up proudly. 'Never had a day's illness in me life,' she told them.

Bertha held out the plate and said, 'Another almond cake, Mrs Brier?'

Ellen took one and bit into it. Jessica shook her head at the proffered cakes and looked at her daughter.

Bertha said, 'I'm going into Hastings tomorrow on the bus. To choose some silk for my dress. I wondered whether either of you would like to come with me.'

Jessica said, 'I'm afraid I couldn't manage it, Bertha. You know how I am.'

Ellen said quickly, 'I could. I haven't been into Hastings for years. I'd enjoy an outing.'

Bertha smiled at her. 'Thank you. I'd be glad of some advice.'

George smiled at Jessica. 'Would you feel up to a walk

as far as the gates while Ma and Bertha are out? You haven't seen the new screen yet and it's beginning to look very nice. I'd be honoured to show it to you . . .' He waited for an answer. 'You could hold my arm and we'd take it very slowly.'

Bertha held her breath. Would her mother succumb to the temptation of a walk with a good-looking young man? She had been a beauty in her youth and it was a long time since she had been so flattered.

Jessica was studying him, her head on one side.

He said, 'I'd really value your opinion, Mrs Maitland, but I know you're not strong. I'll understand if—'

She gave him a bright smile and sat a little straighter. 'I would enjoy a walk,' she told him. 'I fight a constant battle against ill health but with your help I'm sure I could manage it as far as the gates.'

Ellen said, 'Well, that's settled then. As for Bertha's dress – my sister is a good needlewoman. We wondered if we should ask her to make it.'

Jessica drew in a sharp breath. 'But how good . . .' She stopped, flustered. 'I mean, it would have to be . . .'

Ellen said, 'She sews for a living, my sister. Turn her hand to anything, she can. She made my niece's wedding dress and she looked like a princess, didn't she, George? George was there. He knows.'

George nodded. 'It would help her, too, to earn a little money.'

Bertha said, 'I love the idea. I fancy a pale coffee colour and I'll choose a simple pattern because I hate frills and fuss.' She looked at her mother. 'And you will need something new, Mama. We'll have to talk about it. George's cousin says he'll be best man—'

Jessica clasped her hands. 'And Oliver will lead Bertha to the altar.'

Bertha looked at her. 'I did wonder if we should ask Uncle Matty?'

'Matty?' Jessica, horrified, gave her a meaningful glance.

'I don't think so . . .' she began, searching for a convincing reason that would not shame them in front of the Briers. 'I'm afraid he will still be in London . . . on important business.'

'Oh but Mama—'

Jessica gave her another meaningful glance. 'He'll attend the ceremony if he *happens* to be back by then but I don't think we should rely on him.'

An hour later, when the visit finally ended, there were sighs of relief all round. Both mothers felt that they had made a useful contribution, nobody had been upset or upstaged and honour was satisfied.

As George whipped up the horse on the way home, he gave his mother a sideways glance.

'That wasn't so bad, was it?' he asked. 'We all got along well enough.'

Ellen tossed her head. 'Don't talk so daft, George. Course we got along. They're nice people. I never had a moment's doubt.'

As Mrs Letts had predicted, Oliver stayed in bed until after midday and when he reappeared he looked terrible. Bertha was in her room making a list of wedding guests and Jessica was resting when he stumbled out on to the terrace, screwing up his eyes against the onslaught of the sunlight. Chloe looked at him, dismayed. His clothes were crumpled and he was in need of a wash and shave.

He eyed Chloe blearily. 'I'm starving! Mrs Letts has cleared the breakfast things.'

Chloe put down the map of North America she had been studying and looked at him. 'She's also cleared the midday meal. It's nearly two o'clock.' It sounded like a reproof even to her ears.

'You sound like my mother!' He sank on to a chair and closed his eyes. 'I had to see Uncle Matty off in style. I take it he's gone.'

'He caught the milk train to Charing Cross.'

'He called it "doing a runner". He'll never change. Still, somebody might as well live in the flat – though God knows what mischief he'll get up to in town. Run up more debts, perhaps.' He frowned at the map. 'North America? Thinking of emigrating, are you?'

Chloe ignored his attempt at humour. 'My father went there years ago,' she told him. Unwilling to talk about her plans she pointedly refolded the map. She needed to tell him about Dorothy and Albert's change of heart but wondered whether this was a good time. Instead she said, 'Are you sure you shouldn't be in Paris looking for Adele? You obviously love each other and she might find it in her heart to forgive you.'

'Not a hope.'

'No harm in trying, is there? Do you know where any of her family live?'

'I once visited her parents after a quarrel with Adele. I might be able to find it again – and then her mother could throw me out again!'

'Adele might surprise you. Women do forgive. Why not smarten yourself up, go down to Folkestone and cross to Boulogne? You might be talking to her by this time tomorrow.'

Oliver shook his head then followed with a grunt of pain. He clutched his head. 'I shouldn't have done that. My head's thumping. I think I might be sick.'

Chloe rolled her eyes and hoped he'd go somewhere else to do it.

He said, 'Have you seen the baby again?'

Chloe seized her chance. 'I have some disappointing news,' she told him and proceeded to tell him about Dorothy's letter.

His gloom deepened. 'Hell and damnation!' he muttered. 'Sorry. I thought we had sorted out Olivia's future.' He shrugged. 'It gets worse and worse, doesn't it! Well then, I must think again. Do you know anything about caring for a child?'

'Me?' She was startled. 'Nothing at all.'

'You could learn.'

'I have other plans.'

'We could employ a nurse . . . No, maybe not.'

'Jessica brought you and Bertha up so she might well be able to supervise a nurse.' Chloe was aware of a glimmer of hope. 'Are you thinking Olivia might be brought up here at Fairfields?'

'It's an option, isn't it. With Hettie gone . . .'

'Where would *you* be?'

'Here, I suppose, from time to time.' He clutched his stomach, groaned and stood up. 'Excuse me!'

Chloe watched him stagger off in the direction of the shrubbery and then looked away as he began to retch. She tried to imagine what Adele was thinking and wondered whether or not she regretted leaving London so promptly. If she *did* love Oliver she might be having second thoughts. She might even come back. What would *I* do in Adele's shoes? she wondered.

Oliver came back to the terrace and tossed a small purse on to the table.

'I want you to take this to your sister . . .'

'But you've already given her some money.'

'Give her this as well. Ask her to keep Olivia for a few more weeks. Tell her I'm thinking about finding a nurse and . . . and thank them for taking care of her and that I'm eternally grateful. Say—'

'Why don't *you* go?'

He went on as though she had not spoken. 'Say I understand how Albert feels. Tell them we're going to work out something permanent in the next few days. And . . . and give Olivia a kiss from me.'

Chloe struggled to hide her astonishment. 'I have too much to do today. I'll go tomorrow.'

'Thanks.' He rubbed his haggard face. 'I'm not really up to all this. I'm going back to bed. Pathetic, I know, but I can't help it.'

Chloe watched him walk unsteadily into the house. She called out, 'Drink lots of water, Oliver.'

The following afternoon Sid Jakes crouched in the shrubbery beneath the sycamores, watching the house. He had wrapped his large greatcoat around him and his shotgun lay within easy reach. He saw the daughter leave to catch the bus and he saw the companion drive away with Binns. He had it on good authority from a mate in the pub that the son had gone back to London in something of a hurry a few days earlier. And the maid was dead and buried.

So they're safely out of the way, he told himself. Better and better. Eyes narrowed, Jakes spat. He had spent time on this job and his observations were now paying off. Matty Orme would be alone in the house – if you didn't count the old woman, who would be sleeping at three in the afternoon, and the housekeeper, who'd be stuck in the kitchen and wouldn't hear a thing. Orme's luck had finally run out.

'Can't say I didn't warn the stupid old fool!' Ducking further into the shadows of the rhododendrons, Jakes pulled two shells from his pocket and slipped them into the barrels of his shotgun. Rising slowly to a stooping position he looked around.

'Now or never!' he muttered and ran across the grass in the direction of the front of the house. Suddenly he froze in his tracks.

'Sod it!'

A man on a bicycle had ridden into view and now continued, whistling, up the drive. Seeing that he hadn't been spotted, Jakes doubled back into the shadows under the trees and sat down again, rolling his eyes at the narrowness of his escape.

'Hell and damnation!' he growled. 'Just my bloody luck!'

He watched helplessly as the man removed a bucket from his handlebars and went round to the back of the house. Going for water. Jakes ground his teeth with impotent fury.

How many windows was he going to do? If he did them all it would take a year and a day!

Jakes spat again. He was an unhappy man and had a notoriously short fuse. He glared in the direction of the house as the window cleaner reappeared and began to wash down the lower windows.

'You take too long and I'll do you as well!' he muttered.

Oblivious of the danger he was in, the window cleaner carried on with his work until he was interrupted by a large woman who Jakes guessed was the housekeeper, who brought him a mug of tea. They stood together chatting while Jakes cursed helplessly. The minutes ticked past and Jakes heard the half-hour strike from a nearby church. The window cleaner started on the first-floor windows. Another half-hour passed and Jakes heard the clatter of hooves at the back of the house. He'd forgotten there was a rear entrance but it didn't matter. He couldn't be seen. Someone making a delivery perhaps, he thought. But if the window cleaner didn't get on with it the old woman would be getting up from her afternoon sleep and that could be awkward. She might see him from a window and raise the alarm.

'At last! The bugger's on the move!' The window cleaner was wringing out his various cloths. He emptied the dirty water over the roses.

Jakes watched him go with relief and made a rude gesture at his departing back.

'Now!' he muttered reaching for his shotgun and, stooping low, he ran towards the house. He had his plan ready. If the housekeeper answered the door he'd ask for Mr Orme, as polite as you like, with the shotgun concealed beneath his long shapeless coat. If Orme answered it would be a quick blast into the next world.

He rang the doorbell and pressed his ear against the oak door. He heard what sounded like footsteps on stairs. He grinned. That was no lady. This was his man. When the door opened Jakes brought up the gun and fired. Straight

181

at the chest. The man toppled backwards in a shower of his own blood.

He leaned forward to take a closer look. It wasn't Orme. 'Christ!' He had shot the wrong man. Shocked into immobility, he was still staring into the doorway when a young woman ran down the stairs and knelt by the stricken man. How the hell had she got there? He stuffed the gun under his coat.

She cried, 'Oliver! *Oliver!*'

He had killed the son by mistake.

The young woman scrambled to her feet and ran towards him, screaming, her eyes wide with horror. He recognised her now. It was the old lady's companion. She must have gone in by the back way for some reason. Then she looked straight into Jakes' face and he saw recognition dawn.

'I know who you are!' she cried.

He would have to kill her as well.

Having already hidden the shotgun he was now forced to fumble it free of the all-enveloping greatcoat. It took only a few seconds but to Jakes it seemed like an eternity. He brought the gun up and fired again but in those few lost seconds the young woman had reached the door. As the second shot burst from his gun the heavy oak door closed between them.

Jakes was trembling with a mixture of fear and anger as he watched splinters of oak fly in all directions, leaving the door badly scarred.

'Damn and blast!' he said through gritted teeth.

He'd missed his chance, which meant that the stupid bitch was going to finger him to the police. He heard muffled shouts as he stood there, frozen with indecision. The woman was screaming for help but he had no more shells and it was too dangerous to hang around the scene of the crime.

Get out! he told himself and, turning, raced back into the shrubbery. 'Christ Almighty!' He scrambled over the wall and plunged into the wood beyond with questions buzzing in his brain like angry wasps. Where the hell was Matty Orme?

And where had the son come from? He was supposed to be in London. No chance that he would survive a shotgun blast in the chest. Not from that range . . . And how soon would they notify the police? They'd call a doctor first . . .

He needed an alibi. Could he find an alibi? His wife might lie for him but then again she might not. She hated his guts. But he'd find an alibi. They cost money but it would be worth every penny. Dodging in and out of the trees, he now blamed himself for not setting one up in advance. It would be the companion's word against his. There'd be no evidence unless . . . He came to an abrupt stop. Had he left any clues? The cartridges? But no – he had only fired twice so there had been no need to reload. The cartridges had not been ejected.

He cursed as he ran. If he couldn't find someone to give him an alibi he'd have to skip the country. He'd need to find a boat. A fishing boat, maybe . . .

'Bloody well scuppered!' he told himself. All he could do was get away from the scene of the crime as fast as possible. Reaching the open fields, he ran desperately fast, stumbling, panic-stricken, red-faced and furious, in the direction of Winchelsea. He was angry partly with himself and partly with an unkind fate. He had a nasty feeling deep down that this time he may have taken one risk too many.

As the front door slammed, Chloe heard the second blast and thanked God for her narrow escape. She had escaped death by seconds. Shuddering, she bolted the door, fearful that Jakes might attempt to force his way in to finish the job. She had seen recognition in his eyes and knew she was a potential threat to him as a witness to the attack.

She knelt beside Oliver, her heart racing, her mind filled with the darkest despair. Time seemed to stand still, as though in a nightmare. Oliver lay on his back, arms and legs spread wide, his face crushed and bloody, his eyes staring sightlessly upwards. Blood was soaking into his shirt, which had been ripped apart to reveal the torn flesh of his chest.

'Oh Oliver! My dear!' she whispered.

There were small puncture marks across his face and neck from the shot. Was he dead? Could he *possibly* have survived? 'Please God!' she whispered. 'Please don't let him be dead.' And yet she knew in her heart that he was.

She shouted for Mrs Letts and tried to focus her mind but it seemed to be barely functioning.

'Oliver! *Oliver!*'

Picking up one of his hands, she began to rub it. There was so much blood. It seemed impossible he could still be alive and yet she refused to believe the awful alternative. Sickened, Chloe closed her eyes, trying to shut out the sight of his ruined face.

When she opened them again Mrs Letts was hurrying towards her.

'I heard a shot,' she said. 'Oh my sweet Jesus! That's not . . . Oh! God Almighty!' She crossed herself. 'Master Oliver! This can't be happening.' She stood above him, trembling with fear. 'Why? Who would do this? What's he ever done?'

Her panic restored some of Chloe's scattered wits and, scrambling to her feet, she rushed for the telephone. She rang the doctor although she knew there was no hope. He promised to come straight away. Then she rang the police.

'There's been a shooting,' she told them, struggling to keep her voice level. 'No, not an accident. It was deliberate. It was murder. Yes, murder! Send someone to Fairfields – and find Sid Jakes. He's a gamekeeper. Lives around Icklesham. He did it. No, I didn't actually see it but I saw him on the doorstep only yards away . . . He was holding the shotgun. Of course he did it!'

She hung up the receiver and sank down on the lowest step of the stairs. Mrs Letts had lowered herself to the ground and was stroking Oliver's blood-soaked hair. The sight of her tenderness almost undermined Chloe, who was trying desperately to remain in control of her emotions.

'There, there,' Mrs Letts murmured. 'Don't you fret, Master Oliver. The doctor's on his way.'

She glanced up at Chloe. 'I used to see him in his pram,' she said, her voice choked. 'And riding on his hobby horse . . . He loved that little horse. When its mane fell out I made a new one out of wool and stuck it on . . . And when he went away to school I always made him a chocolate cake. He loved that, as you know . . . He was a dear little lad.' She swallowed with difficulty. 'And now he's gone. His poor mother!'

Tears streamed suddenly down her cheeks and Chloe felt her own resolve weakening. If only there was someone who could take over. Someone who could be in charge and would know what to do. She thought of Jessica upstairs, oblivious of the death of her son. But Jessica would collapse under the tragedy and Bertha hadn't yet returned from her shopping trip in Hastings. She would be devastated. Uncle Matty would have to be told and she shuddered to imagine how he would react. Only Chloe alone had that slight detachment that came from not being a family member. It would be up to her, she thought, appalled.

She said, 'Thank goodness it was all over very quickly.'

He wouldn't even have known that he was seconds away from death, she thought. Then she thought of Hettie, who already lay in her grave. That reminded her of Olivia, who was no doubt sleeping peacefully in her cot. Now the little girl had lost her father as well as her mother. Bereft of both parents, little Olivia was truly an orphan.

Chloe hid her face in her hands. She wanted to find a pillow to put under Oliver's head but decided against it. The police wouldn't want Oliver's body to be moved in any way.

Mrs Letts said, 'First Hettie and now Master Oliver. It seems like a dreadful curse is on the place.'

Inclined to agree, Chloe said nothing. Her mind was recovering from the initial shock and beginning to work again. Presumably Jakes had been after Uncle Matty, determined to carry out his threat, determined to take revenge.

185

Mrs Letts said, 'I ought to be doing something but I can't seem to think straight. I suppose a cup of tea . . .?'

'No,' said Chloe. 'We'll both have a brandy to steady us. I'll get it. You stay with Oliver.'

As she poured the brandy, she realised that Bertha would be returning shortly. This tragedy would shatter her new-found happiness.

When the doctor arrived he confirmed that Oliver would have died instantly from his injuries. 'Probably before he even realised that he was going to die.' He sighed heavily.

The police sergeant arrived soon afterwards. Sergeant Tanner was middle-aged, a portly man with greying hair and blue eyes. As he knelt carefully beside the body he drew his breath in sharply. Chloe was relieved to see that he regarded the dead man with respect and something approaching real sorrow.

'This is a dreadful business,' he murmured, shaking his head. 'Taken in the prime of his life, poor fellow. Please relay my condolences to the family.' He glanced up. 'Where are they, by the way?'

Chloe explained and then waited in silence while he conferred in a low voice with the doctor. Sitting nearby, she found that she was shaking uncontrollably in spite of the brandy. If only she could slip away to her room and hide under the bedclothes . . . But escape was not an option. With an effort she straightened up and faced the police sergeant, who was already turning the pages of his notebook.

She said, 'It was Sid Jakes, Sergeant. He was still standing outside the door when I ran down the stairs. When he saw me he tried to kill me as well!'

'Because you were a witness?'

'I assume so. I didn't actually see the shooting but when I saw Oliver lying on the floor Jakes was still there with the shotgun in his hands. I only just managed to shut the door as the second blast came. Otherwise there would have been two victims.'

186

She stopped when he raised his hand to signal that she was going too fast. When he caught up with his notes she explained about Uncle Matty's threatening note.

'You know this note was from Sid Jakes, do you?'

'Mr Orme was quite certain. He knew he was in danger but we couldn't believe anything like this would happen. I wish now we'd listened to him. Even Oliver thought it was unlikely. Now he's been killed instead.' She shook her head, overwhelmed by the immensity of the disaster.

'My chaps are out looking for Jakes,' the sergeant told her. 'He won't get far. Does he think he killed you?'

'I doubt it. The shot made such a mess of the door. I think he must realise his witness is still alive. Does that put me in danger?'

'I don't think so. He'd never be stupid enough to come back knowing we'll have a police presence here. He's more likely trying to put a few miles between us! We'll get him, Miss Blake, and when we do he'll hang for this.' He closed his notebook. 'I never trusted the man. Couldn't understand why anyone would employ him as a gamekeeper – unless it was to frighten the poachers. I suppose he did that all right! But then there was his moneylending and betting and a bit of fencing for stolen goods. Not much he didn't turn his hand to but we could never nail him. Now we can.'

He asked a few more questions about Matty and Chloe explained that he was in London in Adele's flat.

'We'll need to interview him,' he told her. 'Tell him to get back here as soon as he can. We're going to need a statement from him. Now I'd like to go over it once more if you can bear it. Just to check that I've got it right. You say you were about here when you first saw Jakes . . .'

A moment or two later the sound Chloe had been dreading interrupted them. 'That's Mrs Maitland's bell,' she told the sergeant. 'She'll have woken from her sleep. She'll have to be told.'

He frowned. 'Oh dear! More grief. It's a sad business. Would you like me to break it to her?'

Chloe hesitated. She longed to say yes but thought she could break it more gently. Before she could answer, there was a rattle of wheels and a clatter of hooves and they both turned. The police wagon had arrived.

'Ah, that'll be the coffin. I wonder whether we should remove the victim before his mother sees him. I shouldn't like to think of her carrying this awful sight for the rest of her days.' He looked at Chloe.

'I think Bertha should decide that but she's not here. She's gone shopping in Hastings.' Feeling herself sway, she put a hand to her head. So many decisions on top of the shock she had endured. Clutching the banister, she lowered herself to the bottom stair.

'Are you all right, Miss Blake?'

'No . . . but I will be in a moment.' At least she hoped so. Perhaps the brandy had been a mistake.

From upstairs the bell tinkled again. 'I'll tell her,' said Chloe. 'I'll have to. She'll know by my face that something's happened.'

But at that moment she caught sight of Bertha's slim figure hurrying up the drive.

'What's happened to the door?' Bertha demanded. 'Why are the police here?'

Chloe and Sergeant Tanner exchanged a despairing glance. To Chloe he said, 'You go on upstairs to the mother. I'll break it to the sister.'

'But she'll see Oliver like this!'

'Can't be helped. You get along upstairs. You've quite enough to cope with already.'

Chloe nodded and, pulling herself to her feet, somehow found the strength of will to haul herself up the stairs.

She found Jessica in the doorway of her room and took her by the arm.

'Please come back inside. I have something to tell you but I want you to sit down first.'

Jessica paled, alerted by the tone of Chloe's voice and the look in her eyes.

'What is it? Tell me at once. Something's happened. Is it Bertha? An accident? Oh no!' She clapped a shaking hand over her mouth.

Chloe guided her to her bedside chair then sat on the edge of the bed and took hold of her hand.

'There's been a . . . a shooting. I'm sorry but it was Oliver.'

Jessica stared at her. 'Oliver has shot someone? Oh, you must be—'

'No, no. Oliver has been shot. I'm afraid he's badly hurt.'

'Oh!' The word was like a small sigh as the truth dawned. She looked into Chloe's eyes and then drew back. '*Badly* hurt?'

'Yes.' Chloe hesitated and at that moment there was a scream from downstairs.

Jessica said, 'That was Bertha! Does that mean . . . Oh don't tell me . . . Not Oliver. He's not *dead*?'

'Yes he is. I'm so desperately sorry.'

Jessica stared at her, comprehending yet refusing to accept the terrible news. 'You must be mistaken, Chloe. No one would shoot Oliver.'

'It was a mistake. The man thought he was shooting Uncle Matty, because he owes him a lot of money.'

Slowly Jessica's gaze wandered. She looked round the room as though she didn't know where she was. 'But Oliver . . . I mean . . . Where was this? I just can't believe . . .'

Briefly Chloe explained what had happened and as she did so she saw realisation finally dawn in the older woman's face.

'So my son is dead? Has the doctor . . .?'

Chloe nodded. 'The doctor and the police are downstairs. Sergeant Tanner is breaking it to Bertha.'

'Bertha? Oh that poor girl. All her happiness gone!' Her lips quivered.

Chloe could hardly bear to watch her as she struggled to

retain a semblance of composure. If only she would weep. It would be a natural relief.

Suddenly Jessica stiffened. 'Is he still here? Oliver? I must see him. I must hold him. Dear God! My beautiful son. What did he ever do to deserve this?'

Tears blinded her and Chloe stepped closer to put her arms around the thin shoulders. Meanwhile her mind raced. Should she keep the mother from her son? She wished Bertha were with them and, as if in answer to her wish, she heard footsteps along the landing and Bertha stumbled into the room.

Catching Chloe's gaze, Bertha understood that her mother had been told of Oliver's death. She stopped in the middle of the room. Her face was white and drawn and her eyes blazed. 'They're going to catch him, Mama, and hang him! They're going to punish the wretch who did this. If they don't I'll find him myself and kill him with my bare hands!'

Chloe said quietly, 'She wants to see Oliver before they take him away.'

She said, 'He looks terrible, Mama. Don't look at him. There's so much blood and his face and chest . . .' She took a step nearer. 'Wouldn't you rather remember him as he was?'

Jessica was struggling to her feet. 'I want to see my son. However terrible he looks, he is still my son and I will still love him.'

Bertha said, 'Mama, I've seen him. It will be so horrible for you.'

'Help me downstairs,' Jessica insisted. 'I want to see him and hold him one last time.'

By the time Chloe and Bertha had helped her down the stairs Oliver had been covered with a red blanket and the coffin stood open to receive him. The police sergeant watched Jessica anxiously as she knelt beside him and drew back the blanket. He glanced at Bertha but she shrugged.

To Chloe, the ruined, blood-spattered face still came as a

shock and she could imagine how it looked to his mother.

'Oh my dear!' Jessica murmured. 'What on earth have they done to you? But rest easy – he'll be punished. He won't get away with this.' She leaned down and, drawing a handkerchief from her pocket, gently wiped away some of the offending blood. Then she kissed him on the forehead. 'Be at peace, Oliver. No one can harm you now. It's all over and we'll pray for your soul.' She found his hand and pressed it to her lips. 'You had a happy life. I shall remember that. Your childhood . . .' She smiled faintly. 'You were always laughing. A happy little soul.' She tucked his hand away under the blanket and sighed deeply.

The sergeant touched her shoulder and said, 'We must move him now but we'll be very respectful. I can promise you that.'

Bertha helped her up and the three women watched in silence as Oliver was lifted into his coffin. Gently they carried it outside to the waiting wagon and a few moments later they had gone.

'Goodbye, my darling boy,' Jessica whispered and at these words Bertha broke down and sobbed hysterically, clinging to her mother, who made ineffectual attempts to comfort her.

Chloe, exhausted by the drama and tragedy, put her arms around them and wondered how they would get through the rest of this terrible day.

Three hours later Police Constable Godden was pushing his bicycle up the hill and through the arch into Winchelsea. He was feeling rather aggrieved by the fact that a manhunt was in operation around Icklesham and Guestling. A madman with a gun had shot and killed a man on his own doorstep and all hell was breaking loose. Because of his youth he had been selected to go to Winchelsea Beach, where a local fisherman had had his nets stolen.

He had spent nearly an hour on the windswept beach road with elderly Edwin Dengate, taking notes on the theft without so much as a cup of tea or a biscuit. Now he was going off duty.

After passing through the arch at the top of Winchelsea Hill, PC Godden bumped his bicycle up the kerb and wheeled it into the small area known as The Lookout. From here, at the very edge of the cliff, he could look down on to the marsh and across Winchelsea Beach towards the sea. Well hidden from the road, he could snatch five minutes with the clay pipe he had recently adopted in the hope of making himself look older and wiser.

He had just taken the first puff when a sudden movement on the slope below caught his eye.

'What the hell's going on down there?' he muttered and leaned forward to get a better view. Someone was dodging to and fro among the trees. A man. He narrowed his eyes and as he did his excitement grew. A man in a long coat.

'You're up to no good, laddie!' This was something he'd heard his sergeant say and it seemed appropriate. His interest quickened. The man was certainly behaving in a very suspicious way and it occurred to him that this might be the fugitive they were all looking for.

'Crikey!' His heart began to race. Just suppose he was looking at the killer. They'd been warned not to take unnecessary risks but to wait for reinforcements. But he'd be a hero – unless he too was shot and killed. Doubt filled him. He was unarmed and the man was certain to be desperate. He'd murdered someone and that could only end one way – with a noose round his neck, dangling at the end of a rope. So he was hardly likely to give himself up to a very young constable, pipe or no pipe.

'Unless you've got rid of the weapon!' he muttered. Would he be stupid enough to keep the murder weapon with him? Wouldn't he have tossed it away or buried it? PC Godden was torn with indecision. One way he would capture the fugitive single-handed and possibly gain early promotion. The other way he'd end up dead and his widowed mother would have no one.

At that moment an upstairs window opened in the house adjacent to The Lookout and an elderly man stared intently across the marsh.

'Dammit!' Quickly the pipe was knocked out and returned to the constable's pocket.

'There's someone down there,' the man told Constable Godden. 'Lurking about. Shifty like.'

'I've already spotted him.'

'Well aren't you going after him?'

'Not allowed to approach singly.' Fortunately this was true. 'I'm just on my way to report it.'

'Well get a move on afore he legs it. I'll keep an eye on him. See which way he goes.'

Glad that the decision had been made for him, Constable Godden remounted his bicycle and headed for the telephone to ring the police station and raise the alarm.

Eleven

Later that evening Jessica was resting, aided by a sleeping draught. Bertha, still in a state of shock, sat opposite Chloe at the long dining table. In front of them Mrs Letts had placed a bowl of ham and pea soup and a plate of home-made bread.

'We must eat something,' Bertha muttered.

Chloe nodded. 'I'm not hungry but I thought it would give Mrs Letts something to do. She was in a terrible state.'

She ladled soup into her dish and passed the ladle to Bertha. 'Take some. We should let her think she's helped us.'

'Food, the great healer! Or is that "time"?' Bertha swallowed a spoonful of soup. 'Ham and pea soup. This is . . . *was* Oliver's second favourite. After bouillabaisse.'

Chloe sighed. 'This is going to set your mother back years!'

'If she ever recovers.' Bertha rubbed at her eyes. 'George was very understanding about delaying the wedding. I suppose your brother-in-law knows what's happened. He'll have to delay the banns.'

'I think everyone knows by now. A murderer in these parts. Almost unheard of, I imagine.'

'They'll never catch him. I know it here.' Bertha put a hand to her heart. 'He'll slip through the net. You see if he doesn't.'

Chloe cut two slices of bread and took one. 'Eat,' she said. 'We have to keep up our strength . . . And as for catching him, don't forget that they know who he is. Most times

194

there's a murder, they don't know who did it. The police have a head start this time.'

'He'll have friends. They'll hide him. Someone will lie for him.'

'You don't know that. I should think a man like Jakes has more enemies than friends!'

When Mrs Letts came in to remove the soup dishes, she brought in a large shepherd's pie.

'Nice and easy to eat,' she explained, 'and I'll hot it up again if the mistress wakes up hungry.'

Bertha smiled faintly. 'There's enough there to feed an army. If there's any left tomorrow give it to Binns to take home to his mother.'

'Should I give him what's left of the soup? He's hanging around the back door looking as miserable as the rest of us.'

Bertha said, 'Please do.'

Mrs Letts had just brought in a dish of runner beans when the doorbell sent her scurrying to the front door. It was Sergeant Tanner. Bertha and Chloe rushed into the hallway to hear the latest news.

The sergeant, red-faced with triumph, gave them the thumbs-up sign.

'We've got the bugger! Oh! Begging your ladies' pardon!'

Bertha clutched at the banister, too overcome to speak.

Chloe cried, 'Well done, Sergeant! That was quick work!'

'Caught him on the beach heading for Rye Harbour. Trying to get himself over to France. But we scotched that little plan.'

'It's the most splendid news!' Bertha said at last.

Mrs Letts cried, 'The sooner they hang him the better!' and hurried to the kitchen to share the news with Binns.

Chloe said, 'How on earth did you find him?'

The sergeant explained that a young constable had seen a suspicious character hiding in the trees on the cliffside below Winchelsea. 'By the time we'd remustered our men at Winchelsea Beach and caught another glimpse of him he was further on, past Camber Castle. By the time we reached

195

the castle he was on the shingle on the west side of the river mouth, holding up some poor fisherman with his shotgun. Trying to make him put to sea.' He shook his head. 'It was a nasty moment, I can tell you. My chaps were unarmed and we knew Jakes was desperate enough to kill again. When the fisherman saw us closing in he threw himself at Jakes – very rash, that. Brave but rash. There was a scuffle and the gun went off . . .'

Chloe asked, 'Were any of your men hurt?'

'Not seriously, thank the Lord. One lad's got some shot in his left arm but luckily he wasn't too close when the thing went off. That saved him. But Jakes was determined to take out one of my men. He fired a second time and missed and then we knew he'd have to reload so we rushed him. Grabbed him and got him down and put on the cuffs.' He sucked in his breath. 'Very nasty piece of work, that one. We'll all be well rid of him – including his wife. Knocked her about something cruel, from what they say. There won't be many mourners at his funeral – if any at all!'

'So where is he now?' asked Bertha.

'Locked up in the Ypres Tower in Rye – with fetters on his ankles. There's no way that murdering wretch is going to escape his punishment. You ladies can rest easy on that score. He'll stay there until they decide where he's to be tried. Most likely Lewes Assizes. But with your testimony, Miss Blake, he's going to swing for what he's done.'

Bertha said, 'I'd like to be there when he does!' and burst into tears. Chloe turned to comfort her but she evaded her hand and ran up the stairs.

The sergeant watched her go with a look of great compassion. 'Best let her cry,' he advised. 'Tears have to be shed and the sooner the better if you ask me.' He turned his cap in his hands. 'You've had a fair share of grief round here, what with that poor Leeming lass.'

'Hettie. Yes, but so far their child is surviving.'

He nodded. 'Let's hope the worst is over, eh? When things can't get worse they have to get better! Now, I'll be on my way but maybe tomorrow I'll call in and take a witness statement from you. What you saw and all that. Before you start to forget the details.'

Chloe thought she would never be able to forget the terrible details but she simply nodded and saw him to the door. At the front door she asked him to pass on the family's thanks for the way his men had carried out their duties. 'I'd like the fisherman's name and address, too,' she told him. 'I'm sure Mrs Maitland will want to thank him for his courage.'

Walking slowly upstairs to check on Jessica, she tried to imagine where they would all be in three months' time and found it impossible. The only good thing that had come out of the whole mess had been the baby. Could Olivia possibly be the pathway back to happiness for this shattered family? Chloe prayed that she could.

Three days later Matty trudged up the stairs to Oliver's studio with a basket in one hand and his key in the other. At the top of the stairs he turned the corner and gasped with fright. A young woman was sitting against the door, her face half hidden. From her breathing he assumed that she was asleep. For a ghastly moment he wondered if he was somehow responsible for her presence. Had she followed him here? Tracked him down? Had he drunk so much the night before that he had forgotten a liaison with a young woman? Vaguely the name Dora came to him. A big, blowsy woman with frizzy gold hair. Where had they gone? What had they done? The thought sent him reeling back against the wall and in his fright he dropped the basket.

The sound woke her and she raised her head and blinked tiredly.

'Miss Blake!'

She managed a wan smile and held out her hands. He pulled her to her feet and opened the door. Collecting his basket of shopping he followed her into the flat.

'What brings you to—'

'There's been a terrible accident,' she told him. 'I don't

know how to break this to you but Oliver's been killed. Shot.'

He sat down heavily, trying to take in the significance of what she had said.

'Shot? Oliver?' He stared at her, his mouth open.

'Murdered. I'm so sorry.' She sat down close to him.

She indicated his basket, which contained a bottle of brandy, a loaf of bread and a lump of cheese. 'I think you should pour yourself a stiff brandy.'

Ignoring her suggestion, Matty leaned forward in his chair.

'Tell me.'

Slowly the story emerged. Oliver had been shot by Sid Jakes. Horror filled him as the full implications dawned on him.

'He was killed instead of *me*? By *mistake*? Oh God! That's . . . that's obscene! I can't bear it. Not Ollie. Oh sweet Jesus!'

He rocked to and fro, bewildered by shock and grief. Chloe went into the tiny kitchen and busied herself with a teapot and kettle. She returned with a mug of sweet tea, which he sipped obediently.

He said, 'How's Jessie taking it? As if I didn't know. This will finish her, you know. Finish her completely.'

'I hope not.'

'I'm telling you – I know her. She won't survive this.'

Chloe drew a long breath and he looked at her sharply.

She said, 'I've come to ask you to come back to Fairfields. You're in no danger now and we all need you.'

'Need me? *Me*?' He shook his head. 'You know me, Miss Blake. I'm a pretty useless sort of cove. Never been any good to anyone. They'll tell you. Oh I'm good-hearted, I suppose. Life and soul of the party. That sort of thing. But nobody needs me. I'm not that sort of person. No backbone, my father used to say. Weak. That's me.'

She was giving him a strange look but it didn't bother him. His life had been full of strange looks. Only his mother had looked on him with love and even that had been tinged with exasperation. His father had disliked him and had never hidden his disappointment that a son of his should show so little manliness. So little courage. A second-rate cricketer, a third-rate boxer. No one had been surprised when he cheated at exams, betrayed women and turned to drink and gambling.

She said, 'You aren't listening to me!'

'Sorry! I was miles away. Nowhere you'd want to be.'

'I'm asking you to come back and take charge of the family. There's no one else and Jessica is going to need—'

'There's Bertha.'

'Bertha's getting married or have you forgotten? She's waited a long time for that and you mustn't take it from her.'

'Me? Why should I take anything from her?'

'Because you'd be content if she gave up George and devoted herself to Jessica. Because you don't want to take on the responsibility – but you must.'

He gazed slowly round the little flat. He was just beginning to enjoy himself. Free of criticism, he had found himself a cosy little set-up. Not forever, of course, but until Oliver saw fit to throw him out. But now Oliver never would. He frowned. Poor Ollie – and it was all his fault. He, Matty, had brought about Oliver's death. He had robbed Jessica of her son and left Bertha without a brother. Of course he hadn't meant this terrible thing to happen but it had and indirectly he was to blame. He thought of Dora with her large breasts and her funny squeaky laugh. He liked big, cheerful women. Dora would have made him very happy. He could have enjoyed himself . . .

'Matty! You're doing it again,' Chloe pleaded, her voice tinged with exasperation. 'Please listen to me. There's Jessica and there's Bertha and there's Oliver's daughter. Three women, Matty, and they need you.'

He screwed his face into a scowl.

She smiled in spite of herself. 'Don't look like that.'

A thought struck and he brightened. 'They'll have George. You can't deny the blacksmith's a very solid type.'

'George will be away a lot and they'll have their own family to care for, we hope. Bertha and Jessica need *you*. You must see that for yourself.'

'They sent you, didn't they? Told you to haul me back!'

'No they didn't. But Jessica's asking for you. The shock has taken its toll. She's confused and grief-stricken and the doctor's worried about her mental condition. She's having terrible nightmares and doesn't want to eat. I'm afraid she doesn't want to live. I do what I can but I'm not family. You're closer to her.'

Chloe pulled her chair nearer and took hold of his hands. 'This is your chance, you know. You could pull yourself together and help them. Forget the past and start again. Be a different Matty!' She smiled at his woebegone expression. 'Forget gambling and drinking and concentrate on your home and family. You have to come back to Fairfields. It's the only decent thing to do.'

Matty opened his mouth to protest that doing the decent thing had never been his strong point but there was a steely glint in Miss Blake's eyes which he recognised. He tried to imagine himself as a better person. Would he ever be a force to be reckoned with? 'I don't know . . .' he began.

Chloe said, 'You'd have to be very responsible but Bertha and George would be nearby. Jessica would look up to you, Matty. You'd be her rock.'

'What about you? Won't you be there?'

'I'll stay while you need me.'

He sighed. 'You really think I could make a difference?'

'I know it,' she told him.

Two days later, Chloe and Bertha alighted from the dog cart outside the rectory in Icklesham carrying a crib made of willow, complete with bedlinen. They were greeted at the door by Dorothy. Inside they found the parlour spotless with fresh marigolds in a bowl on the window sill. A wooden cot contained Bertha's small niece. Olivia was wide awake, gurgling happily, her tiny hands clutching a small ivory rattle. She was noticeably gaining weight and, to everyone's relief, was thriving in spite of her premature birth.

Bertha said, 'I'm sorry to take her away from you so soon but Mama insists. She is a part of Oliver and Mama cannot bear to be parted from her. The doctor says having the baby in the house will aid her recovery. She is still desperately low in spirit and hardly eats a thing.'

'Poor soul,' said Dorothy. 'I see you've brought a crib.'

'We couldn't take yours. I'm sure you'll be needing it before long.'

'Oh!' Dorothy flushed. 'I hope so. We shan't give up hope.'

Chloe said quickly, 'Uncle Matty is back with us and making a great effort to be of use. He gets up at a reasonable time and is taking an interest in the household affairs, which Mrs Maitland cannot deal with at present. Paying the bills and supervising the staff. I think he rather enjoys being needed.'

As Bertha leaned over the crib, Dorothy hovered anxiously. 'The rattle was a gift from my next-door neighbour. All her clothes are washed and ironed.' Her voice broke suddenly and she turned away.

Chloe put an arm round her but could think of nothing to say. Although Dorothy had already accepted that they must give Olivia up, parting with her would still be an unbearable wrench.

Bertha said, 'Olivia looks very well and happy.' She turned to smile at Dorothy. 'You and your husband have taken great care of her. I can't tell you what a relief it was to know she was in good hands.'

'It was a pleasure,' Dorothy told her. 'She's an adorable child. I'm sorry my husband can't be here. He . . . he was called away. A sick parishioner . . .'

Chloe said, 'I'm sure that you will be welcome to call in from time to time and see Olivia. Mrs Maitland knows how fond you are of her.'

'Most certainly,' Bertha agreed. 'We will always be pleased to see you and your husband. Not that I shall be at Fairfields, of course. George and I have found ourselves a cottage.' Her face lit up at the prospect. 'But Olivia will be in good hands. Mama and Uncle Matty will be her guardians and we have already advertised for a live-in nanny. Olivia is all we have now to remind us of Oliver and we shall all do our very best to make up to her for her double loss.'

Dorothy nodded. 'I'm so pleased. I was afraid Hettie's sister would decide she wanted her. Olivia is such a delicate child – she really needs the best care that can be had.'

Chloe thought of Lizzie and shuddered.

Bertha said, 'Hopefully George and I will have a family and Olivia will have some cousins around her own age. Having no parents is bad enough but being an only child also . . .' She shrugged. 'I think George wrote to your husband with the altered dates for the wedding. Are they acceptable?'

'Yes, they are. I think the whole village is looking forward to it.'

'And Oliver's funeral?'

'All in order. But Albert wondered where you wanted him to be buried.'

Bertha looked up sharply. 'Mama wishes him to be buried in the family plot, next to our father. I've brought the hymns we've chosen and we'd like the choir and the bell. Poor Oliver. So soon after Hettie . . .' Her sigh was heartfelt. 'Who could have imagined that this would happen?' She leaned over the baby. 'Your poor Papa . . . But now we're taking you home.'

Chloe caught a glimpse of her sister's stricken face and decided that they should make the visit as short as possible. 'Well, shall we be off then?' she asked.

Bertha nodded. Carefully they transferred the baby from cot to crib and carried her outside. Binns helped them set the crib down securely in the cart. Before they left Chloe hugged her sister fiercely and whispered a promise that she would be invited regularly to visit Olivia. Dorothy nodded bravely but when the horse set off and Chloe glanced back, Dorothy had her hands over her face and Chloe knew she was crying.

Promptly at twelve thirty the following day Warder Steven Apps opened the door to cell number three and surveyed his prisoner. Light from a window high up in the wall brightened the small room with its stone walls and earth floor. The Ypres Tower had originally been built to protect the town of Rye from marauders but now it served as a gaol.

Jakes, sitting on the end of his flimsy bed, squinted up at the warder. 'Not stew again, I hope.'

'Like it or lump it!' Apps, approaching with the tray, looked at the potato and minced mutton. Gristly meat and lumpy potatoes. He didn't fancy it but then he didn't have to eat it. 'Now you keep well back or I'll take it away and feed it to the dogs.'

He edged forward, keeping a wary eye on his prisoner. Jakes had killed a man in cold blood and fired the same gun at others. Although he was chained to the wall by one ankle he was a burly man and might well find a way to do his warder some harm.

Apps put the tray on the ground and retreated.

'No bread?' Jakes frowned.

'You're lucky to get that. If it was up to me you'd sit here and starve to death.' His distaste was mixed with a morbid curiosity. A murder investigation was a novelty and his family and friends would be full of questions when he went off duty. 'Still, you're going to hang, aren't you. Blasting a man to pieces for no—'

'Got an alibi, haven't I. My wife knows I was with her at the time of the shooting. That's what she'll say.' He reached for the tin bowl and snatched a piece of potato from the plate.

'Ah! But that's not what she says. She says you was out and she didn't set eyes on you all day. Next she knew you were being hunted for killing a man.'

Jakes stared at him. 'She never said that.'

'She did. Made a statement and everything.'

'How come? Eh? The stupid bitch can barely write her name.'

'She said what happened and the constable wrote it for her and read it back. She signed it.' He grinned. 'If you must know, she didn't have a good word to say for you. Maybe you slapped her about a bit too much over the years. Women don't like that sort of thing. They're funny like that. So forget your alibi, Jakes old son!'

'She can't speak against me in court. That's the law. A wife can't—'

'You're for the high jump and I for one—'

He ducked as the tin bowl flew towards him. It struck the wall, spilling the contents, and clattered to the ground.

Grinning, Apps picked it up and reached cautiously for the tray. 'Lost your appetite, have you?'

Jakes regarded him stonily. 'That woman at Fairfields – she'll never identify me. Too scared to notice details – and she slammed the door in my face. So how much did she see? Eh? Not enough.'

Apps laughed at his discomfiture. 'You're fooling yourself! We showed her four photographs – one of them was of you. The one we took when you were first brought in. Remember the fuss you made? Well, Miss Blake recognised you. Picked you out straight away. And she *can* write. She put it all down on paper. How you shot him at close range and tried to kill her an' all. Damning, it is. No, you'll be off to the Assize Court in Lewes before you can say Jack Robinson – and swinging from a rope in a few months from now. You might as well get used to the idea. Try a few prayers. Say a few Hail Marys.'

As he walked out he heard the man curse him and a sudden shiver ran up his spine. The man was evil. He slammed the door and locked it and went back to his desk to await the end of his shift.

* * *

204

Oliver's funeral was delayed by the need for a post-mortem and for the police to conclude their enquiries and collect their evidence. To them, the need for a cast-iron case against Jakes outweighed considerations for the grieving family of the victim and ten days passed before they released Oliver's body. By this time Jessica had rallied a little and the doctor had pronounced her well enough to attend the funeral.

Chloe had marvelled at the change in her once Olivia had arrived at Fairfields. The tiny girl seemed to cast her spell on the entire household and watching her day-to-day progress had helped everyone through the worst of their immediate grief.

Alice Benlow had been selected from the five applicants for the position of nanny and her presence, too, helped the family to survive the darkest days. She was a plump, cheerful woman in her forties who had raised a daughter, now married, and had been a nanny with another family, who sent a glowing reference. At first sight she did not look the perfect nanny, with her careless clothes and unruly curls, but Chloe guessed she would quickly settle in at Fairfields. With her sunny disposition it seemed that Alice Benlow loved the world and everyone in it. 'With the exception of murderers and skinflints,' she told Chloe with a broad smile. 'I do hate a mean man.'

A bright nursery had been hastily prepared, which Alice shared with her young charge. When Olivia was older, Alice would move in to the adjoining room but while Olivia was young, Alice insisted on being close to her at all times.

Olivia, blissfully unaware of her tragic double loss, thrived amid so much loving care and was already a firm favourite. Jessica doted on her, Bertha found her enchanting and even Uncle Matty surrendered to her charms.

On the day of Oliver's funeral it was decided that Alice should carry Oliver's daughter into the church with the rest of the family. The organist played softly as the Maitlands took their places and various friends slipped into the nearby pews and knelt to pray. Albert waited in his sombre vestments and

Dorothy was also present. Mrs Leeming had come but Mr Leeming and Lizzie were absent. George sat with Bertha and his mother. Uncle Matty and Chloe sat on Jessica's left with Alice and the baby on Jessica's right.

Chloe wished that Adele could have been there with them. She had loved Oliver and probably always would. Presumably Adele was unaware that Oliver was dead but the enquiries they had made to find her had led nowhere. Chloe could only hope that she would make a success of her dancing career in Paris.

They sang Oliver's favourite hymns and the choir sang *Jesus, Joy of Man's Desiring*. Albert delivered a touching tribute to the dead man with such obvious sincerity that Chloe's eyes filled with tears. Poor Albert. She thought about his inability to find enough love for Olivia and yet, in a way, it had turned out for the best. How would they have felt if Jessica had demanded the return of the baby after they had decided to keep it? God moves in a mysterious way, she thought, wiping away her tears.

As they followed the coffin out of the church she caught Dorothy's eye and smiled. Her sister looked very pale and Chloe was pleased when George slipped his free arm through hers. Bertha is very lucky, Chloe thought. George was a decent man. Helping Matty to support Jessica, Chloe walked slowly into the sunlight, wishing they could have paid their last respects to Oliver as he lay in his coffin. But the shotgun blast had done too much damage to his face. The undertakers had advised against viewing and the family had reluctantly agreed to have the coffin closed.

As the graveside blessing was uttered, Alice turned to Jessica and, without a word, put Olivia into her arms. A brief smile lit Jessica's face as she lifted the baby and whispered something to her. Chloe, her throat tight, marvelled at the twist of fate that had given them something of Oliver for the future.

She glanced at Uncle Matty and was pleased to see that he

was smiling at the baby. Burdened by his sense of guilt, he rarely smiled nowadays.

Now all that remained was the trial, due in a week's time. The preliminary hearing had been held in the town hall in Rye but the trial itself would be transferred to the Lewes Assize Court. Jessica was determined to attend despite Bertha's best efforts to dissuade her. Chloe and Matty would be called upon to give evidence and the police were confident about the outcome.

A few weeks after the trial, the banns would be called for Bertha and George and everyone looked forward to a happy occasion after the sorrows they had endured.

Saturday the twenty-seventh of July. Poor Oliver was laid to rest today – such a sad occasion for everyone. I'm so full of regrets and guilt I can hardly live with myself. If only I had not interfered. I should have allowed Uncle Matty to steal that salver and then Sid Jakes would have been satisfied. But it seemed so wrong that Binns would have been blamed. At the time it felt like the right thing to do – but how often hindsight proves us wrong.

Dottie looked very pale and ill. I can't imagine how she felt to see someone else holding Olivia. Please God, let her have a child of her own, for nothing else will heal the wound. I wonder if Albert's attitude has caused any kind of rift between them. I will go home again as soon as I can.

Olivia was so good. Not a whimper throughout the service. I am glad that the Maitlands have one or two photographs of her father. She will no doubt treasure them when she is older. Unlikely, though, that anyone has photographed Hettie. Betsy Leeming asked to hold Olivia for a few moments and shed a few tears. At least Olivia will know her mother's family as well as her father's.

As for me, I feel worn out with emotion. The Maitlands are not my flesh and blood and I have been here only a few months but I love them all.

Twelve

On Wednesday the sixth of August at the Lewes Assizes, the number one courtroom was packed. It was a dull day and the gaslights flared, casting a sickly glow. The room smelled of stale air, cheap wax polish and the patchouli oil that the gentlemen used on their hair.

Jessica and Bertha, both still in mourning black, sat at the back of the courtroom with Dorothy. Only yards away, Sid Jakes, wearing his own clothes, sat at the front of the court flanked by two warders. Angus Pye, the crown prosecutor, was a tall, world-weary man who spent of lot of time riffling through his notes. The defence lawyer was Edgar Lightwing – short, middle-aged, with a way of rushing his words. 'All rise!'

The judge came in and everyone rose to their feet then sat again. He had a stern expression and Bertha thought he looked competent. She took hold of her mother's hand and squeezed it reassuringly. 'They'll find Jakes guilty,' she whispered and Jessica flashed her a brief smile.

Outside the courtroom, Bertha knew, Matty and Chloe waited to be called to the witness stand. It was the third day of the trial and various people had been called already. On the first day, witnesses gave evidence of Sid Jakes' good character. These had consisted of his parents and an obliging neighbour. They believed him to be misunderstood, much maligned and blamed for everything that went wrong in the area. Less enthusiastically, his employer had testified that he was 'a hard worker but unpredictable': On the second day the prosecutor had called three people who had fallen foul of Sid Jakes over the year and they all agreed that he was 'inclined to be violent' and 'a heavy drinker'.

The result of the post-mortem was read out and Sergeant Tanner took the stand. He testified to finding Oliver Maitland's body in a state consistent with severe gunshot wounds. He described how and where they caught Sid Jakes as he tried to make his escape. Constable Godden was singled out and praised for his part in the capture.

Today it was Matty's turn to testify and a court official came into the corridor and called him in. He made his way to the witness stand and took the oath. He looked respectable in a dark grey suit with matching waistcoat and a white shirt with a wing collar. A heavy watch chain completed the effect.

Angus Pye, for the prosecution, stood in the middle of the room with a sheaf of papers in his hands. 'You are Matthew Cuthbert Orme?'

'Yes, sir.'

'Mr Orme, it has been alleged that the man who shot Oliver Maitland supposed him to be you. In other words, you were the intended victim.'

'That's true.'

'Perhaps you would tell the court how this mistake occurred.'

Matty spoke clearly but his fingers, clutching the edge of the witness box, were white-knuckled. Not once did he cast a glance in Jakes' direction. He explained the debt and the threatening letter. He told how Chloe had been used as a 'messenger' and how the brick was thrown through the window.

Angus Pye referred to his notes at this point. 'So, to sum up, you maintain that Sid Jakes meant to kill you but shot your nephew instead, because he did not know you had gone up to London on an early train.'

'That is so, sir.'

'You had gone to London to "lie low", as you put it. Meanwhile the accused had come to Fairfield House to carry out his threat to kill you. To murder you with his shotgun.'

'Yes, sir.'

'So the accused had murder in his heart when he came to your home. He had ammunition in the shotgun for the purpose of killing you. It was premeditated.'

'Most certainly it was.'

'You are a very lucky man, Mr Orme.'

Matty swallowed. 'I don't see it that way, sir. I'd rather he'd killed me. Oliver was innocent of any wrongdoing. He had his life ahead of him. He didn't deserve what happened.'

Bertha closed her eyes. Beside her Jessica took out a handkerchief and pressed it to her eyes.

When it was defence's turn, Edgar Lightwing clutched his robe tightly round him and stared at Matty.

'So are we agreed that the accused did not mean to kill Oliver Maitland?'

'That's right but—'

'How could it be premeditated if he did not even know he was on the premises? No doubt he was as surprised as anyone.'

Matty frowned, unsure how to answer.

'Mr Orme, I put it to you that my client had no intention of killing Mr Maitland. Had not planned any such thing. Would you agree?'

'I . . . . Well, if you put it like that. But he did intend to—'

'Just answer the question, please. I put it to you that Mr Jakes was unfortunate on that day to—'

'My nephew was the unfortunate one!' Matty blinked furiously. 'Sid Jakes meant to kill me. He's a murdering—'

The judge banged his gavel. 'Behave yourself, Mr Orme. You will do your cause no good by losing your temper.'

'I'm sorry, your worship. I mean, your honour. That is—'

210

Lightwing smiled thinly. 'No further questions, your honour.' He sat down.

Bertha looked at Jakes, who was grinning at Lightwing. You killed my brother, she told him silently. This court is going to find you guilty and you are going to pay for what you did.

Jessica leaned towards her. 'I'd like to wipe that smile from that monster's face! How can anyone defend him? It's immoral!'

'It's justice, Mama. Hush! They are going to call Chloe.'

They all leaned forward as Chloe entered the courtroom. Dorothy put a hand to her mouth as Chloe took the oath. Jessica patted her other hand. 'Chloe will be fine,' she whispered. 'She's stronger than you think.'

The prosecutor, Angus Pye rose to his feet and stepped forward.

'You are employed as Mrs Maitland's companion. Is that so?'

'Yes.'

'Did you know that Matthew Orme owed a great deal of money?'

'Yes. He confided in me.'

'He had owed it for some time?'

'Yes, but he was going to repay it.'

'Why are you so certain that the accused intended murder when he came to Fairfields?'

'I had heard that he was a violent man. He once frightened me and treated me very roughly. He also attacked Mr Orme. When I saw the threatening letter I knew Jakes would do something bad but I didn't quite believe he would stoop to murder. But I know he did and I know it was him. I saw him and I recognised him from that earlier occasion. He knew it, too, and that's why he needed to kill me as well. If I hadn't managed to close the door when I did . . .' She stopped and swallowed.

'Miss Blake, is the man who tried to kill you present in this court?'

211

'He is. He's sitting there!' She pointed at Sid Jakes.

'I understand you also identified him when shown four photographs?'

'I'd recognise him anywhere. He's a wicked, evil—'

The gavel came down again. 'Please restrict yourself to answering the questions, Miss Blake.'

'I'm sorry. Yes, I identified him from the photographs.'

'And did you pick him out of the police line-up?'

'I did.'

'I'd like you to tell us in your own words what happened on Thursday the thirty-first of July when Oliver Maitland lost his life.'

Chloe breathed slowly in and out. She had been warned not to lose control. She must come across to the jury as a well-balanced individual and not as a woman thirsting for revenge.

'I was at the top of the stairs about to come down when I heard a bang which sounded like a gunshot. I looked down and saw Oliver lying in the hallway and there was a lot of blood. As I ran downstairs I could see out through the front door and there was a man fumbling with his coat. I recognised him as Sid Jakes because I'd seen him before.'

'When was that, Miss Blake?'

'One day when I passed him on the road and our coachman told me his name and that he was a gamekeeper. And again when he grabbed me in the bushes and gave me a message for Mr Orme.'

'A threatening message?'

'Yes.'

'Please continue, Miss Blake.'

'After the shooting I saw him bringing out something from beneath his long coat which I guessed must be the shotgun. I knew he was going to shoot me as well so that I couldn't identify him.'

There was a gasp from the courtroom.

'I didn't have time to run away and there was nothing I could hide behind. The only chance I had was to close the door between us and I ran forward. Luckily the gun appeared to get caught up in the folds of his coat but as I pushed the door to, I saw him raise the shotgun and point it at me. I thought then that I was too late with the door and I was going to die . . . But I didn't.' She turned to look at Jakes and said calmly, 'But no thanks to Mr Jakes. I heard the shot and the door was badly damaged.'

There was a loud murmur in the courtroom and the jurors exchanged shocked glances.

'So you are suggesting there could have been a double murder?'

'I'm sure of it.'

'That will be all, Miss Blake. Thank you. You may step down.'

It was Edgar Lightwing's turn to question her for the defence.

'Miss Blake, when you first saw my client on the road, were you very close to each other for a substantial period of time?'

'We passed each other and I looked at him. He also looked up at us.'

'For how long? Five minutes?'

'Less than that.'

'Less than five? Four then?'

'No. Mr Binns and I were in the dog cart. The horse was trotting so we—'

'So you saw my client very briefly. Mr Binns told you the man was Sid Jakes and you believed him.'

'Of course. Mr Binns was born in the area and—'

'Just answer yes or no.'

'Yes, I believed him.'

'Could he possibly have been mistaken?'

'I don't see how.'

'And when this man you alleged dragged you into the bushes—'

'I'm not alleging it. I'm saying he—'

'Please, Miss Blake.'

He turned towards the judge, who sighed. 'Just answer the questions, Miss Blake.'

'Was it shadowy in the bushes? Were the trees blotting out the light? Perhaps you were too frightened to see him properly. I put it to you that you cannot be sure that your alleged attacker was my client.'

'I am quite sure.'

'You mean the alleged attacker was the same man that you passed on the road and who was named as Sid Jakes by Binns, the groom. He could have been mistaken, couldn't he? You wouldn't have been any the wiser.'

Chloe hesitated. She could see where he was leading but was unable to stop him. 'It was the same man. It was Sid Jakes.'

The defence lawyer tutted with exasperation and threw up his hands as though in despair. 'No more questions, your honour.'

The following day a unanimous jury found Sid Jakes guilty of the wilful and premeditated murder of Oliver Maitland. His lawyer lodged an immediate appeal, which was rejected, and Jakes was hanged in Lewes three weeks later. The verdict and subsequent sentence satisfied the Maitlands' desire to see justice done but nothing would bring Oliver back to them and they would live with his loss for the rest of their days.

Epilogue

June twenty-sixth of the following year dawned bright and sunny.

'A perfect day for her birthday!' Mrs Letts stepped back from the table to admire her handiwork. The cake was covered in frothy white icing and a single candle waited to be lit. A pink ribbon encircled it and the name 'Olivia' had been lovingly inscribed in pink icing.

Chloe smiled. 'It's wonderful,' she told her. 'You've done our little girl proud, Mrs Letts. Can you imagine Olivia's face when we light the candle? She'll be so intrigued.'

Binns, lounging as usual in the doorway, nodded. 'Don't seem like a year, does it? But a lot's happened.'

Carefully Mrs Letts lowered a muslin cover over the cake and returned it to the cool larder. Her round face was wreathed in smiles in happy anticipation.

'I'm glad you stayed on for it,' she told Chloe. 'It wouldn't have been the same without you.'

Chloe's smile wavered a little. Now that the moment had arrived she was secretly full of doubts. Going to America to look for her father had been a long-held dream – but suppose she couldn't find him? Resolutely she pushed the doubt to the back of her mind.

Binns said, 'The christening! Now that was a lovely do. That cake! I still think about it. And Miss Bertha's wedding cake.'

'You're cake mad,' Mrs Letts told him. 'All you think

215

about is food. But I tell you what. I'll make you a cake when you find yourself a wife. How's that?'

His eyes lit up. 'Is that a promise?'

Chloe laughed. 'All you need now is a wife.'

'I'll find someone, you'll see. I've already started looking.'

Mrs Letts said, 'If you stand around here gossiping you'll be looking for another job as well!' and shooed him out of the kitchen.

Chloe said, 'I'm all packed. I'll slip away after the party, before I change my mind.'

She wandered out into the garden, where she found Jessica ensconced in a comfortable chair with Olivia beside her on a rug. There were coloured bricks and a doll but the little girl was clutching her favourite – a white rabbit knitted for her by Dorothy.

Beyond Jessica, Uncle Matty, halfway up a stepladder, was draping coloured lanterns from the branches of a tree. He turned, saw Chloe and climbed down.

'So you're really going to leave us,' he said. 'I don't know how your conscience will let you. We need you at Fairfields.'

She said, 'There's you and Mrs Maitland, Mrs Letts and Alice. You make a wonderful team. I'm expendable.'

Jessica sighed. 'We have to let her go, Matty,' she said. 'It's been her plan all along. Hopefully she'll come back to us one day.'

'Never!' Uncle Matty shook his head. 'She'll be snapped up by one of those ranchers. She'll spend her life on a hot, smelly farm in the middle of nowhere. Nothing but cattle for company.'

'I will not!' Chloe smiled. 'I have no intention of being "snapped up", as you put it. I shall find my father, spend a little time with him and then return to England.'

Jessica ruffled Olivia's hair. 'Well, don't take too long about it or you'll miss seeing Olivia grow up.' She sighed. 'As poor Oliver will.'

216

Chloe exchanged a quick glance with Uncle Matty. Jessica had recovered from Oliver's death but was still prone to occasional periods of melancholy and the family did their best to steer her away from sad thoughts.

Chloe said, 'And there's Dorothy's child to look forward to. My very own nephew or niece. That's something to come home for. The baby will need an auntie and there's only me.'

Dorothy's long-awaited first child was due at Christmas.

'All these babies!' Jessica shook her head in mock dismay. 'It's not too late for Bertha . . .' she began.

'Speak of the devil, Mama!' Bertha joined them, puffing a little.

With a hint of her old asperity, Jessica said, 'You surely haven't been running, Bertha?'

'No, Mama. Would I ever do anything so unladylike!' She leaned down to kiss the baby, who immediately held up her arms. Bertha scooped her up and hugged her gently. 'I was blowing up balloons,' she explained. 'For the party.'

Marriage suited her, Chloe thought. Her figure had rounded out pleasingly and she seemed very content in the cottage she shared with George. Could marriage be that good? Chloe wondered. And would she ever fall in love? It hadn't happened yet. 'But you never know,' she murmured.

'Never know what?' Uncle Matty's sharp ears had caught her words.

She looked at him. 'We never know what the future has in store for us.'

'No, we don't,' he said, 'and it's a jolly good thing we don't.' He took her hands in his and his expression was earnest. 'Make an old man very happy and say you'll come back to us, Chloe.'

'But you won't be needing a companion.'

Jessica glanced up. 'What does that matter? We look on you as part of the family now. You'll always be welcome at Fairfields.'

Bertha said, 'And you must write to us, Chloe. You are an honorary aunt to young Olivia and we shall keep your letters for her to read when she's older.'

Jessica reached out for her hand and patted it. 'Travel is exciting, I'm sure, but you mustn't disappear from our lives. Promise you'll come back one day.'

'I promise I'll come back to you,' Chloe said with a catch in her voice. 'You have my word on it.'